Michael Stewart is from Salford but is now based in Bradford. He has won several awards for his scriptwriting, including the BBC Alfred Bradley Bursary Award. His debut novel *King Crow* was the winner of the *Guardian*'s Not the Booker Award. *Ill Will* is his latest novel.

Ill Will

Michael Stewart

ONE PLACE. MANY STORIES

HQ
An imprint of HarperCollins*Publishers* Ltd
1 London Bridge Street
London SE1 9GF

This edition 2018

1
First published in Great Britain by
HQ, an imprint of HarperCollins*Publishers* Ltd 2018

ISBN: HB: 978-0-00-824815-4
TPB: 978-0-00-824816-1

MIX
Paper from
responsible sources
FSC
www.fsc.org
FSC™ C007454

This book is produced from independently certified FSC™ paper
to ensure responsible forest management.

For more information visit: www.harpercollins.co.uk/green

Printed and bound in Great Britain by
CPI Group (UK) Ltd, Croydon, CR0 4YY

For Lisa and Carter

to the
SEA

LIVERPOOL

RUNCORN

MANCHESTER

Crow Hill

⊗HAWORTH

Penistone Crag

WUTHERING HEIGHTS

⊗ HEBDEN BRIDGE

TODMORDEN

WUTHERING HEIGHTS TO LIVERPOOL
→ Sixty-five miles

1780

You are walking through Butcher's Bog, along the path at Birch Brink. Traipsing across Stanbury Moor, to the Crow Stones. A morass of tussock grass, peat wilderness and rock. There are no guiding stars, just the moaning of the wind. Stunted firs and gaunt thorns your only companions.

Perhaps you will die out here, unloved and unhomed. There was the tale of Old Tom. Last winter, went out looking for a lost lamb. Found a week on, icicles on his eyelids, half-eaten by foxes. Or was it the last wolf said to roam these moors? The ravens will eat out your eyes and the crows will pick at your bones. The worms will turn you into loam. You've forgotten your name and your language. Mr Earnshaw called you 'it' when first he came across you. Mrs Earnshaw called you 'brat' when first she took you by the chuck. Mr Earnshaw telt to call him Father and Mrs Earnshaw, Mother, but they were not your real parents. Starving when they took you in. They named you after their dead son. The man you called your father carried you over moor and fell, in rain and in snow. When finally you got to the gates of the farm it was dark and the man could hardly stand. He took you into the main room and plonked himself in a rocker. By the fire you stood, a ghost in their home. Next to you a living girl and living boy, who spat and kicked. This was their welcome to your new hovel. Nearly ten years ago now. You'd spent weeks on the streets, eating scraps from bin and midden. Kipped by the docks and ligged in doorways. You'd trusted no one, loved no one, believed in nothing.

It was tough in the new place but you'd had it worse. You'd almost died many times. You'd been beaten inside an inch of your life. Gone five days without food. Slept with rats and maggots. Nothing this new place had in store could harm you more than you'd been harmed before. Or so you thought. The girl was called Cathy, the boy Hindley, and you hated them apiece.

Almost ten years ago. But you can still feel her hot spit on your face, and his boot in your groin. None of it ever hurt you as much as her words. Words that cut to the bone. Words that stab you in the back.

You stand on top of the Crow Stones on the brink of the wilderness. It is said that the stones were used for ritual sacrifice. The slit throat of a slaughtered goat. The gushing blood of a lamb seeping into the craggy carpet beneath your feet. The wind tries to blow you off your perch. Blow harder. You are the goat, the lamb, you care not for sacrifice. Let them take you. Let them bleed you. Fuck the lot of them.

For two years your adopted father tried to protect you from Hindley. From his maniac beatings, with fist and boot and club. Sometimes it worked. Until your adopted mother died and your father retreated into himself. The jutting stones of your borrowed home were fitting symbols. The grotesque carvings and crumbling griffins were your companions. But not now. Walking without direction. It doesn't matter where you go as long as you go away from that place of torture, that palace of hate.

They called you dark-skinned gypsy, dirty lascar, vagabond, devil. You'll give them dark, dirt, devil. Cathy wanted a whip. Hindley a fiddle. You'll give her whip, him fiddle. You took a seat at the end of the hearthstone. Petted a liver-coloured bitch. There was some warmth in the room and it came from an open fire. Flames that licked, peat that steamed, coals that glowed, and wood that hissed.

Hindley called you dog and beat you with an iron bar. Mr Earnshaw tried once more to stop him. He sent Hindley to college, just to get the maniac away. And things picked up for a while. Then you watched your father die, watched the life drain from his eyes, his last breath leave his lips. You knelt at his feet and wept. You held onto his lifeless hand, the skin as brittle as a wren's shell. Cathy wiped the tears from your eyes. Hindley came back from the funeral with a wife. She was soft in the head and as thin as a whippet. Always coughing her guts up. Things got bad again. Banished from the house, set to work outside, in the pissing wind and whirling rain. You were flogged, locked out, spent your evenings shivering in a corner while that cunt stuffed his face, supping ale and brandy. Eating and drinking, singing and laughing with his slut.

The wind has lulled now and you listen to its hush. You hear a fox scream and an owl cry. The night gathers in pleats of black and blue. The cold rain falls. You teeter on the brink. It would be so easy to tumble and smash your skull on the rocks. Let the life bleed out of the cracks and let the slimy things take you. No one would miss you. Not even you. The only thing that is real is the hardness of the rock and the pestilent air that festers. You could dive head-first onto the granite. Dead in an instant. Released from the teeth of experience.

You remember another night as black as this. Your love had lost her shoes in the bog beneath Whitestone Clough. You crept through a broken hedge, groping your way up the path in the dark, planting yourselves on a flowerpot, under the drawing-room window. They hadn't put the shutters up and the light poured out. You clung to the ledge and peered in. It was carpeted in crimson and there were crimson-covered chairs. A shining white ceiling fretted with gold. A shower of glass drops hanging on silver chains, shimmering. It was Edgar and his sister Isabella. She was screaming, shrieking as if witches were ramming red-hot needles in her eyes. Edgar was standing on the hearth weeping. In the middle of a table sat a little dog, shaking its paw and yelping. They were crying over that dog, the silly cunts. Both had wanted to hold it and neither had let the other do so. You laughed, you and Cathy. They were like toy dogs themselves, all prim and prettified. Milksopped and mollycoddled.

They stopped yelping. They must have heard you laugh. Then Edgar saw you at the window and started shouting. You ran for it, but they'd let the bulldog loose, a big bastard with a big bastard head, and it had got Cathy by the ankle. It sank its bastard teeth in and wouldn't let go. You got a stone and thrust it between its bastard jaws, crammed it down its bastard throat, throttled that bastard dog with your bare hands. Its huge purple tongue was hanging half a foot out of its mouth, and blood and slaver dripped from its lips.

Then there was a servant running towards you. A big bear of a man. He grabbed Cathy and dragged her in. You followed him. Mr Linton was running down the hallway, shouting 'What is it?' The man grabbed you inside too and pulled you under the chandelier. Mr Linton was looking over his spectacles. Isabella said, 'Put him in the cellar.' 'That's Mr Earnshaw's daughter,' said another. 'Her foot is bleeding.' You cursed the servant, swore like a trooper. He dragged you into the garden, threw you on the grass, then went back to the house and locked the door behind him.

4

You went to the window again. Thought about smashing it in. She was sitting on the sofa. A servant brought a bowl of water. They took off her shoes and stockings. They washed her feet. They fed her cake. Edgar stood and gawped. They dried her wild hair and combed it sober. They wheeled her to the fire. The Lintons stood there staring.

You should shelter. Soaked to the bone and shivering, teeth chatter in your skull. You think about a nook beneath Nab Hill where the earth is soft and the rocks block the wind. It was the first place you and Cathy fucked. She took hold and put you inside her. Her white thighs astride your black hips. Your teacher, your lover, your sister, your mother. She was all you needed in the world. The rest could go to hell.

She stayed at Thrushcross Grange for five weeks. Till Christmas. Hardly knew her when she returned. Turned up on a black pony, hair all done, wearing a fancy hat with a feather in the ribbon. Even her speech was altered. She was dressed in a silk frock. You felt ashamed of your appearance, felt dirty. Your hair was coarse and uncombed. She said you looked grim and laughed in your face. You couldn't stand to listen to that laugh, couldn't stand to be so black next to one so white. You ran out of the room, burning with shame. Your flesh was a fire of disgust. The next day the Lintons were invited to the house. You were banished to the outbuildings. They called you dog, called you devil. You'll give them dog, give them devil.

Your thoughts are jumbled. They whirr like the storm around you. They make a flaysome din in your skull. Shelter. There's a cave under Penistone Crags. A roof over your head. A hole to lig in. Get out of the storm. Where are you? Somehow you are lost. The moor so familiar, but you don't recognise the landscape. You make out black shapes, skeletal outlines of withered hawthorns.

Whinstone and mud. The ground keels. You are somewhere. You are nowhere. You are here. The night is as black as your shame, as black as your face. You are wandering like a blind man. You don't know anything any more. Not what's up. Not what's down. You don't know who you are, where you came from. You don't even know your own name.

On the Straw with the Swine

I woke the next morning with my head on a pillow of mud, Cathy. I could hear the worms crawl through the earth beneath. I imagined them poking their blind noses through the loam. I ached all over. Every bone was a bruise. Everything I touched and everything around me was cold and wet. I watched an ant crawl over the back of my hand, clambering over each hair as though it were a hillock. It was a bright June morning. The sun was shining, making the dew glisten. I stood slowly, painfully, and looked around. I recognised where I was. Somewhere between Harbut Clough and Shackleton Knoll. Not far from the prominent stoop where you first kissed me on the lips. Lips so soft. Kisses so sweet. The lark and the linnet sang to us.

I walked along a faint path, past Lumb Falls, towards Abel Cross. My head was pounding and my mouth was parched. My eyes stung and my legs throbbed. I was shivering. I picked up pace. Got to gather heat. I walked past a cluster of farmhouses and stone outbuildings. By a mistal I could hear the milch cows lowing inside. Maybe they would let me have some barley bread and buttermilk. No, got to keep on going. I contoured over the hillside, Crimsworth Dean in the distance. The forest beneath, a verdant roof of leaves. I could see at the top of the woods the outline of Slurry Rock jutting out like a boar's fang. I walked along the grassy bank of the beck until it sloped gently down to the water. I stooped to drink where the flow was strong. I let the cold of the water flurry in the cup of my hands, then supped greedily. My mouth and throat unclagged as the cool liquid slooshed.

I could live out here, a wild man in a cave. I didn't need anyone else, want anyone else, have anyone else. I could catch rabbits with snares I'd make myself and cook them on the fire. I could make a rod out of willow and fish for trout and pike. I could make a bed out of fresh heather and, like the titmouse, I'd gather the soft heads of cotton grass to line my nest. Fuck people, I didn't need them. People only brought you pain. Better to stay away from people. At least until I had a plan.

I thought about you with the Lintons that day, when they came to visit. I vowed to get you all or die attempting it. Supping mulled ale from silver mugs. I was a stain on their polished tray. I was the muck on their well-scrubbed floor. Leave them to it. I had turned my back on them and gone inside to feed the beasts. Fuck 'em. Fuck the rotten lot. Spoke to no one except the dogs. And when you had all gone to church, I went onto the moor. Fasted and thought. I had to turn things around. I had to get you back.

I came in through the kitchen door, went to Nelly and said, 'Make me decent.' I was younger than Edgar but taller and twice as broad. I could knock him down in a twinkle.

I wanted light hair and fair skin. Nelly washed and combed my curls. Then she washed me again. But she couldn't wash the black off my face. Then I saw you all, descending from a fancy carriage, smothered in furs. Faces white as wealth. I'll show the cunts, just as good as them, and I opened the door to where you and they were sitting. But Hindley pushed me back and said, 'Keep him in the garret. He'll only steal the fruit.' How ashamed I'd felt that day. How cold and lonely I'd been in that garret with just the buzzing of the flies for company.

I stopped by a ditch and picked some crowfoot. I looked at the white petals and the yellow centres. Some call it ram's wort; it is said to cure a broken heart. How pretty it looked with its lobed leaves, and how desolate. I crushed it up and threw it on the ground. I had no use for pretty things. Bring me all that is ugly and I will serve them all my days, the henchman to all that is loathsome. I laughed at my own grandiosity. What was I? Even less than the muck on my boots. Which weren't even my boots, but Hindley's hand-me-downs. How he'd gloated over that. Another detail he could use to show the world that I was beneath him. Almost everything I owned had once been his property. I had nothing that I could call mine. Not my breeches nor my surtout, not even the shirt on my back. I walked a little further through grass and moss and rested by a rowan tree. It is said that witches have no power where there is a rowan tree wood. Do you hear me, Cathy?

My mind snapped back to that day. That cunt Edgar had started, saying my hair was like the hair of a horse. I'd grabbed a bowl of hot sauce and flung it right at him. Edgar had screamed like a girl and covered his face with his hands. Hindley grabbed hold of me, dragging me outside. He punched me in the gut. When I didn't react, he went for the iron weight and smashed it over my back. Go down. Kicking me in the ribs. In the face. Stomping on my head. Then he got the horse whip and flogged me till I passed out.

I gripped the root of the rowan to help me to my feet. I needed something to eat to stop the pain in my gut. I saw some chickweed growing by a cairn and clutched at the most tender stems. It tasted of nothing. I found some dandelions further on and chewed on the leaves. They were a bitter breakfast. I carried on walking. Something of the plants must have nourished me because as I walked I could feel some of my strength restored. The sun was getting bigger and higher in the sky and my wet clothes began to steam.

Cold stone slabs. When I had woken the next day from Hindley's flogging, Cathy, I discovered that he'd locked me in the shed. I was aching all over, bruises everywhere, caked in dried blood. It wasn't the first time he'd beaten me senseless, nor was it the first time he'd shoved me in the shed. I could cope with the beatings, and the cold stone flags for a cushion, but the humiliation still stung like a fresh wound. A razor's edge had a kinder bite. I could hear you and them in the house. There was a band playing, trumpets and horns, clatter and bang. I could hear you and them chatting and laughing as I lay in the dark, bruised and battered, my whole body a dull ache and a sharp pain. I swallowed and tasted the metal of my own blood. How to get the cunt? I didn't care how long it took. I didn't care how long I had to wait. Just so as he didn't die before I did. And if I burned in hell for all eternity it would be worth it. At least the flames would keep me warm and the screams would keep me company. Kicking the cunt was not enough. He must suffer in every bone of his body and in his mind too. His every thought must be a separate torture. He must have no peace, waking or asleep. His whole life, every minute of every hour of every day, must be torture. Nothing less would do.

I'd been walking for a good hour and my clothes were almost dry. I'd walked off the stiffness and the pains all over my body were abating. But not the pain in my head. That was growing. I walked through Midgehole and along the coach road to Hebden. I'd walked it before, once with my father and several times with Joseph. With horse and cart. I was hungry again and thirsty. The chickweed and dandelion breakfast not enough to sustain me for long. I hadn't eaten a proper meal since yesterday morning, and only then a heel of stale bread with a bit of dripping. Along the roadside was a row of cottages. Sparrows flitted from the ivy to the hedges. A cat sat and watched. The world was waking up. I saw a man load up his horse and cart with woven cloth and earthen pots. It was market day then. Rich pickings for some. Perhaps there would be opportunity to work for some food or like the vagabond you all think I am, I might find a way to steal some victuals.

By the time I got into town, the market was already open. Merchants stood by their stalls. Some of them shouted their wares. Others made a show of their articles. There were 'pothecaries selling cure-alls, potions for this, creams for that. There were herb sellers. Grocers standing by stalls piled high with fruits and vegetables. Some sold meats: hunks of hams, racks of rumps. Others sold cheeses: wheels and wedges, finished with mustard seeds and toasted hops. Baskets, breeches, a brace of grouse. Hats, shawls, second-hand wigs, a heap of dead rabbits. Cordials and syrups, jams and sauces. Woollens from the hill weavers. Pewter dishes, earthen plates, porridge pots and thibles. I could smell lavender, thyme and burdock, and other sharp smells I couldn't discern. The stallholders shouted over each other, so that you couldn't make out what they were saying, just the bark and screech of their voices. Did I want this? Did I want that? A quart for a quarter. Four for a penny. Half for ha'penny. I didn't want much. A lump of cheese or a slice of beef would do me. I wandered around, waiting for my opportunity, but there were too many eyes about.

I bade my time before I found a way to swipe an apple. I tucked it under my coat and walked off, waiting until I was around the corner before I took a bite of the sweet flesh. The apple was wrinkled by winter but to me it tasted delicious. As I took bite after bite of the fruit, I wondered if my revenge would taste as sweet as that ripe pulp. I watched children laiking. They ran after a ball around the town square, playing catch, then piggy-in-the-middle. A small child squealed as the older taunted him. I remembered playing piggy-in-the-middle with you and Hindley. He'd always throw the ball too high for me to catch, even if I jumped. But you would throw it low on purpose and pretend it was a bad throw. From those outward actions, our inner feelings grew.

I thought back to the day his slut gave birth to a son. She was ill, crying out in pain, and it was such joy to watch Hindley suffer. That week, as she lay dying, the cunt was in agony. How I laughed behind Hindley's back. Thank you,

God, I said under my breath, or thank you, devil. I'd prayed to both, not knowing which would hear me first. All my prayers were answered. I knew what Hindley loved the most and it was his slut. I knew what would hurt the cunt the most – the slow, painful death of his slut.

The doctor's medicine was useless. My spell was stronger. I learned from your witchery and from your arcane power. My anti-medicine had worked. I watched her cough and splutter. I watched her chuck up blood. I watched the life drain from her face. I watched the wretched slut die in front of the cunt. I went to the funeral so I could observe his agony some more. How I'd wanted to laugh when they'd lowered the coffin into the ground and tears had rolled down his cheeks. Each tear was a sugared treat. And afterwards in the church hall, he was inconsolable. The curate had patted him on the back, said he was sorry for his loss, and offered him some brandy. But Hindley was unreachable in his grief. Only I knew how to reach him. Later that night I'd put my ear to his chamber door and listened to him sob as though it were sweet music.

Hareton was the bairn. The fruit of Hindley and the slut's union. You were fifteen, all curves and skin. I taunted Hindley so that he beat me. Called his bairn a witless moon-calf. And I laughed when he fired and lost his temper. So that his beating brought no satisfaction. Fuck the lot of them: Isabella, Edgar, Hareton, Hindley. I'll make them pay. I'll make them all suffer. I'll make a purse from their skin. They called me vulgar, called me brute. But they had no inkling of the depths of my brutality. I spoke through gritted teeth: mock me now, but one day I will sup from your silver cup. And it won't be ale I'll sup, but a broth of your tears and blood.

I stopped a way from the market and watched women haggle with the stallholders. I gnawed the apple to its core, crunched the pips between my teeth, and slung it over a hedge. Truth was, I didn't have any idea what to do next. I had no friends, no food, no money, no home. All I could trade was my labour. I didn't want to work here in Hebden, too close to you and them. Even if I didn't see you, or Joseph or anyone else, word would get back. I needed to go further, to a new parish. A place called Manchester, halfway between home and Liverpool, where Mr Earnshaw had brought me from. We'd discussed it together after Sunday service one time. There was lots of work by. Big mills being built and new machines invented. We'd talked about how we could run away, find work and make a fresh start, free from Hindley's tyranny.

I went back to the marketplace. More people were milling about now and it was easier this time to steal another apple and a chunk of bread. I stole a wheel of cheese and a meat pie, put them in my pockets. I climbed to the hill above the town. The sun was still in the east and I needed to walk west as that was the direction of Manchester. I just needed to keep the sun behind me until noon, then keep the sun in front of me till dusk. I could see Lumbutts Farm in the distance. I made my way across moor, through Bird Bank Wood and Old Royd. And eventually into the village of Todmorden. The road followed the river, where the houses were built into the steep clough, which climbed high on both sides. The effect of this was to make the way ahead darker than the way back. Parts of the clough were quarried and there were heaps of stones waiting to be faced at the mouths of the delves. I needed money and lodgings. I was far enough away now from Wuthering Heights. Although I'd walked here by myself before, when you were laid up at the Lintons', I knew that it was far enough away from Wuthering Heights that I'd not be spotted here. Joseph said the men who lived hereabouts had hairs on their foreheads and the women had webbed feet, but I suspected that was just idle laiking. I could ask for work. Summer. Plenty of farm labour. It was midday when I arrived in the village. I sat down by the green. I ate the pie. First the crust, then the filling. I wandered around until I found a tavern on the corner of a cobbled street. There was a sign outside that I could not read, but the painting on the sign was of a jolly fellow in a bright smock, and the place looked friendly enough. After some deliberation, I plucked up the guts to go inside.

It was dark and smelled of stale beer, colder inside than out. There was a fireplace but no fire, it being the wrong time of year for flames. I marked the stone floor and the low wood beams, the wooden benches and seats. A few farmers were standing around a horn and rope, playing ring-the-bull. A group of labourers were leaning on the bar. I asked them to excuse me as I made my way to the barrels. They were in no rush to move but shuffled out of the way nevertheless.

'What can I get you?' said the landlord. A large, ruddy-faced man with ginger whiskers. He was standing by a massive barrel of ale, laid on its side, with a tap at one end. I had no money.

'I'm looking for work.'

'You what?'

'I want a job.'

'Round here?'

'Or hereabouts. I'm a hard worker. I don't shirk. I can do any amount of farm work: digging and stone-breaking, wall-building, graving, tending foul. Whatever there is I can turn my hand to it. Do you have work yourself? Cellar work, maybe? I can lift barrels all day.'

'No. No work here, pal.'

'Would you mind if I asked your customers?'

'What do you think this is? Either buy some ale or fuck off.'

I looked around the room. At the hostile faces, white faces. White faces looking me up and down. I didn't fit, wasn't welcome. I looked at the labourers and saw the muck on their knuckles like ash keys. I looked at the farmers and saw the mud on their boots. Yes, there was work hereabouts, but not for me, Cathy. Turn around. Get out.

I wandered around the village. Not much to see. There were signs of life all right. But no life for me. I made my way to the river. If I followed its flow, it would take me in the right direction. There was a faint path by its banks, more of a rabbit run, or a badger track. I carried on walking, at the edge of what I knew. I'd never been further than this point. Not since I was a small boy, in any case, when I was taken from one place to another, then to somewhere else to be abandoned at the dockside. My memory of my early life was like a landscape shrouded in a thick mist. I remembered streets near water. I remembered rowing boats and ships with massive sails. I remembered a warm room full of strong smells and harsh sounds, a strange man with a knife, beckoning me. He was smiling at me but something about him was unsettling. He smelled of grease and sweat and his teeth were black. There were many shiny surfaces but everything else was a blur. I didn't even have a clear memory of Mr Earnshaw. The first thing I remember clearly is you, Cathy. I remember our first meeting, and our friendship growing stronger each day. Until it grew beyond friendship into something else. I remember the first time we fucked, and after, lay in each other's arms, looking up at the sky, watching the clouds form into faces. Counting crows. Joseph was out, loading lime past Penistone Crags. Hindley was on business. When we got back home, I marked the occasion in the almanac on the wall. A cross for every night you spent at the Lintons'. A dot for those times spent with me on the moor. I showed you the almanac. You said that you found me dull company. You said I knew nothing and said nothing. You said I stank of the stable. Then Edgar turned up, dressed in a fancy waistcoat and a high-topped beaver hat. I left you to your pretty boy.

As I followed the beck west, I dreamed as dark as the brackish waters. I wanted to kill them all, but like a cat with a bird, leave them half-killed, so I could come back later, again and again, to torment them. You as well, Cathy. You were not exempt from my plans. The sun was directly above me now and I could feel its heat. I took off my coat and bent down low so that I could cup some water from the beck. I saw my black reflection staring back. I took a drink. It cooled me. I sat by the bank and brooded. I watched water boatmen and pond skaters dance across the surface of the beck where it gathered and pooled. I watched beetles dive for food and gudgeon gulp. Blue titmouse and great titmouse flittered in the branches above. I watched a shrike impale a shrew on the lance of a thorn. I didn't know how long it would take me to get to Manchester. Another day or two, perhaps. Surely there would be work there for a blackamoor. I'd heard we were more common in those parts. I stripped off and dived into the beck, washing all the filth from my body. The water was cool at first but as I swam, it soon warmed around me. My flesh tingled and my skin tightened. I splashed water on my face and rubbed at the mud in my hair. I lay back, let the water take my weight, and looked up at the sky. I floated like that, staring up at the white whirl of clouds, with no thought in my head. The clouds drifted, gulls flew by. I closed my eyes and tried to keep my mind as clear as the sky, pushing out all thoughts.

Across the blank blue of my mind I heard a voice: There's money to be made in Manchester town. And I remembered Mr Earnshaw say that a man from humble stock could make a pretty penny in the mills and down the mines. And I heard your voice, Cathy. That it would degrade you to marry a man as low as me. Oh, I'd get money all right. I'd show you. I'd shame you. Words that burned. Words as sharp as swords. Words you could only say behind my back. I'd shove those ugly words down your lovely throat.

I swam to the bank and climbed out. I sat by the edge of the water and watched toad-polls flit by the duckweed and butterflies flap by Rock Rose. A butterfly and a frog. They both had two lives. Why couldn't I have two lives? Like that toad-poll at the edge of the beck, already sprouting legs, about to break through the film of one world into another, I was on the cusp of the life that had been and the life that could be. I could rise from the depths. I could crawl into the light.

I lay naked as a newborn and listened to rooks croak and whaaps shriek. I let the sun and the breeze dry my skin, then I got dressed. I stuck my hands deep in my pockets, retrieved the rest of the pilfered vittles, just crusts and crumbs, and scoffed the lot. I lay back on the cool grass to rest for a minute or two. I watched twite and snipe, grouse and goose. I didn't want to think about you or them but it seemed that my mind was set on its course. I couldn't stop it thinking about them and you. What they had done. What they had not done. What you had done. What you had not done. It would degrade you. I would degrade you.

I watched the peewit flap their ragged wings and listened to their constant complaining, tumbling so low as to almost bash their heads on the bare earth. Perhaps they had young nearby and were warning me away.

Out here, surrounded by heather and gorse, with the blue sky above me, I felt free. I closed my eyes and felt the sun's rays on my face. The sun felt like you. Like your heat next to my skin. Like your breath on my neck.

When I woke the sun was further on. I felt dozy. Must keep going. I got up and shook the grass from my clothes. I plucked cleavers from my breeches. I stretched my limbs and joined the path by the river once more. I walked through fields of sheep, fields of wheat, fields of beef. Fields of milk, mutton and mare. Over meadow, mire and moor. I climbed over dry-stone walls. And clambered through forest. Eventually I approached another village. I arrived at a packhorse track and walked along it. I passed cottages and barns. Mistals and middens. There was a sign on the road but I couldn't read it. Although I knew the alphabet, you never completed your tutelage. There was always something in the way with language. We had a more direct connection, Cathy. A pure link. That's what you said, and I believed you.

It was a small village with two taverns, a butcher's, a baker's and a chapel. All clustered around a green where a tethered goat grazed. I went into the first pub and asked for work. I went into the second pub and asked for work, and in every shop. Everywhere I enquired the answer was the same: no work for the likes of you. My limbs ached. My eyes felt as though they were full of sand. I sat on a bench in the graveyard. I was tired and it would be dusk soon. No roof to offer me shelter. I sat and watched two old women tend to a grave. They pulled out weeds and arranged some flowers. They scraped away the lichen from the engraving so that the chiselled letters were fresh once more. They nattered and gabbed. So-and-so has his eye on so-and-so. Will he do right by her or will he use her as his plaything? Looks Spanish. When's summer going to start proper? Who was that strange fella in church last Sunday? Not seen him before. Not from these parts. Old Mr Hargreaves is dead. Finest weaver in the county. Found him in his own bed. Half-undressed. On and on they nattered, about this and that. By these women was an open grave.

The women noticed that I was watching them. They looked at me suspiciously. They pointed and whispered. But I didn't care. Let them talk. Let them think and say what they liked. They meant nothing to me. There was no one alive who meant anything to me now. Not even you, Cathy. I was nothing, and no one. I focused instead on the black rectangle to the side of the women. Its blackness falling down into the ground. Where did it go, this blackness? To hell? Perhaps I should climb into this hole. I thought back to Joseph's fire-and-brimstone catechisms. Was hell really all as bad as he would have it? With sinners in perpetual torment? You showed me a picture in a book, Cathy. A man with horns and a pitchfork and a big grin on his pointy face. He looked more comical than evil. Evil hides behind the door. It lurks in the shadows. As I thought about hell and evil, I saw people congregate. There were men and women gathering around the black rectangle. There were four men carrying a coffin on their shoulders. They were dressed in black and the men and women surrounding the hole were dressed in black. A veiled woman was crying. I could see her face shake beneath the veil and tears fall onto her dress. It was good to watch her cry and watch the rest of them grieve. Let her weep in her widow's weeds. It was music and food to me.

I thought about her wedding to this corpse who had once been a man. Perhaps in this very church. Everyone done up again, only this time in white and brightly coloured garments, the lavish pretence, the gilded facade. Pretending to marry for love, when really it was for wealth and status. Love didn't need a marriage chain or a poncey parade. Love baulks at ceremony and licence. They talk about tying the knot but love unties binds. It lets the bird out of the cage. The bird that is freed flies highest. The cage is best remembered enveloped in flames.

You told me you would never get married. That we would always be together. You promised. How easily your words betray you. Marriage is for dull people, we both agreed.

And people are dull, except for when they grieve. I watched the priest and the party of mourners, watched the mound of earth at the back writhing with worms, starlings stabbing at the flesh. I watched the men drop the coffin, using ropes to lower it slowly into blackness. More people weeping. Some of them beyond tears. I supped on their misery. Every death is a good death. All flesh is dead meat. I had cried when Mr Earnshaw passed away, but now I wished I hadn't. I was glad I'd listened to his last breath. Seen him choke. Will he go to hell or to the other place? I hoped he would burn and his blood would boil in the red flames of the inferno. I cursed cures and blessed agues. At last the wooden box was lowered into the ground completely and the ropes thrown in after it. Swallowed up by blackness. How long would the fine oak casket last until the wood splintered and decayed, and all the slimy things ate beneath the grave?

When all of the party had gone back the way they came, with heads bowed and handkerchiefs on display, I stood up and approached the open grave. I stood over the black hole and peered in. The coffin was surrounded by clay, with black soil on top of the box, which the pastor had chucked in. I imagined, in the place of the coffin, you and I, Cathy, lying next to each other. With six feet of earth above our heads. For all eternity. That way you would keep your promise.

I left the churchyard and wandered around the village and the looming moorland until it was fully dark. I was looking for shelter. I came across a farm surrounded by outbuildings. I found an unlocked barn, lifted the latch and swung open the door. Inside there were pigs, nudging and jostling each other. They smelled of their own shit. In the corner, by the swine, was some loose straw. It wasn't exactly a four-poster bed but I could make my rest out of that, I thought.

I left the barn and wandered some more, not tired enough to lie down on God's cold earth. I walked down a tree-lined track, back into the village. As I did, I heard music in the distance, a cheerful jig, and, drawn to the noise as a moth is to a lantern, I tried to find its source. I wandered along cobbled roads and muck tracks until I came to a village hall. It was a large barn, painted white, with light pouring from its windows. The music was coming from inside. I walked around the back. There was a small leaded window and I peered in. There were lines of lanterns and a huge fireplace with a roaring fire. There was a long table laid with food and drink. There were people lined up dancing: men and women of all ages. The women wore colourful frocks and bonnets. The men wore smart breeches, bright waistcoats and fancy hats. The hall was decorated with brightly coloured ribbons. There was a fiddle player in a cocked hat, playing a frenetic tune. I watched the group dance and sing and sup flagons of ale. I watched them smile and laugh and talk excitedly. The men held their women in their arms and drew them close to their bodies. I felt sick at the sight of them.

Then I saw a black, repulsive face staring back at me. Half-man, half-monster, just as Hindley said. My reflection in the glass pane. A black shadow of a man with not a friend in the world nor a bed to rest, barred from life's feast. I wanted the night sky to swallow me up, to be dust. I could never be one of those people in there. My life would never be one of mead and merriment. Condemned to stand outside the party. Not like you, Cathy, with your fancy frocks and fancier friends. With your ribbons and curls and perfumes. I wandered back to the farm, crept into the animal barn, and lay down on the straw with the swine.

Flesh for the Devil

That night I dreamed we were on the moor; the heather was blooming, and you were teaching me the names of all the plants of the land: dog rose, gout weed, earth nut, fool's parsley, goat's beard, ox-tongue, snake weed. Your words were like a spell. I watched your lips form the sounds. I saw your tongue flit between your perfect teeth. Witches' butter, bark rag, butcher's broom, creeping Jenny, mandrake. We looked around at the open moorland, but it had all been hedged and fenced and walled. There were men, hundreds of them, burning the heather, digging ditches, breaking rocks. There were puritans, Baptists, Quakers, inventors, ironmasters, instrument-makers. Our place had been defiled. The flowers of the moor had been trampled on. The newborn leverets butchered. The mottled infant chicks of the peewit had been crushed underfoot. Guts in the mud. You were in the middle of the mob, a heckling throng, staring around. I held my hand out but I couldn't reach you. You were lost to me.

The next thing I was aware of was someone taking me by the shoulders.

'What the bloody hell do you think you're doing?'

I was in the barn with the swine, and a lump of a man with a bald head was shaking me roughly. He wore big black boots and a leather jerkin. He looked more like an ogre than a man. It was morning and light from the open barn door poured in.

'I'm sorry, sir.'

I was too weak from sleep to fight the brute.

'What do you think this is, a doss-house?'

'I had nowhere to stay,' I said.

'That's no excuse.'

'I was tired,' I said.

'Get up and get out. This isn't a hostel for gypsies.'

'I'm no kettle-mender.'

'What's your name?'

I thought for a moment; I wracked my brains.

'Come on then, lad, speak up. Have the hogs gobbled your tongue?'

I remembered that young boy at chapel, Cathy, you were friendly with him. Died of consumption a few years since. I always liked his name. It was good and whole and clean.

'My name, sir, is William Lee.'

I'd stolen the name of a dead child. A boy we laiked with before and after sermon.

'Well then, William, Will, Billy, that doesn't sound gypsy to me, I give you that. What kind of work can you do?'

'I can dig, build walls, tend fowl, tend swine. Any work you have.'

'Are you of this parish?'

'I'm an offcumden, sir, from the next parish.'

'I do need hands, as it happens.'

'What for?'

'I've a wall that needs building. And stone that needs break-ing. A bloke did a flit after a drunken brawl a few nights back. I'm a man down.'

'I'm that man, sir. I'm a grafter.'

'Sure you're not a pikey?'

'I'm sure.'

'I don't employ gyppos.'

He took me over three fields, two of meadow, one of pasture, to where there was a birch wood and a small quarry. As we stood by the delph I realised, in fact, that he wasn't as large as I'd at first thought. Though still heavyset and big of bone, he was not the giant my waking eyes had taken him for.

'This is where you get the stone. There's a barrow there. Don't over-fill it, mind. I don't want it splitting.'

He showed me where it had been parked for the night. Next to the barrow were several picks and wedges, as well as hammer and chisel. Then he walked me across to another field where a wall was partly constructed.

'And this is the wall. In another hour or so there will be some men to join you. Some men to break stone and others to build. The one they call Sticks will tell you what to do.'

'Thank you, sir.'

'The name's Dan Taylor. I own this farm.'

With that the farmer walked back down to the farm buildings and I sat on a rock. I amused myself by pulling grass stalks from their skins and sucking on the ends. I gathered a fist of stones and aimed them at the barrow. I watched the tender trunks of the birch wrapped in white paper. A web of dark branches. The leaves and the catkins rustled in the breeze. I waited an hour or two before the first of the men arrived. He was skinny as a beanpole and his hair was dark. He had a bald patch to the side just above his ear, in the shape of a heart. His beard grew sparsely around his chops. He told me the farmer had spoken to him about me.

'Well, William Lee, you do as you're told and we'll get along fine, laa. The name's John Stanley. Everyone calls me Sticks.'

He unfurled his arms the way a heron stretches out its wings and offered me his willowy hand to shake.

We broke stone for a time before two more men appeared and joined us. When we were joined by another two men, Sticks put his pick down.

'Right, men, we're all here and there's lots to do. Looks like the weather will hold out despite the clouds.'

He pointed up. There were patches of blue but mostly the sky consisted of clouds the colour of a throstle's egg. Not storm clouds though.

'Good graftin' weather,' one of the men said.

'This is William Lee. He'll be working with us today. Me, William and Jethro will work here to begin. Jed, you barrow, and you two start walling. We'll swap after a time. Come 'ed.'

We set to work again.

'You from round here then, laa?' Sticks said as he loaded up a barrow with freshly broken stones.

'The next parish. About thirty miles east.'

'So what brings you to this parish then?'

'I'm just drifting. No particular reason.'

'People don't just drift. They always have a purpose. You're either travelling to somewhere or running away from someone. Which is it?'

'Neither.'

'Suit yourself. Give me a hand with this.'

I helped him lift a large coping stone.

'Had a southerner here last week. From Sheffield. Think he found us a bit uncouth. Only lasted two days. Could hardly tell a word he said, his accent was that strong.'

'You don't sound like you're from round these parts your-self,' I said.

He had a strange accent and not a bit like a Calder one. He had a fast way of talking and a range of rising and falling tones that gave his speech a distinctive sound.

'You travel around and you take your chances. I've done it myself. Got turned out of one village one time. The villagers threw stones at me and called me a foreigner. It's getting harder and harder for the working man to make a living.'

'Why's that then?'

'Because a bunch of aristocrats are stealing the land beneath our feet. They'll turn us all into cottars and squatters. Before you know it there won't be any working men, just beggars and vagrants, thieves and highwaymen, prostitutes and parasites. Mark my words, laa.'

'Is that so?'

'The days of farm work is coming to an end. They've got Jennies now across the land that can spin eighty times what a woman can spin on her tod. A lot of the labourers hereabouts have gone off over to Manchester, doing mill work, building canals. I've done canal work myself, built up the banks, worked on the puddling. Dug out the foundations. It's back-breaking work, I'll tell you that. It's said that on the duke's canal the boats can travel up to ten miles an hour. And not a highwayman to be seen. Done dock work as well, in Liverpool. That's where I'm from, you see, laa.'

I liked the way he pronounced 'Liverpool', lumping it up and dragging it out.

I thought about where I had come from. All that I knew was that Mr Earnshaw found me on the streets of that same town. Perhaps I would go back there. Seek out my fortune in that place instead. I wasn't fixed. No roots bound me to the spot. Where there was money to be made that's where I was heading. Enough money to get you and Hindley. If I were to make the journey, I could use Sticks's know-how.

'I'm heading that way myself,' I said.

'Be careful how you go, laa. It's not safe to walk the roads. A man's liable to be picked up by a press gang or else kidnapped and sent to the plantations. They're building big mills over in Manchester. But you won't get me going there. Worse than the workhouse. Have you heard of the men of Tyre?'

'No.'

'Pit men. They cut the winding ropes, smashed the engines and set fire to the coal.'

'Why?'

'To protest against their working conditions. It's not natural to never see the sun. A pit is hell on earth. A mill is not much better. Folk call it progress. But there's trouble brewing, mark my words.'

'So what brings you here then? Why did you leave Liverpool?'

'Oh, I travelled about. Done this and that. You know how it goes.'

We worked on all morning with Sticks chelping in my

ear. At lunchtime the farmer brought bread and ale. I asked for water.

'What's wrong with ale, lad?'

I had no intention of turning into a Hindley.

'Nothing, sir, I just prefer God's water.'

'Well, there's a stream up yonder you can drink from. Or there's the well in the yard.'

After we'd eaten we swapped around. Me and Sticks set to work on the wall. Behind us was a birch wood and down the valley the farm and the outbuildings. We could see the thatched roofs from where we grafted. I shifted the stones into different sizes, heaping them into sets, saving the large uneven stones for the coping. I enjoyed the work even though it was slow going, like piecing together a puzzle. Each stone had to be carefully selected so that it sat just right with its mates. We started with the largest, heaviest stones, for the foundation of the wall, working up so that it got slimmer as we built. Every now and again we would strengthen it with through stones that hitched the two sides. We chose the flat side of the stones to face the wall, filling in the gap between the two sides with the odd-shaped smaller stones left behind, then the large, boulder-like ones as coping to top the wall and make it solid. The sun was up and the larks were singing way above our heads. So high in the sky I couldn't actually see them. I saw a puttock being attacked by two crows and later the same crows attacked a glead that was twice their size. It's just one battle after another, I thought. Even in these placid skies.

'Had a problem with rats last week. The barn was overrun with them. Had to get the rat-catcher in with his dogs. Took him the best part of the day to flush them out and even then he didn't get them all,' said Sticks as he looked to place the stone in his hand.

'Well, where there's hens there's rats,' I said.

'You're right there.'

'And where there's swine there's rats.'

'True enough. Where there's folks there's rats,' he said and laughed. 'Seems, sometimes, folks and rats are the same thing.'

We worked on in silence for a time, selecting the right stones, placing them, then finding a better stone for the job and starting again. For every three we laid we'd have to go back a stone. After we had built about half a yard, Sticks stopped working and took out his clay pipe. He sat on one of the stones and stuffed the bowl of the pipe with tobacco. He snapped off the end of the pipe and took out a striker and a brimstone match. He held the striker to the match until the sparks caught. Then he held the lighted match to the bowl. He puffed out smoke and smiled at his success.

'What's your vice then?'

'Eh?'

'Do you play cards at all?'

'Sometimes.'

'We usually have a game after supper. Ace of hearts, faro, basset, hazard. What's your preference?'

On rainy days I'd played hazard with you plenty of times, Cathy. When the storms outside raged even too ferociously for our tastes. But the other games I'd never heard of.

'I'll probably sit this one out,' I said.

'No head for gambling, eh?'

'Need to earn some money first.'

'There's a tavern up the road. There's skittles and ring-the-bull every night if that's more your tipple.'

'I'm not much of a player.'

'There's a cockfight at least once a week, sometimes a fistfight. If you've no taste for blood there's always dancing.'

'I'm not much of a dancer.'

'Suit yourself. But if you work hard you've got to play hard. The one goes with the other,' he said.

He finished his pipe and put it in his pocket. We worked on all through the afternoon. By the end of the day we'd built up two yards of wall. We cleaned our tools with rags and stored them safe for the evening, then we traipsed down the hill for supper. Sarah, the farmer's wife, served up oatmeal, bacon and potatoes. She was such a wee thing that I couldn't help but picture her union with Dan Taylor and wince at the prospect. Like an ox on top of a stoat. The farmer rolled out a barrel of beer. He untapped it and poured the beer into large flagons. He handed them around.

'Not for me, thanks.'

'That's half your wages.'

'I don't drink beer more than I need to slake my thirst.'

'Ah, spirits more your choice?'

'I don't drink spirits.'

'I'll have his portion,' Jethro said, a short, stocky man with red hair.

'Well, don't think I'll be paying you otherwise,' the farmer said.

'Leave him be,' said his wife. 'Can I get you anything else?'

'Water if you've got it, please.'

'There's buttermilk?'

She fetched me an earthen pot of buttermilk.

The farmer seemed pleased with my work and said that

he would take me on. For all my labour I was to be paid five shillings a week and a gallon of beer a day. I would drink what I needed to slake my thirst and sell the rest to the other labourers at thruppence a pint. If I could sell four pints a day, that would be another shilling, doubling my wage to ten shilling a week.

After I'd eaten I took a walk roundabouts. The farm consisted of a barn, a parlour, a dairy, peat-house, stables and mistal. There was also a chicken coop away from the buildings, with a fenced-in run where the birds could scrat. A dozen hens and a handsome cock. The window of the dairy had the word 'Dairy' carved into its lintel. I'd seen this before when we'd been out walking one time, Cathy. I remember you telling me that this was to ensure it would not be liable for the window tax. Another way the rich robbed from the poor.

I walked up the lane. A mile from the farmhouse, there was a short turn by a clump of sycamore. The lane was narrow and next to this a church. It was a small, steep-roofed, stone building, with a few arched windows in a stone tower, rising scarcely above the sycamore tops, with an iron staff and vane on one corner. There was a small graveyard, enclosed by a hedge, and in the corner of this, but with three doors opening in front upon the lane, was a long crooked old cottage. On one of the stone thresholds, a peevish-looking woman was lounging, and before her, lying on the ground in the middle of the land, were two girls playing with a kitten. They stopped as I came near and rolled out of the way, while I passed by them. One of the girls laughed, and the other whispered and pointed. The woman said something in a sharp voice. I wondered what she'd said and who she was. I felt that in some way I was being judged. Though they seemed far from a position of authority.

34

I wandered around the other side of the farm. Past the farmyard was another huge barn, a wagon-shed, the farmhouse, and the piggeries I'd ligged in the previous night. Close to was a mountain of manure that steamed and festered. The farmyard was divided by a wall, and milch cows were accommodated in the separate divisions. It was quite a place the farmer and his wife had. I wondered how he'd come by it. By hard graft or by cunning theft? Or by being born into it? Which is another kind of theft.

I made my way back to the outbuilding where the men were at their leisure.

Sticks asked me where I'd been. I told him about my perambulations and of the sharp-tongued woman.

'That's the wife of the farmer's son,' he said in hushed tones. 'Be careful how you tread with the pair of them. She goes by the name of Mary and he goes by the name of Dick. I don't know which is worse. I saw her crack a man's skull open with a hemp-wheel last summer. He's tapped different. He doesn't lose it like she does. If he clobbered you over the head he wouldn't raise his voice, or change his expression. There would be no sign of anger at all. Got to watch those ones, laa. The farmer's no soft touch either. He'll have you up at four o'clock in the morning and he'll work you till dusk. You'll earn every shilling, I'll tell you that much. I've done all sorts in my time. At six years old I were a bird-scarer. I've been a gardener, land surveyor, bookkeeper for a brewery. Every type of manual labour. Doesn't matter what you do, the master's always got the upper hand.'

The farmer's wife fetched more victuals. After bread and

cheese and porter, the men brought out their pipes. One of them took a spill and lit it from the fire, lighting first his pipe, then passing it around. There was some conversation on the hardness of the times and the dearness of all the necessaries of life. There was talk of reform.

'Why bother? It'll only end up the same, either way,' Jethro said.

Sticks butted in. 'Listen, laa, why should the wealth be in the hands of so few? And why should they get to say how it goes, when we don't get a say at all? Have we, as grafters, no right to get what's fair? I'm talking about the courts of this land. They're corrupt. Have you no opinion about that, soft lad?'

'Opinions cost lives. That talk is high treason,' Jethro said.

He pointed out that the penalty for which was to be hanged by the neck, cut down while still alive and disembowelled.

Jethro pulled a fork from the fire with a faggot on the end and blew on it to cool it. 'And then, as if that's not bad enough, his entrails burned before his face. Then beheaded and quartered.' Just in case Sticks hadn't got the message, he took the faggot and bit into it.

'But apart from that, what's the punishment?' Sticks said.

There was much laughter at this.

'Look, all I'm saying is that every man should have a vote. Whether lord or labourer, jack or judge,' said Sticks. 'Give every man his own acres so that he's not beholden to any landlord. And give him a voice. Give him a say-so over his own matter, that's all I'm saying.'

There was more grumbling and protestation.

'I'm talking about universal suffrage, for heaven's sake. God made us all equal.'

'You won't get that without a civil war, I'm telling you that.' Jethro again, between bites of his faggot. 'Mark my words, there's them at the top and there's men like us, and there's no changing it.'

'We've already had a war and where did that get us? Bloody nowhere, that's where,' said another man.

'The only way you're going up in this world is swinging from the gibbet,' said yet another.

I let the sounds of their arguments drift over me. I had no interest in universal suffrage. Only in a particular form of suffering: yours and Hindley's.

They talked some more, then the cards came out and I watched the men play.

'Is that gypsy boy laikin'?' Jethro said, pointing to my corner.

'He's no gypsy,' Sticks said.

'His skin is gypsy.'

Different games of cards were played and money changed hands. Jethro was well oiled by this point, and throwing his coins around. I watched him stroke his red hair distractedly as he chucked his money about. I saw him lose his hand, once, twice, then a third time, and in so doing, lose that week's wage. I must learn to play this game, I thought. Jethro sat in his chair in the dark, smoking his pipe and supping ale. He was muttering under his breath, 'What will she say? What will she say?' Sticks, who was the winner, was smiling and laughing, dealing one more hand. Here was another man reaping where he had not sown and gathering where he had not strawed. There are more ways than one to skin a rabbit, Cathy. Ask a weasel.

'I'll tell you what,' said Sticks to Jethro, 'I'll give you a chance to get even. How does that sound?'

Jethro pretended not to hear and sat in the dark sucking his pipe, which had now gone out.

'Tomorrow even, bring that cock you were bragging about. I'll bring one of mine, and we'll have a little skirmish.'

Jethro grunted.

'Suit yourself, then.'

But despite Jethro's apathy, the next night after supper he disappeared for half an hour, returning with a cock in a willow cage. Inside was a black-and-red bird of some considerable size. A proud fowl with a penetrating gaze and a lustrous plumage. The men gathered around the cage to get a closer look. There was nodding of heads and a general air of admiration. Dan Taylor turned to Sticks.

'Well then, get your battle stag, let's see a bit of cocking.'

Sticks nodded. He stood up and shook the straw off his breeches. He walked off and returned with a cage containing a mottled brown-gold rooster, a similar size and weight to that of Jethro's. It looked like the comb and wattle of both birds had been dubbed, so there was just a lip of red on the head of the birds, and a line of red under the neck. A party of men gathered around. I was introduced to Dick, Dan's eldest son, and took an instant dislike to him. He had the same petty meanness in his eyes as Hindley. He was smaller than his father, with black hair and red skin. Where his father was broad and meaty, Dick was all bone with muscles like knots in string. The outline of his skull beneath his skin protruded. The men talked about which cock would win and bets were laid.

'My money's on Jethro.'

'Mine's on Sticks.'

'Tha's more a dunghill than a gamecock.'

Some men shuffled the bales of hay and straw so that an enclosed area was formed and the birds were released. The men jostled to get the closest. I watched the fight from some distance. The men were positioned at the furthest extremes of the makeshift arena. Before the fight the birds were slapped and their feathers ruffled to agitate them. At first the men held their birds by their back ends, lifting them up and down and towards each other. The spectators shouted encouraging words. The men approached each other so that the birds, still being held, could peck and squawk at each other to further agitate them. Then when the birds were fired up, the men let them go and they flew at each other. The feathers on the backs of the birds' necks were stiff like a turned-up collar and what was left of their combs were gorged. Their tail feathers stood proud and they held their chests out. They faced each other, their necks protruding. The black one bobbed his head and the brown one followed. I imagined these cocks as me and Hindley. With me as the black one and Hindley the brown.

Then the brown one flew up, making a piercing squawk, striking out with his spurs. The black one retaliated by jumping over his opponent. They turned to face each other again. There was a stand-off before the birds squared up once more, strutting and sticking their chests out, clucking and squawking. A flapping of wings and the birds flew up. The black one was on the back of the brown, but then the brown bird flipped over and the table was turned. More strutting, then they squawked and pecked some. They started to spar more aggressively and it was hard to follow the action. There was screeching and blood. Feathers and dust. I couldn't make out the details. The men cheered on.

I noticed Dick Taylor, standing apart from the men, not joining in or cheering, but smiling inwardly. His black eyes seemed blacker in his red face. Unlike the other men, his pleasure didn't seem to come from the game itself. His joy was derived from the suffering of others. After a time, the commotion was over but I couldn't tell who had won in the chaos and confusion. Both birds seemed to be bleeding badly. Neither was the victor. Dick was still smiling as money changed hands, the smile only a skull makes from the grave. I realised it was a different kind of battle I wanted with Hindley. Where the scars are worn on the inside. Whoever the loser and whoever the victor, their cuts would heal in time and they would be ready to fight again. But I didn't just want Hindley dubbed, I wanted to watch his very spirit crushed.

~

With the exception of the red-skinned Dick, and the politically minded Sticks, the farm labourers were a simple enough bunch of men. As long as they had work during the day, ale and bread at night, card games and somewhere to lig down, they seemed agreeable. We all slept together in the barn, with a chaumin dish burning flaights. The arrangement being not that much more than I'd found in the hog barn, but I couldn't really complain. It was dry and it was warm. We ate together in the kitchen in the morning. Cages hung from the ceiling beams with songbirds trapped inside. A blackbird, a nightingale and a throstle. An oak chest, a chest of drawers, a long table that accommodated us all around it, and chairs for us to sit on. The floor and tops were strewn with bowls and tins, jugs and mugs, syrup tins and porridge thibles. In the back kitchen the food was stored, beer brewed and oatcakes baked. The farmer's wife was helped out by Mary, the peevish wife of Dick.

I decided I would stay here for a while. The work suited me and I enjoyed the company of this Sticks character. Or at least he didn't lock me in with the beasts or take a whip to me. I kept my head down, sold my ale rations to the other men, and saved my pennies. I was biding my time until I had enough bunce to move on to Manchester town, maybe even Liverpool. I would save four pounds. That seemed a sum that would keep me from destitution and set me up wherever I found work next. I calculated that I could be back on the road again in eight weeks, if I kept clean.

We worked all week on the wall and by the Sunday it was finished. We stood back and admired our work. The wall was good and strong. No wind and no beast would break it. I looked around at the landscape all around me. Meadow, pasture and field enclosed by stone walls and beyond that moorland. Walls that reached up steep cloughs and bridged over fast-flowing becks. Walls that marked who owned what and marred the land they squatted upon.

It was the end of the first week and the farmer insisted that I accompany him to church. As you know, Cathy, I am no lover of the chapel, but it was easier to keep the peace. He loaded up a coach with the members of his family and me and Jethro and a few others followed on foot. Sticks refused to accompany us, saying that he could worship his God any place he liked. He didn't need churches. When we got to the place of worship, we were expected to walk up the church and bow to the parson. The squire and other parish notables sat in state in the centre of the aisle and erected a curtain around their peers to hide them from the vulgar gaze of the likes of me and Jethro and the other men. The minister talked of virtue and charity. But I had neither virtue or charity, just bile and contempt. God was not my friend. I sought only the company of the devil. Indeed, I had much in common with him, for had he not been cast out of heaven and was he not now wandering the earth in search of his revenge?

~

Days went by, then another week. I had saved a full pound as I'd planned to do and was a quarter to my goal. There were more walls to build and we worked steadily every day, taking it in turns, using hammer, wedge and chisel to break stones in the morning, then hand and eye to build the wall in the afternoon. The next day, we'd swap it around. It helped to break up the monotony of the job. I mostly partnered with Sticks and we grafted with me listening and him talking. His conversation ranged from the political to the personal within the same breath.

'Have you heard of the tithe awards, laa?'
'What's that?'

'A tenth of produce given to the rector of the land. One pig in ten, one egg in ten, one cow in ten. But the mill dun't have to give a tenth of their produce. What do you think about that then?'

I shrugged.

'I tell yer, it's unfair is what it is.'

'I suppose it is.'

'We've got to fight for a fairer system, laa. No one is going to make the world fairer, only us. By hard graft. You've got to fight for everything you get in this life. Even love. My first love was Mary. Fourteen years of age. I was seventeen. What a beauty. Like a painting. At the very first sight I was taken, I remember it like this morning. I had a feeling so strong for her that I forgot what I was supposed to be doing. I just wanted to be with her all day, morning, afternoon and evening. As soon as I'd finished my work I'd be there, like a dog. It was just like in the songs, when a temptress puts a spell on a man.'

Oh, I knew that feeling all right, Cathy.

The wall-building was slow but satisfying work. I liked holding the stones in my hands, turning them over. I liked their weight and hardness. Something that was solid and dependable. And it was good to stand back at the end of the day and look over what we'd achieved.

When the wall was done there was more work for me. Dan had stable work I could do and to which I was accustomed, and plough work to which I was not but soon became so. Every morning I rose before four of the clock and would go into the stable. There I would cleanse the stable, groom the horses, feed them, then prepare my tackle. I would breakfast between six of the clock and half past the clock. Then plough until three. I took half an hour for dinner, attended to the horses until I don't know what hour, when I would return for supper. After supper, for extra bunce, I would either sit by the fire to mend the shoes of the farmer's family or beat and knock hemp or flax, or grind malt on the quern, pick candle rushes, or whatever the farmer bade me do until eight of the clock. Then I would attend to the cattle. There was not much time for leisure, but the pennies were piling up and I kept a bag of them hidden in the woods in the hollowed-out trunk of an elm.

The other workers began and ended each day by thanking God, but I would do no such thing. And so this became my routine for the next few weeks. The work was hard but I grew strong and my thoughts turned again to my plan. I now had two pounds. I was halfway there. Perhaps in Manchester I could set myself up and be my own master. Every night I would wander to the hollow and count my pennies. Once I had counted them, I would pile them all carefully back into the bag and hide it in the hollow as a squirrel does an acorn. It was a disturbed night in the barn with the other labourers, as some of them snored or else talked in their sleep. When slumber did visit me I dreamed about you. Sometimes I would wake with you on top of me, but when I reached out to touch your skin you turned into air. In another dream, I came into your chamber and you were there in bed with Edgar and he was leering at me. Other times I'd dream I was with Hindley, with my hands around his throat, squeezing the life out of him, and I would wake with a jolt and the disappointment of an empty grasp.

I would lie on my back, trying to block out noxious smells

and the noisy racket, filling my head with plans of revenge. Yes, I would make my fortune in Manchester or Liverpool, but at some point in the future, I intended to return to you, an improved gentleman. I remembered the adage of the hare and the tortoise. I would take my time. I would savour my vengeance. I would linger as it lied.

With this in mind, one day I got into conversation with Sticks and asked him what I could do to improve my situation.

'You need to read and write, laa.'

'I know my alphabet,' I said.

'That's a start. But you look around you at those who can read and write and those that can't. Every labourer here is illiterate, me excepted. Do you think the squire is illiterate? Do you think the parson is? Or the doctor or the lawyer or the judge?'

'So why do you choose the life of a farm labourer if you can read and write?'

'Like I've said to you before, laa. There's them that's running to something, and them that's running away.'

'Which one are you?'

'No matter, laa, no matter. Look, you want to improve your station in life then you start with your letters and your words. Everything comes from that.'

Sticks was right: if I were to gain dominion over Hindley's mind and over his estate, and also gain your true respect and be a worthy adversary to Edgar, I would have to go beyond the rudimentary lessons you taught.

'So how would I go about it then?' I said.

'I tell you what, laa, there's a Sunday school that's been set up in the village by the Methodists there. Been going a few years now, and it's not just for bairns.'

Sure enough, when I went into the village the following Sunday I was informed that there was indeed a school for youths of both sexes, from fourteen to twenty-one years of age, and that it was in a commodious room at number four Sheppard Street. I attended one of the sessions. There were about twenty pupils sitting on the floor as there were no chairs. Most of them looked to be farm labourers. The teacher was a Methodist called George, simply dressed in black with a white silk scarf. His skin was pale and his hair was short and parted on one side. He copied out some passage from the bible in neat handwriting, using chalk and a slate, and said it was our duty to learn to read it for ourselves. He turned to us and picked up a bible. He held it aloft.

'God gave you eyes and a brain. This book is not just for priests and nobility, it is for you and your kin, and it's your duty to read the truth within.'

He called us 'children of wrath'. He chalked up the letters of the alphabet on the board and we had to join in as he sang them out. It was a joyless and repetitive experience. I tallied that the classroom was not for me. I tried to take instruction but something in my head resisted. I was familiar with the alphabet in any case and would as much be able to self-learn given a book or two and some time. I went on three or four separate occasions and was by then further on with my learning but not sufficient as I'd hoped. When George was taken up with tutoring one morning, I took hold of one of the bibles in the room and secreted it inside my surtout. I knew its stories well from Joseph's sermons, and figured this would help me to sightread. I waited for the lesson to come to an end, then walked out of the school bidding George good day and saying that I would see him the following Sunday, even though I had no intention of going to the school ever again.

So, the next Sunday, after telling the farmer and his wife that I was off to school, I walked up and onto the moor and, after some searching, I found a shallow cave where I could self-school. It was a good spot, a long way from any path, and well hidden. I spent every spare hour I had there. When the workers were playing cards and drinking ale, I would sit with my book. I brought blankets and made the space comfortable. I found a flint and steel in one of the barns, collected kindling and wood, filched a few flaights from the lower barn, and there I'd stay, with a fire to keep me warm, nicely sheltered. Once or twice I even spent the night there, waking at dawn and sneaking back into the barn while the others were still sleeping, joining the rest of the labourers without anyone the wiser. But mostly I studied. It was hard-going to begin with. I opened the book on the first page and commenced my learning. The first word was easy. I knew the sound of 'I' and 'n' and could put them together. 'The' I also knew. The third word was my first challenge, but by saying it aloud in stages, I got there. First 'beg' then 'inn' then 'ing': 'beginning'. Many hours those first few pages took me and I was glad I had no company to hear my clumsy efforts. A Hindley or a Joseph would soon have made me regret my efforts, sure enough.

It was all God said this and God said that. And God made this and God made that. I always liked the story of the Garden of Eden. And I was pleased when I got that far. The story was familiar to me but it was good to reacquaint myself with its lesson. Though it was not the orthodox one. God lied to Adam and Eve. He said that if they ate the forbidden fruit then they would die. But the fruit was not poisonous and they did not die. In any case, God had made the tree and made the fruit. Then the serpent came along and talked to Eve. But the serpent did not lie because he said that if they ate the fruit they would know good and evil and the snake was right. They did learn good and evil when they ate the fruit. God lied. The devil told the truth. When they were cast out of Eden, I thought that this was for the best. Who would want to stay in Eden under the authority of a tyrant? I was on the side of the snake. For wasn't the snake also a child of heaven?

I recalled that day when we clambered down Duke Top, through the wooded clough past Cold Knoll, resting in the heather near Lower Slack.

'What's that?' you whispered.

I didn't see it at first, so well hidden was it in the undergrowth, but as my eyes adjusted, I saw it, a viper's nest, the mother with her babies underneath her belly. They were all curled around each other for warmth. The mother bobbed her head and flicked her tongue. She saw us watching her and coiled protectively around her brood. We sat and watched, as stiff as rocks, not wanting to disturb the scene. We hardly even dared to breathe. At last we crept away, leaving them alone again. There was something majestic about that creature and we had both been bewitched by her finery.

And I read of Cain and Abel, of Cain slaying Abel, and I realised that Cain had acted in haste and could have punished his brother much worse by not killing him. In this way Abel escaped his true punishment. I was determined that Hindley would not escape his. On I read, it getting easier verse by verse and chapter by chapter. So that by the time I got to Exodus my reading was accomplished. I read all the culinary advice God offered Moses. I read the Lord's commandments and vowed to disobey them all: I would steal, I would bear false witness, I would covet my neighbour's oxen, and I would kill if I felt like it. But better to kill a man's spirit, to crush it entirely, while saving his flesh for the devil.

The Man with the Whip

One morning towards the end of August, after I had finished my work in the stable, the farmer approached with a scythe and said he needed me to do some different work.

'No time to stand there idle, lad. The hay needs cutting. I need to gather as many hands together in yonder hayfield.'

He handed me the tool. I walked up to the hayfield where a small gathering of farm workers loitered. Men and women and children. We waited for Dan's instructions, then we got to work. We grafted all day, me in shirtsleeves, swinging the scythe so that it cut the stalks, then catching up armfuls of moist, reeking grass, and tossing it out to the four winds. Each swathe of cut grass was shaken out with a fork, then turned and turned until it was as dry as a bone. From dawn till dusk, a file of servants and hirelings toiled in the field. Some of these hirelings were no older than bairns.

There was a girl working beside me, with very pale blonde hair and striking grey eyes. She couldn't have been more than ten or eleven years of age and there were no signs yet of comeliness. She was dressed in a simple white frock and her feet were bare. She was surrounded by people and yet seemed all alone in that field. Like there was an invisible wall all around her. She looked at no one and spoke to no one. She grafted but never seemed to toil. When all the hay was cut, we gathered it in stacks, ready to be carted to the top barn. At the end of the day we went down into the yard and found places to sit, while the farmer's wife served barley bread, cheese and ham, and the farmer rolled out three barrels of ale.

'Will you partake?' he asked the girl with the white-blonde hair, who was sitting on a bale of hay, eating her bread and cheese on her own.

'I will not,' she said, without looking up at the farmer.

'Please yourself,' the farmer said and went to the next worker.

This made me smile. I went over to her and sat at the end of the bale.

'Not a disciple of ale then, are we?'

'I don't mind.'

'And you've no thirst on after all that work?'

She didn't react or even look at me.

'I know where there's a stream nearabouts. And I know where there's a well.'

She grunted and stuffed a chunk of barley bread into her mouth.

'I'm William Lee,' I said.

She nodded without looking up and without offering me her name. This also made me smile. I tried to engage her in conversation but she was having none of it, and when

I'd finished my scran I got up and shuck the hay from my breeches.

'Well, nice to meet you,' I said. 'Even though you've not much to say for yourself.'

She just nodded.

Young in years but old in temper, I thought and chuckled inwardly. I took myself to my den, where I read some more from the book. I read about the righteous Job, of which I'd heard many times from Joseph. He was fond of quoting from the book and fancied himself as a bit of a Job figure. The Lord hath given and the Lord hath taken away. He called it the grandest thing ever written. But reading it for myself was a very different experience. I saw Job and God in a different light. I despised Job's piety, and God's malevolence. I saw in God a Hindley-like tyrant. God killed Job's children and he didn't even have the guts to do it himself. Instead, he got Satan to do it. At least Hindley had the balls to kick me in the face with his own boot.

~

The next day, while mowing with my scythe, I saw Dick, the farmer's son, in the field yonder. I had little to do with him, but even so, I had picked up that there was something wayward about him. Sticks had been right about that. I'd had one altercation with him a few days ago, when he had accused me of taking tobacco from his tin. When I pointed out that I didn't smoke, he had just laughed and said that I could have taken the tobacco to sell to another man.

'There's money in shag, we all know that.' I merely

shrugged. But he had squared up to me and said, 'I don't like you, William Lee. I don't like the way you carry off. Every gypsy I've ever known has been a liar and a thief.'

I stared into his black eyes but there was no life there.

I'd felt the heat of anger rise in my belly, but Sticks had been standing nearby and had signalled for me to leave it. I'd kept my mouth shut and wandered up to my den. Sticks was right. It wasn't worth losing my work or my head over. I would just add him to my list. Beneath you and Hindley.

Now here was this Dick fellow, making his way to where we were cutting hay. There was a file of us, grafting. It was late on, and although she'd kept up until now, the girl with the white-blonde hair had got behind. I saw Dick approach her.

'You need to keep up,' he said, 'no place here for stragglers,' and he pushed her.

'I'm going as fast as I can,' she said.

'Well, it isn't fast enough,' he said and pushed her harder. She fell over. Dick laughed.

She stood up and brushed herself off, then she said something to him that I couldn't make out. We'd all ceased working now and were watching this. Dick stopped laughing and his face went pale. The bones of his skull seemed to protrude more prominently. He was going to say something but seeing he had an audience, he marched off. As he walked past me, I heard him mutter under his breath, 'I'll teach her to curse.' But there was no more incident after that and we worked on throughout the afternoon.

Some of the workers sang songs to pass the time. Saucy and bawdy numbers in the main. Songs about drunken monks and tragic sisters, cruel brothers and comely shepherds' daughters. I listened to a song about a farmer who, in paying off a compact with the devil, tries to rid himself of a shrewish wife. The man offers his wife gladly. But the woman proves too much for Old Nick and he returns her to the farmer. There was another song about a young woman who gives up her true love for a wealthy landowner. She marries the landowner, who she doesn't love, and lives an unhappy life. The man she really loves goes off to make his fortune, but perishes in the wilderness. At last the girl realises she needs to be with her sweetheart and she goes off to find him. Instead she finds his corpse. I wondered when you would come to your senses, Cathy, and realise what a fool you'd been.

Although many of these songs were known to the other workers and through repetition of their verses became known to me, I did not join in. I had a voice that was hardly made for talking let alone singing. But listening to them made the work more bearable and I was thankful for them. Afterwards we downed tools and scoffed supper. I took hold of a flask of water and tucked it inside my coat, saving it for later. It was the end of the seventh week and I now had three pounds and ten shillings saved. I was almost there and was thinking about my departure and how this flask would come in useful for the journey. Just one more week, I said to myself. I would make my way west. To Manchester town.

When the pipes and cards came out, I took my leave. I walked across the fields towards the wooded area where my bag of pennies was hidden. I groped in the hollow until I retrieved it. I took out the pennies from that evening's sale and put them with the others. I counted up the new total. Three pound and eleven shillings. In fact, I could be on the road in just five more days. I'd been spending quite a lot of time there of an evening, listening to the evensong of titmouse, finch and warbler, catching sight of an owl from time to time, either at its plucking place or roosting in the trees. I was struck by its eyes, which were made of the same cold grey glass as those of the girl with the pale blonde hair. The haymaking was nearly over. Just the top field now left to reap. The farmer had talked of further work, bringing in the harvest, but I had almost saved up my pennies now and was nearly ready for the road. The big town beckoned.

There was no showing from the owl, nor was there much evensong to soothe my ears, but the night still felt young and I was not tired. Nor was I in the mood for my usual book-learning. So I walked through the wood and onto the moor, past my makeshift den. The ground became tussocked and sopping. There were paths made by rabbits and foxes across the morass. I thought back to our moor, patterned with these types of paths. Some days we would follow them, me and you, Cathy, and they would stop dead. We used to say that those paths led to another place, beyond the physical world. A witching place from where you drew your magic. Past cottages, barns and turbary roads, turf and peat cuts healing over like scabs. Packhorse tracks, homesteads, landholdings. When all signs of human life vanished, that's where we would stop and sit. Sometimes we'd watch fox cubs play or hares box. Other times, we'd lie back and look at the paintings in the sky that were far superior to those done by human hand and brush, for they were ever-changing from one thing to another. I'd see a castle, but you'd see a dragon's eye. I would see the branch of a tree stretch into a withered arm, which would change again into a fish, then a bear. I'd point out the shape and try and get you to see what I could see, but you'd already spotted another thing of wonder and you were pointing it out to me: a rat, a bat, a frog, a fox.

The sun was slipping down past the horizon and the sky was closing in. The grass had given way to heather and I could hear the grouse croak like old crones cackling. Wet green moss grew like a soft woollen blanket, leggy heather, bracken, moss and sedge. Tangled sphagnum. Cotton-grass and bilberry. It was a moor like our moor where we used to watch the hatching of the peewit, whaap and sea pie. I remembered the moor as the place we had lived in and by. To run away to the moor in the morning and remain there all day. The moor was our school and our refuge. It was a place of solace and a place of wonder. Finding the gamekeeper's heap of dead crows, or his gibbet of weasels. Once we came across a stoat trap, with a stoat still in it, miraculously unharmed, and we let it go, watching it scurry through the grass. A morning chorus of uncountable larks, uncountable beauty. Watching glead soar and hawks hover. In winter, snowdrifts deep enough to blanket the bog. In summer, the white tufts of cotton-grass waving over the same marsh. Yellow gorse, red poppies, purple heather. Every moss, every flower, every tint and form, we two noted and enjoyed. Even the smallest waterfall or heather-stand was a world of joy. The moors were an eternity where life was boundless and our bliss was endless.

No punishment could rob us of those moments. No braying deterred us. You plucked some white stalks of gorse and said they were bones. Our bones, whitened by the weather.

We watched a puttock wheel in the mist and listened to the cackling moorcock flap through redding heather.

I felt such a strong yearning for those days, when it was just you and me and the moor, Cathy, that I felt it as a physical pain. Why had you let Edgar come between us? What did he have that money couldn't buy? I ached for you. It was a sharp pang in the middle of my breast. Sometimes the longing got so bad that I could hardly breathe. It felt as though a viper was coiled around my heart, squeezing the life out of me. And I couldn't unclasp it. I was suffocating. I was drowning. I was choking. All I wanted in the world was you. Now you had left me, abandoned me, and for what? Gold and silver and trinkets that meant nothing to you. I wanted to scream out: No, please, don't leave me. I cannot live without you. I wanted to tear myself in two. I lay on the ground, felt the tears sting and let the acrid water drip from my eyes.

It was fully dark when I eventually came around. I made my way back to the farm by moonlight, dropping down from the moor on the other side. As I scuttled along the path in the silver light of the moon and the stars, I heard a distinct screaming. Not the screaming a vixen sometimes makes when she calls her mate or the long harsh screaming of a barn owl, but another sound. I thought for a moment that it was the screaming of a wild cat.

I stopped and cocked my head, listening more intently. As I did, I realised that the sound could only be one thing: the piercing scream of a person in pain. I followed it and found myself outside the building where the hay was stored. There was candlelight leaking from a crack in the door. I placed my eye there and saw a peculiar scene. The girl with the white-blonde hair and grey eyes was standing in the middle of the room. There were two men: one was the farmer's son, Dick Taylor, the other I did not recognise. He was stocky with a thick mop of yellow hair, like a corn rig. The farmer's son had hold of the girl with one arm, and his other hand was over her mouth. The man with yellow hair was uncoiling a length of rope. He took out an axe and I saw the metal blade glint in the light of the tallow candle. He chopped two lengths of rope. The axe cut through the thick rope as though it were a single blade of grass. He took one length and tied it to a wooden pillar, then took hold of one of the girl's arms. He tied the rope firm around her wrist. Then he took the second length and tied her other wrist to a wooden post on the far side of her. I could see the panic in the girl's eyes.

When she was firmly tied, the man who had hold of her stuffed a handkerchief in her mouth and tied another around her face, preventing her from screaming out. The man with yellow hair went to the back of the barn. I couldn't see what he was doing but when he came back he had a black leather bull whip in one hand. The farmer's son took out a knife and used it to cut the girl's frock. He then tore it so that the entire length of her back was exposed. Then the man with yellow hair uncoiled the whip and cracked the air. He smiled at the farmer's son.

'Give it to me,' Dick Taylor said.

'Spoilsport.'

The man with yellow hair handed over the whip to the farmer's son. The farmer's son put the knife on the ground. He cracked the whip himself a few times and smiled. Then he walked up to the girl, turned around and counted his strides back. On the sixth stride he stopped and turned to face her. He stood quite still for a moment, then cracked the whip across the girl's flesh. She flinched in pain and her eyes bulged. Her skin split where the point of the whip sliced at the flesh and blood leaked out. I saw it pour from the wound and felt a heat rise within. I thought about Hindley and the whip he had used on me. I knew how it could cut through flesh and I felt the girl's pain as if it were my own. And then a kind of mania spiralled in my head. My thoughts were travelling upwards like a puttock in the sun, to be replaced by a cold, hard, black feeling.

I shouldered the door and burst through. Both men turned around to face me. I picked up the axe from the ground and ran at the farmer's son, who was still clutching the whip. He pulled the whip back and tried to crack it across my face, but as he did I lunged at him with the axe, grabbed for the whip, and chopped his hand clean off at the wrist. He screamed and blood gushed from the wound. I went for the other man but before I could get hold of him he ran out of the barn, closely followed by the bleeding farmer's son. Then I was on my own with the girl. The severed hand was on the ground on top of some straw, twitching. It was still clutching the whip. I untied the girl and removed the handkerchiefs from her face and mouth.

'Are you hurt bad?' I asked.

She was standing quite still, staring at me impassively.

'I've had worse,' she said.

'Why were those men whipping you?'

'They said I'm a witch.'

'Why?'

'They just did.'

'They must have reasons?'

'People talk through me.'

'What people?'

'Dead people.'

'Then you are a witch.'

I took the flask of water from inside my coat and handed it to her.

'Here, drink this.'

She pulled out the cork and supped from it.

'Why did you stop them?'

'I don't like whips.'

She handed the flask back.

'We can't stay here,' she said. 'They'll come back. With more. What you did – it will not go unpunished.'

'Come,' I said. 'I know a place we can hide till dawn. Then we can head over the moors, away from this town.'

I cleaned the blade of the axe, wrapped it in a coarse rag, and tucked it down the back of my breeches. I found the knife further on and stashed that in my surtout.

'Where are you heading?'

'West.'

'Can I come?'

'You can come as far as you need to get away from those men. But no further.'

The last thing I needed was a travelling companion to slow me down.

I took her hand and we walked out of the barn. I could hear some commotion in the distance. Then I heard voices.

'It's this way!' someone shouted.

They were coming for us already. I held onto the girl's hand harder and together we ran up the lane and into the wood. I led us through a thicket and over brambles until we came to a tree that we could easily climb. It was close to the elm where I stashed my pennies. I reached for the nearest branch and used it to steady me as I wedged my foot into a nook. I levered myself up into the tree, then pulled the girl close to where I was crouched. I held her tight and told her to shush. I heard voices and the snapping of twigs. We were being followed by a mob armed with torches, pitchforks, scythes, knives and pickaxe handles. I could see their silhouettes and the orange flames. The men searched the wood.

'Must be here somewhere,' someone said. 'Can't have got far.'

'I'll lynch the pair of them.'

'Watch out. He's got an axe.'

Three men approached our tree. I could make out the tops of their heads from where I was crouched. One was the man with yellow hair. He leaned against the trunk immediately below us. I held my breath and put my hand over the girl's mouth. She was rigid with fear. I could feel her heart beat against my belly. I clung onto her. The men were panting.

'Stop a minute, I need to get my breath.'

'Which way?' the yellow-haired man said.

'They must be here somewhere.'

'Is Dick all right?'

'I don't know,' the yellow-haired man said. 'He's lost a hand.'

'They'll lose more than a hand when I get hold of them,'

another said. I recognised the voice: it was the farmer, Dan Taylor. 'No one does that to my son and lives to tell the tale.'

'Might have climbed a tree.'

'Lift that torch up.'

A man came over to where we stood, torch in hand. My surtout was a dark brown colour and the girl was tucked inside. I ducked my head behind a branch as the light from the torch came closer. As they raised it I held my breath again.

'I can't see anything.'

'Lift it higher.'

I could feel the girl's heartbeat quicken. I could feel beads of sweat trickle down my back.

'What's that?'

'Where?'

'Those are eyes.'

I clenched my eyes closed. I stayed as still as a statue.

'There. See?'

'It's only an owl, you fool.'

'I thought for a moment . . .'

'Ha!'

'You've got to admit, the girl's eyes are a bit like that.'

'Come on, they must be further in.'

The men went deeper into the forest. I waited until the lights from their torches diminished and the night was black again, and took a deep breath. Thank God for my friend the owl, who had returned to the wood at just the right time. I whispered to the girl, 'Come on, let's get out of here.'

We climbed down. I'd been tensing every muscle of my body and only now was I aware of it. I retrieved the sack of coins from the hollow in the tree and I took the girl to the makeshift cave. There was just a sliver of moon to guide us, obscured by mist. I put the bag of coins in my pocket.

As my heartbeat slowed, the reality of the situation struck me, and I kicked myself. I was still nine shillings short of my target. Why had I acted so rashly? For a girl I barely knew? Now I had an angry mob baying for my blood.

'What's your name?' I said in the dark.

'Emily. What's yours?'

'I told you the other night: William Lee.'

'What do we do now?'

'Get the fuck out of here.'

The moon was cloaked by cloud and the sky was black. Further protection, I thought. Their torches would burn out soon, and they wouldn't be able to see anything without them. We managed to find our way to the cave, stumbling here and there as we did. I reckoned that we were safe here until dawn. It was far enough from the farm, and they'd never find us in the dark, even with torches, as they wouldn't think to look around these parts. The cave was in a steep dip and well hidden. I got a fire going, knowing that it couldn't be seen from any angle. Even so, I burned the flaights rather than the woodpile, as they burned with a lower flame. I passed her the flask again.

'Here, drink.'

'Have you got anything to eat?'

'You'll have to wait till morning.'

'I'm starving.'

'You'll last. Let me have a look at the wound.'

She turned her back to me and I examined it in the light of the fire. It had ripped deep into her flesh. The wound would heal but it might get infected. I wondered if it needed stitching. It was too dark for me to make a poultice but I knew where there were some soothing herbs and I'd fix her a remedy in the morning. She was shivering. I gave her the shirt off my back. One of Hindley's hand-me-downs.

'Here, put this on.'

She took hold of it as though it were something dead and festering.

'It fucking stinks.'

'Put it on.'

She did. It drowned her but I figured it would keep her warm. Her chest was as flat as an oatcake. I thought about your chest at her age, already budding with womanhood. I put my rough surtout on, itching from the coarse stitching. I felt it scratch at my shoulders.

'You could show some gratitude,' I said.

'Eh?'

'You know, such as, thanks, William.'

'What for? A stinking shirt?'

'I saved you from a braying back there. Perhaps worse.'

I waited for a response but there was none. I watched the flaights glow in the fire, giving off hardly any flame.

'We'll be safe here for now, but we'll have to be on our way first thing. Get your head down. You need to sleep.'

'Do you think that man will die?' she said.

'Which man?'

I don't know why I asked because I knew full well which man she was talking about.

'The man whose hand you cut off. The farmer's son. Dick.'

'Perhaps.'

64

'I hope so,' she said. 'I hope he bleeds to death. My only regret is that I won't be there to watch.'

I hoped so too, Cathy. I took the blanket and wrapped it around her shoulders.

'Go to sleep.'

'Where you heading?'

'I told you: west.'

'Why?'

'That's my business.'

'I've never been west. Been east lots of times. York mostly. And south. Went to London with my dad. They had a big fire there, you know, a hundred years ago. Burned most of it down. My dad told me all about it. Said it was started when a baker forgot to put out his oven. Took them forty years to build it back again.'

She chattered away for some time. She reminded me of you at that age. Full of mischief and as nosey as the devil.

'What did you say to Dick to make him snap?'

'He's heard rumours, that's all.'

'I meant in the field, when you were cutting hay.'

'I can't recollect exactly. He was having a dig. Fucking cunt.'

'Who taught you to curse?' I said.

'No one taught me nothing. I'll say what I fucking well like.'

I was surprised to hear such flaysome speech from one so young, but not at all offended. In fact, it amused me. It had always been me with the filthy tongue. I remembered Nelly saying she'd never heard such blaspheming and Joseph saying that he'd scrub my mouth with lye. Now I had some competition.

Eventually she lay back and closed her eyes. I watched the

light from the fire flicker across her face. Less than a minute later I could hear her breathing deepen with sleep. How innocent she looked in slumber. I remembered watching your sleeping face, for hours, mesmerised. How innocent your face had looked as well, a long time before Edgar changed you for the worse. The fire was nearly out and I stared into the red embers. As I did I saw the girl's blood. I saw the glinting bit of the axe spotted with gouts of red. I felt the bite of the axe through Dick's thick wrist. Clean steel. Wet red blood. I saw Dick's arm without its hand. I saw the blood pump from the wound. Had I killed a man? I wondered. It was only what he deserved. I wouldn't be losing any sleep over it. I took the remaining blanket and wrapped it around my shoulders. I lay back and listened to Emily snore. Whether I'd killed the man or not, the act of violence had felt pure, and in the moment of it something had released itself within me, the way the wind blows the stones clean.

Throttling a Dog

I woke twice in the night, the first time from a dream in which I was being chased by the villagers. The second time I was being flogged by Hindley. I felt the sting of the whip and turned to see his malignant glare. I was shivering. The wind had picked up and was blowing rain into the cave. I looked over to the girl but she was sleeping soundly. I wrapped the blanket tightly around me. The cloth was damp. I hugged the damp blanket but sleep would not come. Emily tossed and turned. She cried out, 'No, no, fuck off.' But she didn't wake up. I must have drifted off because the next thing it was almost morning. It seems she woke first because when I opened my eyes she was standing over me. It gave me a shock. The sun was behind her, peeking over the horizon.

'What are you doing?'

'Wondering when you'd wake up,' she said.

I stood up, stiff all over. It felt as if the rain had crept into my joints. I walked around in an effort to cast off the stiffness. Last night's fire was a pile of ash. I heard a lark high above our heads. I looked up, but the sky was still dim and even with my head stretched fully back, it was too high in the heavens to observe. How easy it is for birds to escape. How effortlessly they find freedom. While we remain manacled to the earth.

'We'd better make a move,' I said. 'Let me have a look at your wound first.'

'It's all right.'

'Let me look.'

I pulled the shirt up so that I could examine the cut. It had healed some overnight and didn't look as though it would need any further treatment. I'd seen Mr Earnshaw stitch up one of the hogs when it had cut itself on a jagged piece of metal, but I'd never done it myself, so I was glad it didn't need stitches. I collected together my few possessions, but I left the bible where it was. I'd got what I wanted from it and was not interested in its moral lessons. I made sure I had the flask, the axe, the knife and the bag of coins. I rolled up the blankets and tied them separately with some string.

'Come on. We need to get moving.'

'I'm hungry,' she said.

'If you want to eat, you'll have to wait till we get to the next town.'

'How far is that?'

'I don't know. I know one thing: we can't go back to the village. There will be a witch-hunt for you and when word gets round there will be a manhunt for me.'

'Obviously.' She looked at me with contempt.

'Here, carry one of these,' I said.

I handed her the smaller of the two blankets.

'Let's get moving.'

We headed west with the sun still a golden line behind us. As we walked it rose but was obscured by clouds. The ground was damp with dew and last night's rain, and a lingering mist carpeted the moor. The view opened up to a green-and-grey patchwork quilt. Below us, field after field, fence after fence, wall after wall, hedge after hedge, land that was once open and free, according to Sticks. A few years ago this had been common land. Now it was all sectioned and marked like a slab of mutton ready to be butchered. Sticks had told me how it had been stolen from its people. How they'd been kicked off the land of their birth, evicted from their cottages, which were razed to the ground. The wind was strong and blowing against us, and the cold crept under our skin.

'Walk quicker.'

We traipsed along rabbit paths and beside becks. Through fields of mud. The sky was clearing but there were still lots of grey dark clouds and the grass was sodden from the rain. But the wind was blowing eastwards and the clouds were moving away and things were brightening. The rooks and crows above us called out across the moor. In the distance, on a bare branch, a raven preened its glossy wings.

We trekked for some time, walking on paths made by farmers, labourers, dogs and cattle, all churned up by boot and hoof. Sometimes paths made by rabbit and hare. Sometimes no path at all. We did not choose the easy route; instead we walked as the crow flew, keeping to the tops so that we had a vantage point.

'Can we stop now?' Emily said, after a while.

'No, we've only just got going.'

'We've been walking for hours.'

In fact, I didn't think it was more than an hour, but without a timepiece it was hard to say.

'We'll stop at the next town.'

'Where's that?'

'I don't know.'

'We should nick a couple of horses,' she said.

'One lot of trouble is enough.'

'What difference does it make? Trouble is trouble. And the quicker we get away from it the better. That's what I say. If my dad was here now, he would have found a stable, nicked a couple of decent nags and had them saddled. You wouldn't see us for dust.'

'He's not here. And we're doing things my way, not your dad's.'

'I'm just saying.'

'Well, don't.'

'Smart fellow, my dad. Knew a thing or two. Not a bit like you.'

'What are you saying?'

'I'm not saying anything.'

'I know what you're getting at, so button it.'

'We rode from London to Leeds in three days one time. You need to keep your strength up when you're on the run. No sense in wasting energy. My dad used to say that there are two ways of doing things: the easy way and the right way. No sense in doing it the right way when there's the easy way.'

'When we get to the next town we can stop for something to eat and drink. We can sit down and rest for an hour.'

In fact, my plan was to ditch her once we got there. I was responsible for me and no one else, and that was the way I wanted it. No hangers-on and no freeloaders. We dropped down off the moor and followed a stream until we approached a hamlet. We walked through a small graveyard. Even in a remote spot like this, the dead linger. It was good to see the rabbits making burrows beneath the graves. Flowers sprouted from between the stones. Harebells, lupins, foxtail and forget-me-nots. Daisies, milkweed and love-in-the-mist. A dog rose clung to the wings of an angel. The stones were marked as they always had been, but now I could read their inscriptions: 'here lyeth a good Christian', 'sacred to the memory of', 'a good wife', 'a dear husband', 'a cherished son'. But I had no one. No one to love and no one to mourn me when I was gone. I was no one's son or brother, and no one's husband. And it suited me fine.

We passed the backs of people's houses, washing pegged and drying on the line, heaps of sticks and wood ready for chopping. I thought maybe we could stop here, but aside from a few houses and outbuildings, there was nothing. Our path narrowed, the clouds thickened. I could hear the braying of cows in the distance. As we got closer I could see the farmer with a stick counting them in ready for milking. The lowing of cattle was soothing. Hooves, bracken, cow parsley, the verdant hawthorn, twisted and prickly. Thick peat smoke billowed from the chimney of a farmhouse. Tentacles of ivy grasped the trunk of a wych elm. A dead grouse in a draining ditch. And still the flaysome wind blew in our faces. I felt a wet drop on my cheek. I looked up at the clouds that were darkening again. Another wet drop on the back of my hand. On the nape of my neck. Then the rain poured down.

'I'm getting wet,' Emily said.

'Keep walking. When the sun comes out you'll dry soon enough.'

'This farm stinks of shit,' Emily said.

There were heaps of horse manure and swine ordure. The air was thick with the rich stench.

'How do you think farmers go on all the time when it stinks of shit?'

'You get used to it.'

'I wouldn't want to get used to it. Shit should stink of shit, it shouldn't ever stop stinking of shit just 'cause you get used to it. It stinks of shit for a reason. You're meant to stay away from it.'

'Put a peg over your nose.'

'I haven't got a peg. Why would I have a peg? You don't half talk bollocks sometimes.'

Fences, walls, hedges. We climbed over a stile and across another mud-clad field.

'My knee's giving me gyp,' Emily said.

'What do you mean, your knee's giving you gyp? How old are you – ten, or ten and sixty?'

'It keeps locking.'

'It will be fine.'

'Then why does it keep fucking clicking?'

I shrugged.

'Why don't we stick to the roads? It will be easier on our feet. This isn't even a proper path. I don't know what you'd call it, but not a path in any case.'

'The roads aren't safe. They'll be on horseback. This is the only way we can be sure they won't find us.'

'Horses can travel across country, you know. We used to do it all the time, me and my dad.'

'But not by choice,' I said. 'They won't want to risk laming them.'

'They could take it steady. They won't lame them if they take it steady, not even on this route. I'm telling you, me and my dad travelled loads of miles over worse than this without laming the horses. You've just got to be careful how you go.'

Past birch, beech, bracken and bog, black mounds of mole-hills. We saw a long wire between two posts and hanging from the wire were the moldwarp corpses, their velvet grey fur wet with mizzle. Their huge white teeth and claws, glittering. Waiting to be skinned.

'My dad had a jerkin made from fifty moleskins. He got it off a nobleman. Lord so-and-so. Though he didn't look noble standing in a ditch.'

We walked through more fields until the moor opened out again and below us the river snaked and frothed.

'You a gypsy?' Emily said.

'No.'

'You look like a fucking gypsy to me.'

'Well, I'm not.'

'My dad said that gypsies were thieves.'

'Did he?'

'And that they kidnap girls and eat babies.'

'You'd better watch your step then.'

'Thought you weren't a gypsy?'

'Look, just keep your mouth shut, right?'

A white linnet settled on a prominent stoop about ten yards ahead of us. As we walked on, it took flight again, flitting down the path where it settled, bobbed its tail and watched us approach. As soon as we got within ten yards it flew onwards, and so on for half a mile or more.

'What's that bird doing?' she said.

'Showing us the way.'

'No, it's not. You don't half talk some tiff.'

We passed a post that a goshawk must have used as a plucking place. Beneath a scattering of feathers was the flesh and elastic of the meat membrane.

'If you're still hungry, you can eat that,' I said.

'Don't be disgusting.'

'Beggars can't be choosers.'

'Yes, they can. I'm not eating that. I'm not that desperate.'

In fact, I was only half-joking. The meat was fresh and likely to be better than any we got in the next town. We walked on in silence, past half-quarried boulders furry with green moss, abandoned slabs of granite slippery with mud, until we came to a working delph and we stopped and watched the bearers break stone. There were four men with pickaxes, wedges, chisels and hammers. I thought about Joseph and me up at Penistone Crag, him lecturing me on hell and damnation, and the sins of the flesh. But I had only ever experienced the pleasures of the flesh and the pain of boot and whip.

'Do you think they get much money for breaking stone all day?' Emily said.

'No.'

'Then why do it?'

'It's honest toil.'

'It's a mug's game, if you ask me.'

'What other work is there?'

'There's lots of things you can do. I mean, you've got a choice. You don't have to whack bits of rock all day. You're not telling me that's a good way to spend your time?'

'Someone's got to do it.'

'That's all well and dandy, William Lee, as long as that person isn't me.'

More farm buildings, old barrows, spades, shovels, hoes, pitchforks. Past fern and bramble. The rain was luttering above us. And a relentless patter on leaf and grass. The blades were lying flat.

'My feet are hurting.'

'I can't do anything about that.'

'Let's just stop.'

'We're not stopping.'

'Why not?'

'If you want to stop, you can stop, but I'm keeping on going.'

'I need some boots,' she said. 'Ones with laces. Then my feet wouldn't hurt. And I need stockings.'

I ignored her. I had a blister but I didn't say that my feet were hurting too, as I didn't want to think about my own pain. Best to push it to one side. Ignore it and it would go away. Physical pain was easy to master. The pain inside was much harder to bridle.

'I need a new frock too,' she said. 'They've wrecked this one.'

'I need lots of things,' I said. 'Need doesn't get.'

'You can't expect me to wear this stinking shirt all the time. It doesn't even fit. I mean, where did you even get it from? It's falling to bits. Look, the stitching is coming away at the sleeve.'

I thought, there's nothing wrong with this girl that a few

good clouts around the ears wouldn't fix. But hadn't I been clouted often enough? And what good had it done me?

Beneath our feet the earth yielded to our tread. I didn't think it was a good idea for her to go barefoot but I didn't say anything. The moss tramped down and the grass gave in. We ploughed on. We came across a heap of sticks, twigs and branches. Someone was going to have a fire tonight if the pile dried. Out here, in the middle of nowhere, it seemed like an odd spot. Perhaps it was for two lovers, who came to the moors to escape.

The rain fell in angry drops. I thought about God in his heaven, looking down on us, and how he was lauded, but it was the devil beneath us who had a nice fire to keep us warm.

Emily stopped and rubbed her feet.

'I'm wet,' she said. 'And cold. My feet are sore.'

'Keep walking. It's only water.'

We trudged on and as we did the rain slowed to a patter, then stopped altogether. I could feel the heat creep from behind the clouds. I thought about your sweet breath on my neck, Cathy. I thought about when we put our lips together and you passed the air from inside you into me. You said, 'That's us.' It's true, Cathy, I missed you. I missed your caresses and your soft kisses. But fuck you, you bitch.

I tried not to think of that cunt Linton writhing naked on top of you, like some sick worm, kissing you, fucking you, his cock inside you. I looked around instead and tried to forget you. Puttock, twite-finch and white-crow. I listened to the whooping call of the whaap. I focused on the black-and-white flash of the sea-pie, and the ragged flapping of peewit. And in this way I extricated you from my thoughts.

Above us, the high-pitched screech of the peewit heightened with the ragged flapping of their wings. Around us, the green fern, the purple heather, the ripple of the wind on the surface of peaty puddles. Then our view opened out onto a bigger moor, but not our moor, Cathy, one far more bleak and barren. It was black. Broken only by the heavens above, and the majestic flight of a heron, its head tucked into its neck like a bib. Its beak like a spear. Our feet squelched where the sheep had churned up the ground beneath us.

'This bit reminds me of the moors past Pickering,' Emily said. 'You been there?'

'No.'

'You ride out of Pickering to Cropton Forest. Or in your case, walk. We spent the night there once, me and my dad. It's a nice forest. You come out the other side and you get onto a Roman road. My dad said it was nearly two thousand years old. It's as straight as a washing line. Takes you all the way to Goathland. There's a big waterfall there. We stopped at a tavern one time. There was a billiard table but we didn't play. My dad got the cards from behind the bar, and we played noddy all night . . . Ow! I think I've broke my ankle.'

She was limping. We stopped. She sat down on a boulder. I took her foot in my hand and turned it around. I'd seen more meat on a wren. And the bones were nearly as delicate as that tiny bird. I could crush her foot in my fist.

'It's not broken,' I said, 'just sprained. Best thing to do with a sprain is to keep on walking.'

'What do you know?' she said. 'Are you a doctor now?'

'I've had sprains before. I know what I'm talking about.'

'If I had boots they'd support my ankle. I could tighten the laces. How far do you think we've walked?'

'I don't know. Maybe five or six miles.'

'It must be further than that.'

We carried on walking, with Emily, still limping, just behind me.

'How far is Manchester?'

'Maybe ten miles or maybe forty.'

'That's helpful.'

I had no real idea, Cathy. I just knew that Mr Earnshaw had walked to Liverpool and back in three days. It might be just over the hill for all I knew, or several days away.

'I'm thirsty,' she said.

'We'll find a stream.'

'Where's the flask?'

'It's empty.'

We walked downwards, over tussock grass until we came to running water. We stopped and I stooped down, making a cup with my hands. I drank. The water was fresh and cool.

'Here, have some.'

She stooped where I had stooped and did the same. I looked down at the spiky green moss all around us. I reached for it and plucked a stem. Despite its spiky appearance, it was soft. You called it star moss, Cathy. I recalled you picking some and saying that it looked fierce but that the things that look fierce are often gentle. I filled the flask and corked it. We carried on our way.

'This is boring. Why won't you talk to me?' she said.

'Talk to you about what?'

'Anything. Just say something.'

I've really got to get rid of this brat, I thought. The next place I could drop her, I would.

'Tell me who you are, where you came from. I don't know – anything.'

But Cathy, how could I tell her that when I didn't know myself?

'You tell me your story. If it's good, I'll tell you mine,' I said at last.

'Right then.'

She paused before commencing.

'My dad was a highwayman.'

'Was?'

'He was hanged by the neck last year. Knavesmire gallows. He hung for three days, shrieking in pain. A kind gentleman came in a passing carriage. He stopped and took out a pistol. Shot him through the brains.'

What would you make of this girl, Cathy? She could certainly tell a tale.

'What about your mother?'

'My mother was a whore. She died giving birth to me.'

'And was it your dad who taught you that trick?'

'What trick?'

'The dead-people-talk-through-me trick.'

'It's not a trick.'

'No, course it's not.'

Although not fully credulous, I did think, Cathy, that it might have been a trick, but it might also have been witch-craft, or demonic possession. You'd told me once that the devil could possess the mouths of mortals. And make the sounds of others.

'And was he always a highwayman?'

'He was not, no. We had our land stolen from us and we were made outlaws. At first we tried to live by honest crust. We found work in a coal mine. I was employed to drag bunches of furze along the galleries to send off the choke damp. It's not as glamorous as it sounds. The fire damp was dealt with by the fireman, who was my father. He wore wet leathers. Didn't half look funny in them. He carried a pole with a lighted candle at the end, with which he exploded the gas. It was a risky job. Water was the next problem. We lined the shafts with sheepskins and wooden tubbing. When the water drained into the sump of the pit bottom, we had to set up a chain of buckets. It was a right pain in the arse. We rode the shafts by clinging to a winding rope. I saw heads split in two and young'uns fall from the ropes to the bottom of the shaft. They never bothered to shift the corpses. Left them down there to rot. We moved the coal by panniers, slung across the backs of horses, or wagons moving along ill-made roads. Horse gins drew the coves to the top shaft. It was hard slog. I tell yer, you think farm labour is tough, but it's nothing compared with mine labour.'

'So what happened?'

'Eh?'

'If you were in regular employment, the two of you, how did he end up an outlaw?'

'They say he was a bad'un. That he had bad blood running in his veins. They said even his bones were bad. That he had badness in the marrow. He didn't like the work. It was dicing with death, he said. He didn't want me down the pit. Said it was no work for a girl. Least not his girl. He had higher

80

hopes for me, he said. He got into an argument about pay. The gaffer was trying to dock his wages over something or other. Said he'd been shirking.'

'And what happened?'

'The gaffer ended up down the bottom of the shaft with the young'uns. That's all I know. We had to make a run for it. He said it was good riddance. No better than the work-house. One night we kipped at an inn and we came across a counting clerk in a drunken stupor. My dad stole some keys to the man's strongbox and rifled it. That were two hundred pounds and after that my father got a taste for fine living. He bought a prize mare and saddled her. He purchased a sword and a good set of pistols. He got me a fine frock and some leather boots. We worked the Great North Road. There were regular stagecoaches. And mail coaches. He felt no guilt about it. He said the rich had stolen his land from him and now he was taking from them. He was only getting what was his.'

You'd told me about the outlaws and highwaymen of this land, Cathy, and I have to say, we both had a sneaking admiration for them. I remembered you reading out stories from the local paper that Mr Earnshaw would bring back on market day, of the outlaws of the road and of the riches they had acquired. It was rare that anyone got hurt and it all seemed like harmless fun to us. Listening to the girl recount her story, I became fascinated by a life of crime once again. In truth, the highwayman was a man of my own heart. He was a freebooter, a libertarian, a don't-give-a-fuck bastard, who scorned conventions. Why should life be lived as a crushing tedium and unrewarded toil? Why should the haves live in splendour and the have-nots in squalor? Although I did not envy the highwayman his vices – neither drinking, gambling nor whoring were my game – I did envy his freedom. But here I was now, on the open road, as free as any highwayman. I loved the stories you told me of Robin Hood. Of how, not by force but by cunning, he had outwitted his enemies. In this man who haunted the thickets and forests of England, I saw myself, and we talked about how we could live on the moors, feasting on its bounty of rabbit, hare and grouse. We wouldn't need society or any of its laws. We wouldn't need anyone, just us.

'It wasn't all stealing though,' Emily said. 'One time we came across a farmer who'd had fifty pounds robbed off him, and my dad said to him, show me the way the robber went and I'll get the money back for you. So the farmer did and my dad went after the robber. The thief denied having stolen the money until my dad put a pistol to his head. He bloody well coughed up then, I'll tell you. True to his word, my dad handed the fifty pounds back to the farmer. You see, the farmer wasn't a rich man and my dad only stole from them that deserved it. He hated thieves who stole from their own. The farmer only had that money because he'd just sold his cattle at the market. He needed that money to prevent his family from being homeless. He had to raise enough money to pay his rent. Not only that, a few nights later, my dad went to the farmer's house when he and his family were sleeping and placed a bag of gold on his doorstep. Imagine that, going to bed poor and waking up rich.'

As Emily chattered away we walked across some of the most barren moors I have yet seen, where not even a stunted hawthorn could find purchase. There was darkness at the heart of this moor, that I could feel creep under my skin and seep into my bones. I found Emily's stories helped, not only to pass the time, but also to soften the feelings of melancholy that the landscape evoked. The wind picked up and the sky darkened. We could see black rain fall like rods in the distance. Then sheet lightning and thunder so loud it sounded as though the sky was cracking open. Thankfully, the storm soon passed over, leaving a shower in its wake. Even this dried up.

For many miles we walked where there was nothing of any significance to note. Then we came to huge grey boulders strewn here and thereabouts, as though they were giant dice tossed by a gambling god. We passed over a part of the moor that was covered in grass so white that it was almost like bone. And I thought about the straw in the stables where I'd been locked from time to time when Hindley got it into his head that beating me senseless was insufficient punishment. I thought about turning to Emily and recounting the stories of Hindley's whip and boot and the outbuildings that were so often my prison, but she had plenty on her plate and the land was bleak enough without making it bleaker.

Fortunately the view changed. The black barren peat moor softened as heather sprouted. Then all we could see for miles around was purple. The heather blooming in every direction, alive with bees collecting nectar from the cups of the flowers. Dropping down off the moor, we could see around us, in every direction, farm buildings, fields, coppices and forests. The beck below. I remember when we talked about how the moors were really the scars left from the trees that had been cut down and uprooted. What we were looking at was a once-fresh wound now hardened. If the trees were still here, we would have no sense of the landscape at all, and no moor. We came to a cobbled path. More fields, fences, walls and hedges. The hoarse rattle of a long tail. The path opened out onto a bridleway with steep stone walls either side. The ground now was sandstone and grit. The wall was covered in moss and the path stretched out above us back onto the moors.

'On another occasion,' Emily said, 'we overheard a conversation at a village pub where we were staying. There was talk of a wealthy bailiff who'd made a lot of money by extracting it from the poor. We went to bed that night, letting the landlord lead the way with his lamp, then we climbed out of the window. We pursued the bailiff, who gave us every farthing. My dad returned the money to those that deserved it. He liked to rob usurers and lords and any other cunt that had wealth that wasn't theirs.'

'So where did it go wrong then?' I said. 'Sounds like you were on a good number.'

'Sometimes a man's luck runs out,' Emily said. 'And so it did with my dad. After one particular robbery of a powerful judge, a reward was put out. My dad had folk looking out for him, watching his back, but there were other folk who saw that they could profit from him. Someone squealed, we don't know who. Some men came one morning and arrested him while he was eating his breakfast. They brought him to court in leg-irons, but he wore one of the smartest suits you've ever seen and carried a nosegay as big as a birch-broom. After he was hanged, I was picked up by a beadle. The parish of settlement sent me to the workhouse, but I jumped off the cart before they got a chance to get me there. Since then I've roamed the land, living on naught but my own wits.'

'That's some story,' I said.

'Now it's your turn,' she said.

'Well, I've nothing like that to tell. Most of my story I'm ignorant of. And that which I do recall will not sufficiently entertain you, I suspect.'

'Tell me anyway. I want to hear it.'

I shrugged. I had no tongue for talk.

'Where are you from?'

'I don't know.'

'Why do you want to go to Manchester?'

'To earn a crust.'

'To do what?'

'I'm going to make something of myself.'

'How can you make something of yourself when you don't even know who you are?'

I shrugged again. But she had touched a nerve. Perhaps in Liverpool town I would find my mother. I barely dared to think such thoughts. Did she even know I still existed? Had she been too poor to rear me and thought Mr Earnshaw could provide for me where she could not? It was the one thing that made sense. The only way a mother would give up her child was for the good of that child. I was convinced my mother had done the best by me. And how sweet it would now be to find her and hold her in my arms. To kiss her on her cheek. She would cry with joy and sorrow. Joy at finally finding me but sorrow at all the years she had missed. I would wipe away her tears. I would hang at her neck. Then we would sit and talk and fill in the missing years for each other. She would tell me my real name. Who my father was. She would tell me of my origins. How sweet that conversation would be.

'Come on then. Tell me,' Emily persisted.

I told her of my life with you at Wuthering Heights, Cathy. I told her about the death of Mr and Mrs Earnshaw, my adopted mother and father. And of Hindley's tyranny. I told her about Joseph's catechisms and our life together. I told her about Nelly nursed me back to health. She was particularly taken by the tale of the time you lost your shoe in a bog and we had ended up on the grounds of the Lintons, outside looking in. I told her about the dog I'd throttled with a stone. How I'd pushed it to the back of the brute's throat, choking it. How you had been taken in and fed soup, and how I had been expelled. Thrown out onto the wet ground, to wander moor and mire in the dark. I told her how since that moment, Edgar had come between us.

'He sounds like a right dick.'

I told her about his fancy clothes and foppish hair, and how he'd made fun of my appearance. As I told her I felt the humiliation burn my skin again, as though it were still fresh. I told her of my final night at Wuthering Heights and the overheard conversation.

'So why did you run off then?'

'They thought I was in the stable but I was standing by the kitchen wall. I heard everything. She told Nelly that Edgar had proposed to her. And that she had accepted him.'

'Why would she do that?'

'She said because she loved him. Because he was handsome and cheerful. She told Nelly that she wanted to marry him because he was going to be rich.'

'But what made you run off?'

'After what she said. That it would degrade her to marry me.'

'You soft bastard. Even more reason to stay and get what's yours, or else make misery for those who scorned you. If I were you, right, I'd fuck 'em both over.'

It was difficult to argue with her reason. For one so young she had an old head on her.

We watched a blood hawk above us, its wings fixed to the sky, its eyes pointing downwards, looking for its prey, the whole moor its larder. And I thought how I would like to be up there looking down. On you, Cathy. And everything that you had no right to have. Fuck you for saying I would degrade you. Damn your soul to hell.

'How far now?' Emily said.

'Maybe ten miles. Maybe more. Maybe less. I don't have a map. And I don't know where we are in relation to anything else. Try not to think about it. The more you think about it the longer it will take.'

'So why did you put up with it?' she said.

'Put up with what?'

'With Hindley. With his beatings. With him locking you away. Starving you. Whipping you. And with that Edgar humiliating you. If you were bigger and stronger, why didn't you bray the pair of them?'

Why indeed, Cathy? It was difficult to explain to this girl how years of ill treatment affect you. How you get used to it. Harden to it. Become indifferent to it. How part of you even thinks that you deserve it. That they are your social superiors, and you are their servant, to be used and beaten at their whim. In reality there was nothing but the mind's manacles that prevented me rising up and supplanting them. But even your efforts, Cathy, to bring me out of my slavish stupor had ultimately failed. In the end, the worm is happy to be trodden on.

'That was the law of the land,' I said at last.

'The law can be bought,' Emily said.

'And if you have no money?'

'Then you get money.'

We came across another field of sheep. We stopped for a breather and watched the lambs leap and frolic, jostling each other, and then when things got too rough, returning to the safety of their mothers, nestling up to the soft, warm fleece. Even though they had outgrown the teat. We carried on walking and soon we could see the farmer in the distance. As we got closer we could see that he was wearing a bloodstained smock. The sheep bleated, the wind howled and the lambs gathered for slaughter.

'See,' I said. 'The lambs offer their necks to the knife.'

'Are you saying you're a lamb? 'Cause you're not right. You've got to stop thinking like that. Don't be a loser. No one's going to give it you on a plate, you know. You've got to get it for yourself, see. Like me and my dad. Be the lion not the lamb.'

Strong words from the girl, I thought, Cathy, but words that rang true and burned like the smith's branding iron. Words I needed to hear. Despite being called a devil, I had been the lamb – too ready to lie down and take my punishment. But now I would become the lion. I would fight for what was mine.

The sun was fully clear of the clouds now and the moors were transformed. Huge pools of light brightened the bracken, making it almost golden in patches. Shifting shades darkened the heather. As the sun shone, I saw that it made the granite rock sparkle. Tiny jewels, white, red, gold and silver, twinkled at us. We watched the cows chew the cud and they watched us. I wondered where they'd come from. Somehow they looked wrong on the moors, as though they didn't belong. We walked for miles without seeing a soul, trudging through thick black peat bog. Then we saw an old woman, wrapped up in shawl and bonnet, supporting herself with a stick. She dragged one leg behind her.

'Where are you going?' she asked.

'We're heading west. How about you?'

'Just to the next town. My brother. He's sick.'

'Is it much further?' Emily said.

'Where to?'

I kicked Emily on the shin. 'Oh, just to the next farm,' I said.

'Not far, over yonder.' The old woman pointed. 'Mind how you go, it's boggy thereabouts.'

I thought it best to end the conversation there. The less she knew about us the better, if she was bound for the town we had left. The last thing we needed was her spreading word of the direction we had come. It wouldn't be hard to give a description of us. With my dark skin and Emily's white-blonde hair, we were an easy pair to paint a picture of. We bade her good day. We watched her trudge through the peat and as she did I reflected that everyone has someone to care for them, Cathy, except me and the girl.

'From now on, leave all the talking to me,' I said.

'I only asked.'

'Well, don't.'

We carried on, wading through peat bog. Rain and oily mud. The water had penetrated through my boots now and was squelching between my toes. The blister was stinging. I wondered if I should go barefoot like Emily. But then I thought it was probably best with boots than without. They'd dry out. And although they were Hindley's cast-offs, I was grateful for them.

We had set off in the morning with the sun behind us, casting our shadows in front like giants. Now it was afternoon and the sun was in front, drawing our shadows behind. On and on we walked, mile after mile, hour after hour, sometimes along a path, and sometimes not. But always heading west.

We came across a farmer. He approached us with a hammer in his hand.

'Good day to you, sir,' I said.

'Where do you two think you're going?' he asked.

'We're heading west.'

'There's no path through here. You'll have to turn back.'

'Sir, if you let us on our way, we will be gone in no time at all. We will do no harm to you or yours.'

'I don't think you heard me proper, sunshine. Turn around and get the fuck off my land.'

I felt the heat rise within once more. How easy it would be to take out the knife and plunge it into the man's neck, or crack the bit of the axe through the top of his skull, like smashing an egg. But then I took stock. No sense being hung for a calf when it was a milch cow I was after.

We walked back to where we had entered the farmer's field, climbed over the wall and made our way around his land. It was a sizeable chunk, his estate, and it was an inconvenience to circumnavigate it. I thought about coming back at night and burning his house while he and the rest of his family were asleep. In the distance we saw the spear–like spire of a chapel surrounded by thin mist.

'See, over there, that's where we're heading. We can get something to eat there and rest. It's not far now.'

'You would say that.'

Conjuring the Dead

In less than two miles we came to the next town.

We dropped down onto a firm road with ditches either side for the rain to run off. I remembered you telling me, Cathy, about a blind man who had made hundreds of miles of roads like this. You told me how he had dug out the soft soil, laid bunches of ling and heather on the bed of the earth, covered these with stones, and dressed them with a layer of gravel, so that the rain would drain away, with ditches either side. I wondered if this road was the work of the same blind man. A man who had been born without his primary sense, who had, despite this disadvantage, achieved greatness. It was a turnpike road and we had to pay a toll. I begrudged this but handed over the money.

'It's turnpikes like this made it hard for my dad, you know,' Emily said. 'He hated them. It's getting harder and harder for the honest highwayman to earn a crust. With folk squealing, and now bloody turnpikes with their hedges and fences, that's what he used to say.'

The town contained a tannery and a blacksmith's, as well as a number of shops. We went from one to another. I bought some wheat bread and some cheese and butter, using up a portion of the money I'd saved from the sale of the beer. I reflected that the remainder wouldn't last me long, even less with this limpet clinging to me. I'd have to lose Emily if I wanted to eke out what little money I had. Pretty soon I would have to find a new way of earning some bunce. I took the food outside and we found a bench close to a green where some goats grazed. We sat and ate our grub. I watched the girl shovel in the bread and cheese, so that her mouth was overfull and crumbs tumbled out onto Hindley's shirt. She had the manners of a pig. It was nice for once not to be the slovenly one.

'You can finish that, then you'll have to be on your way,' I said.

'What do you mean?'

'I told you last night. You can't come with me. You'll be safe here. The men won't find you.'

'But I haven't got any money.'

I took out some pennies from my pocket and handed them over.

'Here. Have these.'

'That won't last me five minutes.'

'You're not my responsibility.'

'Don't be a cock.'

'You are the responsibility of this parish now.'

'They'll put me in the workhouse. Or worse, prison.'

'You'll get by. You've got your wits about you.'

'But the beadle will come like last time.'

'What do you mean, last time?'

She wiped some cheese away from around her mouth.

'I was arrested for vagrancy. I was thrown into prison. I can't tell you what a miserable time it was, William Lee. Vagrants and disorderly women of the very lowest and most wretched class of human being, almost naked, with only a few filthy rags that were alive with vermin. I'm lucky to be here at all. Many only got out of that place in a coffin.'

'Look, it's not my problem. I said I'd bring you to a place of safety and that I've done.'

I stood up, brushed the crumbs off my coat and turned to walk away.

'Stop. Don't go yet. I can help you.'

I turned back. 'What do you mean, you can help me? How can *you* help *me*?'

'I've told you, dead people speak through me.'

'Even if that were true, what use would that be to me? I've enough trouble to settle with those still living, never mind trouble with the dead.'

'How long do you think you can last with a few pennies in your pocket?'

'That's no concern of yours.'

'You won't last more than a week or two with what you've got, I'm telling you.'

'I'll manage.'

'People pay me to talk to their dead.'

'How do you mean?'

'The lately bereaved. I can get money off them.'

'Show me.'

'I will, but not here. I need peace and quiet. It's not easy to do.'

I had no need for the girl and indeed it would be better for the both of us to go our separate ways. If we were being followed, by staying together we were loading the dice in their favour. And yet I saw that she was vulnerable on her own. Still, she had been so before I came along, and would be thereafter. In any case, I had enough on my plate. But it would amuse me to see this feat.

'You can come with me until we get somewhere quiet. Then you can show me your trick.'

'It isn't a trick.'

'Whatever it is, let me see it for myself.'

'Then you'll consider my offer? It's something we can both make money from.'

'I'm making no promises.'

We turned away from the town and took to the road once more. We crossed over field and meadow until we were sheltered by a coppice.

'It's quiet here,' I said. 'Show me.'

'It doesn't always work,' she said.

I stood and waited. At first the girl looked flustered.

'Give me a moment,' she said.

I stood and waited some more.

'All right,' I said, 'that's your moment. It's been nice knowing you, Emily.'

I turned to walk away.

'Hang on. I can feel something.'

I turned back.

She closed her eyes and began to breathe rhythmically and slowly. In. Out. Her breathing became deeper, stronger. I drew closer. Her arms lay flaccid by her side, but then I noticed the fingers trembling involuntarily. She leaned forward and started to mutter. I couldn't make out what she was saying. At first I felt the urge to laugh but I suppressed it. The muttering moved closer to a groan and the urge to laugh came to me again. She started to shake. She raised her head. Her feet were twitching and the ends of her fingers were quivering, as though they were dancing over the keys of a piano. She stopped breathing. I counted. One, two, three . . . I got to ten and she still hadn't taken a breath.

'Emily, stop messing about. You're going to cause yourself damage.'

Still nothing. This is stupid, I thought. She's fooling no one with this game. Maybe it worked on children her own age, but I wasn't falling for it. I'd had enough of her folly and I went to shake her, but as I did, she took in a slow raspy breath that seemed to be drawn from the bowels of the earth. She opened her eyes. The same pale grey-green irises, but somehow changed. As though the candle inside had been snuffed out. She stared at me unseeing. She glared through me into another world. Her eyelids flickered erratically. She began to talk but with another's voice. It was the voice of an old woman and it sounded broken and frail. I felt a shiver travel down my spine and the hairs on the back of my neck stand up.

'William Lee.'

The accent was foreign and not one I recognised. I didn't respond.

'William Lee, William Lee, William Lee.'

Still I didn't say anything.

'You are not William Lee.'

96

I felt a jolt this time, like a cold metal pike poking through my spine. I shuddered. Despite myself, I was drawn closer.

'How . . . how do you know?'

'Because I know who you are.'

'Who are you?'

'The one who knows who you are.'

'Who?' I said, more urgently.

'Can you not guess?'

'Is that you? Can it really be you?'

'Yes, it is me, son.'

I felt my heart tingle with recognition.

'Mother? Where are you?'

'I am passed. I have crossed over.'

'Are you in heaven?'

'You have nothing to be afraid of.'

'What's my real name? Where am I from?'

'Your real name is not your real name. You are from far away.'

'But where? I'm going to Manchester, Mother, to make something of myself.'

'You came to Liverpool with me when you were very young.'

'I don't remember.'

'We were on a boat.'

'Were we?'

'Only I died before we got to the docks. I'm sorry, son. I wish I could be there with you. I want you to know that I'm watching over you. Always. I didn't mean to leave you on your own in this world.'

'I know, Mother. I understand.'

I felt hot tears spill from my eyes and run down my face.

'Go back to Liverpool and look for where you came from. That's where you'll find who you really are.'

With that Emily closed her eyes again and collapsed on the floor. I wiped my own eyes with the sleeve of my coat. I went over to where she had fallen. I picked her up and shook her.

'Wake up.'

I shook her again. At first, nothing. Then she opened her eyes.

'Are you all right?'

'Yes, yes, I'm fine. Did someone speak to you?'

'Yes.'

'Who?'

'Someone who said she was my mother.'

'What did she say?'

'It doesn't matter.'

I was shaking badly. I put the girl down on the ground and sat beside her. I closed my eyes and tried to gather my thoughts, but it was my emotions that were welling up inside me. I felt like a just-found orphan again. I was back by the fire, with Hindley glaring at me, and Mr Earnshaw telling him to stop scowling. 'Where's your manners, son? This boy is less fortunate than you. He has no mammy or daddy. He has no home. I want you to treat him as you would your brother, do you hear me? You'll see, you'll be best friends before you know it.' But the boy stood in the shadows and glared. I was dumb with fear.

I opened my eyes again. There was a crow in an ash tree close by, cleaning its beak on a branch. Then it unfurled its slick wings and took flight. I watched it soar over the moors.

'Well?'

I regained my composure.

'Well, what?'

'Do I pass?'

Had I been taken in? I wondered. Had my dead mother really spoken through the mouth of this girl? Certainly I knew that the dead could pierce the skin separating their world from ours. You had told me yourself of the ghosts that lingered in ancient places and the spirits who wandered the earth in search of solace, but had this girl the power to summon them, or was it a trick? When she spoke it was with another's voice. How could a girl speak with the voice of another? It had to be real.

'How do you do it?' I said at last.

'I don't know.'

'Is it a trick?'

'What kind of crooked character would use someone's grief for their own amusement? What do you take me for, William Lee? I promise you it's not a trick. All I know is that I have been blessed with a power. A power that can comfort and console both the living and the dead.'

What had the voice told me? Not who I was, but how I could find who I was. But I knew that already. Was it possible through practice or through a peculiar talent to fake spiritual possession? It had felt real at the time, sure enough, and the emotions the visitation had engendered in my soul – there was nothing fake about them. Real or not, I supposed it didn't matter; all that mattered was how well it could convince. It had convinced me. It would convince others.

'I don't know, Emily.'

'I can make us a lot of money.'

'So why do you need me?'

'I said I could make money. I didn't say I could keep money. A girl like me, travelling on her own, I don't stand a chance against the cutpurses and the freebooters. I need protection.'

I reflected on my lot. The pitman had his marrow, the smith his striker, sawyers worked in pairs, but I was on my own, Cathy. If what the girl had said was true, if my mother had spoken through her, then my mother was dead, and there was no one on earth waiting to take me in their arms. Perhaps me and this girl would provide some sort of company to each other. If she was as good as her word, then maybe it could work. She would need someone strong to protect her earnings. On her own, she and her money would be easily parted.

'You can stay for as long as you pay your way. I'm willing to give it a go for now.'

'I won't let you down.'

'If you do, you're out.'

The girl shrugged. 'So where are we heading?'

I thought for a moment. Manchester was no longer my desired destination. We could go there to rest, but we would move on to where Mr Earnshaw had found me in the street.

'Liverpool.'

'What for?'

'I've got some unfinished business there.'

'Where is it?'

'We head west until we get to the coast.'

'That's where Liverpool is?'

'Yes, I think so. It's a big town with a port where ships come and go. Hundreds of boats sail there.'

At the same time as I was talking to Emily I was

remembering. The boats, the bustle, the ocean. I recalled what Sticks had told me.

'I was a navvy, laa. I built up the banks of the Irwell and helped construct the locks. After that I worked on the duke's canal. Digging, puddling, the lot.'

'What's the Irwell?' I'd asked him.

'Don't you know, laa? It's a waterway. Goes all the way to the coast. It's where all the goods from around the world come from.'

'There's a canal, Emily. From Manchester to Liverpool. It's just been built. We can follow its length along the towpath. It shouldn't be hard to find.'

'Sounds like a plan. Shall we get something to eat?'

'You've only just eaten.'

'It gives you an appetite.'

'What does?'

'Conjuring dead people.'

'I wouldn't know.'

'Well, take it from me. You stick by me and you'll go a long way, William Lee, see if you don't.'

I thought about the last man she had probably said that to and saw him hanging from his neck. We both stood up and made our way back to the road. It was a well-constructed turnpike, and, with the sun in front of us, I reckoned it must be heading into Manchester. I was sick of trudging through fields of mud and moors of peat bog. We weren't far from the town, I figured, and far enough to be safe from the men who would have turned back some time past. I wondered how easy it would be for the farmer's son to steer a horse with only one hand. It would be difficult work, I wagered. Good. He had either bled to death or was now so handicapped by his amputation that finding us was an impossible task. We could relax, I decided. As we walked I felt something touch my sleeve. I looked down and saw that is was Emily. I shrugged her off.

For the most part the road was good. There were rough-looking wagons drawn by sturdy horses. Draymen, delivering tun and butt, hogshead and barrel. There were farmers' carts, piled high with hay, and finely carved coaches, ornately decorated. There were those who travelled on foot like us. Farm labourers who had finished their shifts, tinkers peddling their wares from one town to another. A coach pulled by four grand horses, coloured ribbons plaited through their manes, white, red, yellow, blue, riding past us. A coach driver sat high up front in uniform. Three men sat at the back in top hats, and at the front, three women in fine dresses carrying brightly coloured umbrellas above them.

'We'll be rich like them, one day,' Emily said.

'How do you work that one out then?'

'With my brains and your brawn we'll go a long way.'

'Cheeky bleeder.'

'I'm serious. We can make a lot of money, me and you.'

'Can we now?'

'We can buy a shop.'

'What sort of shop?'

'A cake shop.'

'Don't get ideas.'

'We'll start small, but we can get bigger as word spreads. We can employ bakers and cake-makers. People to serve behind the counter. We can oversee it all. Eat as many cakes as we like. Fancy cakes, with caraway seeds and oil of sweet almonds. Red cherries, loaf sugar, cinnamon and rose water. Icing and whipped cream. Custard and syrup. Pretty soon, we can open up another shop. Then another.'

I didn't want to correct her by telling her she had no place in my future. I had no interest in cakes, or shops of any kind. But then, part of me thought, maybe she has. Maybe I can take her back with me to Wuthering Heights, as Mr Earnshaw had brought me, where she can live in comfort, in front of the fire. Maybe find something useful for her to do, like tend fowl, but nothing too burdensome. The more I walked the more I mulled it over. It would wind Hindley up and push Hareton out of the picture. This made me smile. As I thought it through, I could see it as a possibility. I felt Emily's hand in mine. I didn't shake it off.

Tripe and Black Pudding

The journey to Manchester town took a day and a night, and we slept under the stars. We found a sheltered area beneath a blackthorn and I made a fire to keep warm. We suppered on faggots we'd purchased along the way. As we lay looking up at the many constellations, I taught Emily what you had taught me all those years ago. I pointed out the Dog Star and the Northern Cross. I showed her Leo and told her the story of Hercules strangling the great beast with his bare hands. I pointed out the swan and the bear and the ram and the bull, and all the other animals that filled the night sky.

When we got to Manchester town there was much commotion and mulling about. I was taken first by the sights, then by the sounds, and finally by the smells. In truth they must have hit my senses at the same time, but the magnitude of the vision I saw before me was too much to take in. The town in front of us was like nothing I had ever seen. It was more like a picture from one of your story books. A fairy-tale kingdom with palaces and princesses. Ladies and gentlemen of fine attire. Some wore fancy clothes, silk coats and embroidered waistcoats. Brightly coloured frocks, coloured ribbons and outlandish nosegays. Men with coloured strings through their breeches. My nose was assaulted with their perfumes. But also there were those in tattered rags, ravelled dugs and barefoot.

The buildings towering above us, reaching up to the clouds, were fit for giants. Like the Nephilim that Joseph spoke of. Doorways and arches that reached up to accommodate Goliath. Spires that pierced the blue canvas of the sky. Stones patterned with grotesque carvings and the roofs set with domes and decorated pikes. My ears were pricked with the clamour of industry. The clanking of metal plates. The clatter of iron-rimmed cartwheels on cobbles. Walking sticks, silver-tipped, tapping on the bevelled sets. Shouting, laughing, wailing. Street sellers hoarse with their own boasts. Pigeons and gulls grabbing at crumbs spilling from hand baskets and carts. Squawking and screeching. The stench of burning coals, of rotting offal and festering fruits. Piss and shit and vomit. A beggar sleeping in the gutter. A painted chaise pulled by fine mares. I saw the driver crack his whip and drive his vehicle over the fingers of the beggar, slicing through two of them as though they were breakfast sausages. Not stopping to help the man, but cracking the whip for his horses to go faster. I grabbed hold of Emily. This was a place where you had to keep your wits about you. The vision before me was one part heaven and one part hell. I could barely decide what to make of it.

We walked down a street signposted 'Shudehill', then along another signposted 'Withy Grove'. There was such an array of accents, from every corner of the kingdom, and even from the Emerald Isle. I remembered that was one of your other theories to my origins, Cathy. You said that the Spanish Armada had planned to attack England but that there had been a severe storm and that some of its vessels were wrecked on the west coast of Ireland. I was the son of a Spanish duke and an Irish gypsy. The duke had been saved from the storm by the gypsy girl. She had pulled him out of the water half-drowned and revived him, then she had nursed him back to health in her caravan. She had fallen in love with the duke. Then one day, some sailors came for him and he was called back to his ship and she never saw him again. Only now she was carrying his child. I used to laugh at some of your ideas, but I was comforted by them too: I was from somewhere, I was someone, I wasn't just an orphan.

As we walked further into town, past Cannon Street and along Market Street Lane, there was an overpowering stench of industrial refuse and of open sewers. Children played among the garbage and privy middens. There were buildings everywhere; some looked like they'd only just been built. And all around these were buildings in different stages of construction. Some were just a few walls and others were wanting roofs. Others again were merely marks on the ground. There were skeletons of buildings waiting for their flesh and skin. There were builders, sawyers, carpenters and various men at work. There was a hubbub and a swarm. There was gin being sold from wheelbarrows in the street and, later we learned, privately in garrets, cellars and back rooms. We saw many partakers stagger around in their bibulous stupors. We saw Methodist ministers reading from the Bible and other religious scripture; harlots selling their bodies; and beggars, their flesh rotting with distemper, covered with scorbutic and venereal ulcers. Among all this, stalls of every description selling their wares. Sweetmeat stalls, rope makers, chair menders, knife sharpeners. There were lanterns for sale and brimstone matches, sealing wax, silver buckles, snuffboxes.

There were a great many shops. We approached the most sizeable. Inside there was an impressive variety of articles: tea, coffee, loaf sugar, spices, printed cottons, calicoes, lawns, fine linens such as you were now accustomed to wearing: silks, velvets, silk waistcoat pieces, silk cloaks, hats, bonnets, shawls, laced caps, and a myriad of elegant things, Cathy. In short, all the finery that you were now taking for granted. There was a druggist selling pomatum, fever powder, angel water, Jesuit drops. Hemlock for tumours and burdock for scurvy.

We came across another shop that sold every kind of offal. Many items to fill our appetites. There were red herrings, bloaters, cow-heel, sheep's trotters, pigs' ears, tripe and black pudding. The black pudding looked the most appetizing and I asked the shopkeeper what it consisted of.

'It's a sausage made of blood.'

'What blood?' Emily asked.

'Pork blood. There's oatmeal in there too, and pork fat. It's a health food,' she said. 'It'll keep your strength up.'

I liked the idea of feasting on blood, and in the absence of a good supply of Hindley's, we bought two slabs and the vendor wrapped them in paper and lathered them with malt vinegar. We took our food outside and ate it. The taste was unlike anything I'd ever had before but very pleasant. Emily had eaten hers before I was even halfway into mine.

'Lovely,' she said, licking her lips. 'I could eat another one of those.'

'We've not got much money left now,' I said. 'We'll have to get to work soon.'

But there was too much to see in these bustling streets and we wandered around for hours. Along Deansgate and King Street, there were soup kitchens and Irish vagrants. There were people living in sheds made of clot and clay and others made of brick. There were rats running in and out of the building and dogs running wild. We saw many a deformed infant, with knees swelled or ankles swelled, one shoulder lower than the other, round-shouldered or pigeon-breasted. Or in some other way deformed. There were younger infants still, hardly able to walk, with rag dummies in their mouths. We saw children not much older than four or five, leaving a cotton mill: small, sickly, barefoot and ill-clad. Children on street corners selling pins and needles. Women selling tapes and laces, fruit and cakes. I bought myself an orange and Emily a gingerbread man. I cut my orange in two and sucked the juice out. It was only the second time in my life I'd ever tried one, the first time being when I stole one from a bowl that was meant for the Lintons. So its sweetness was still a novelty. I watched Emily savage her gingerbread man, gobbling down his head first, then his legs.

'They taste better if you eat them like this,' she said. 'Before they get a chance to complain and run away.'

Then we saw before us, Cathy, such a peculiar object of misery, that my own history of affliction seemed as fortune.

Emily turned to me. 'Look at that boy. What the hell happened to him?'

'I don't know,' I said.

I couldn't stop staring at this poor freak. He had neither a hat for his head nor a buckle for his shoes. He was no more than twelve years of age but much shorter than Emily. A cripple on crutches, little more than three feet in stature. His legs and feet were as crooked as twisted willow branches. His hair looked like a hog's bristles and his head like a black cinder. My own was as white as Edgar's in comparison. He was blind and used his crutches as feelers, testing the ground before taking a step forward, like a snail with its tentacles. The boy coughed with such a hacking sound, I thought he was going to hawk his guts up. I saw him spit blood onto the cobs. I overheard a conversation between two men who were standing beside us.

'He's still employed in his work. Would you believe that?' the first man said.

'And what work would that be then?' said the second.

'He's a sweeper of chimneys.'

Emily moved closer to me and clutched the arm of my coat.

'Poor bastard,' she said, under her breath.

No torture Hindley rent on me could compare to the daily torture this boy suffered at his place of work. I glanced around. Everywhere I looked I saw routine cruelty and every-day misery. Alongside which there were fancy coaches and gentlemen and ladies, in and out of tailors' shops, milliners', candle shops and fine bakeries. So much wealth and privilege alongside so much privation. Not one of these gentle folk stopped to assist, or even seemed to notice this miserable wretch.

I watched Emily eye a wealthy family with envy. They were standing outside a milliner's, looking in the window.

Their daughter appeared to be about the same age as Emily. Her father was wearing a black tricorne, with a knee-length red silk coat. He had a gold-tipped walking cane, and two gold chains dangling from his waistcoat. His wife had a dress of green silk and a hat decorated with feathers. The girl wore a powder-blue silk dress, quite simple in design in comparison with her mother's dress. Likewise, her hat was a simple white with a powder-blue ribbon. Still, it looked expensive. I saw Emily clock all this.

We roamed the streets all day until at last I said that we needed to find somewhere to lig for the night. Our money would run out sooner than I'd anticipated. Everything here was twice what it would have cost in Keighley. I wondered if we could go to work. Now was as good a time as any. We walked along the river, past the cathedral, until we found a large graveyard on the outskirts of the town. There we waited.

'I think we should use different names,' Emily said.

'How do you mean?'

'Just as a precaution.'

I looked about the chiselled graves; some were headstones, and some lay on the ground. Some were fresh and others pock-marked with lichen. I read out names: 'Edward, Arthur, Henry, Obadiah, Solomon.' I watched Emily scan the stones as well.

'I'll be Clarissa,' she said.

'Pleased to meet you, sister, my name is Obadiah.'

The first four mourners we approached dismissed us in various ways. One called us minions of Satan, another called us devil's spawn. I was starting to think that our business was doomed to failure.

'Well, we've given it our best shot,' I said.

'No, we've not. Takes longer.'

'One more go then, Emily.'

'Let's try it different next time.'

'How?'

'I'll stay concealed till you give me the word. You work them round a bit. Then call me over.'

'What difference will that make?'

'Just try it.'

I shrugged. I supposed it was worth a go.

Eventually we saw an old woman approach a grave and stand in its shadow, muttering under her breath. The mound of earth in front was newly turned. We did not approach but watched from the shade of an oak. She was dressed in black widow's weeds, which even from this distance I could see were cut from an expensive cloth. She wore a long black headdress that covered her back, which was trimmed with a white lace edge. Then she commenced sobbing. She took out a white handkerchief from under her shawl and wiped her eyes. I waited until she had spent some of her grief and the tears had dried. Emily waited in the shadows.

I tentatively approached the woman. The grave was grandly carved and of an ostentatious decoration. I noted the name cut into the stone: Tom Hardy.

'Good afternoon, madam. I am very sorry for your grief. Please accept my condolences. Mr Hardy was a fine man. We all thought the world of him, I just wanted you to know that.'

She looked at me properly for the first time, studying my attire.

'Did you know him?'

'Not so well, madam, but a little.'

She observed my scuffed boots and the loose stitching on my surtout sleeve.

'Did you work for him in the mill?'

I was thinking on my feet – so he was a boss of some sort.

'That's right, madam. It was a pleasure to work for your husband. He made our labour light. My name is Obadiah Bell. Pleased to make your acquaintance.'

We shook hands and she told me her name was Elisabeth Hardy.

'He was a kind man,' I said. 'Some of the other managers at that mill are cruel taskmasters. I've seen some dock a man a day's wage for being a minute late to the job. But not Mr Hardy. He was an honest man and decent. I only wish the world had more men like him.'

'I knew the mill would be the death of him,' she said. 'It was all he could think about. It wasn't enough to make a profit – he wanted to improve conditions for the workers. Shorter hours, better pay. He even talked about fitting bigger windows so that the workforce could enjoy the light of the day. He said it was the devil who toiled in the dark. Such long hours. I know that's what killed him. He said he couldn't claim to have built the first mill, but he could claim to have built the best mill. The one that was closest to God.'

'I've worked for tyrants in my time, madam. What can I say? Men more like monsters, who thought nothing of people, only of pounds, shillings and pence. I've had to leave some jobs just to save my own skin. To stay would have been to perish. God bless your sweet husband.'

'I wish my Tom had realised that to do good, one has to start by doing good by oneself.'

'If only he had realised, madam. May I introduce you to my sister? We are both grief-stricken ourselves.'

'I'm sorry for your loss.'

'Our parents are both dead. Burned to death in our family home, just a few days ago. They are just now buried yonder.'

'That's awful. You poor things.'

I beckoned Emily over.

'This is my poor sister, Clarissa Bell.'

I observed the woman's reaction.

'I know what you are thinking: there is no family resemblance. In truth, she is not my sister by birth but the only sister I have known. Her parents took me in off the streets when I was still a bairn, and they became my parents also.'

A good lie embellishes the truth, Cathy.

'Pleased to meet you,' Emily said.

The girl and the woman shook hands.

We spoke gravely of our respective deceased before I brought the conversation to the place I wanted it to be.

'My sister has a peculiar gift but one that may serve to comfort you in your grief.'

'Oh really, what is that?'

'The dead speak through her.'

The woman looked shocked. She took a moment to compose herself, then said, 'I've heard of this gift. Some say it is the work of the devil.'

I lowered my voice. 'Some do, madam, that's true. But tell me, if it be the work of the devil, would it offer such comfort to the virtuous?'

113

'Well, I don't know. I just know what the minister said.'

'And what was that?'

'That sorcery and witchcraft is the ken of Old Nick.'

'But this is neither sorcery nor witchcraft, madam.'

'How can you be so sure?'

'Didn't Jesus raise Lazarus of Bethany four days entombed? Would you call that witchcraft? Would you accuse Jesus of sorcery?'

'No, never.'

'And isn't the devil's job to meddle in the affairs of men? To bring down those with virtue so that they reach his level? And if that is so, why would he waste his time, offering solace to good Christian folk like yourself?'

'That's true,' she said, but then shook her head in doubt. 'I don't know. I just don't know.'

'It takes a lot of strength out of my sister to perform the rite. But it makes her happy to comfort the bereaved. It is God himself who has given her this gift. The Lord has blessed her.'

'But I've been told that sometimes the devil does good work in order to turn us to his side.'

'Would it not be a great comfort to be able to speak to your dear Tom again?'

'Yes. It would.'

She nodded gravely. I could see my words were having an effect. That we were winning her over. She was at the point of change and I just needed to push now ever so carefully.

'The dead also pine for the living. Tom wants to speak to you. My sister is the vessel for his voice.'

'Are you sure it will be all right?'

'I promise you.' I took her gently by the arm. 'Please, step under this tree and we'll see if she can be of assistance, for she is not always able to perform the rite. It is dependent on so many things. Let's pray that the powers work inside her, God willing.'

We walked over to our secluded spot under the cover of the old oak. Jack Nicker and Betty Tit twittered about the boughs.

'Do you have anything about your person that belonged to Tom, by any chance?'

'This,' she said.

She unlatched a gold chain from around her neck.

'I had this made a few years ago. It's Tom's old watch chain.'

She handed it to me and I gave it to the girl, who clutched it in her fist. It was a spontaneous idea, but I know how people can attach themselves to things. Emily closed her eyes and her arms went flaccid by her side.

'I hope she can offer comfort,' I said to the woman. 'May the good Lord bless us today.'

For a moment nothing happened. We stood under the tree and waited. Then Emily began to shake. She bowed her head.

'Is she all right?' the woman whispered.

I put my finger to my lips. 'Please, she needs silence to perform the rite,' I whispered.

Emily went into her trance as the dead crept into her flesh. Her extremities tremored with the feeling of another. Until she raised her head level with the old woman's and opened her eyes. Again, I witnessed the same transformation. The same eyes, but not the same eyes. These were the eyes of one who had passed. The old woman standing before me gasped. I gave her a reassuring nod. I noticed that the graveyard had fallen silent. No birds now sang.

This time when the girl spoke it was with the voice of an old man.

'Beth, is that you, my love?'

The woman grabbed my arm to steady herself. She turned to me. 'Can this be true?'

I nodded. 'Believe your own ears.'

The woman was speechless. She shook her head.

'Beth, it's me. I am here.'

The old woman turned to me once again for reassurance.

'Please, it's all right. Talk to your husband.'

She turned to Emily. 'Tom?'

'Yes, my love?'

'Oh, Tom, is that really you?'

'It is.'

'But . . . how can it be?'

'I am come. I speak through another.'

'Oh, Tom!'

Tears flowed freely from the woman's eyes and she dabbed at them with the handkerchief.

'Oh, my love. Please don't weep for me. I see you at my grave and I see you weep and it makes me very sad. For I am in a better place waiting for you to join me.'

'Oh, Tom, it's so good to hear your voice. I've been so lost without you.'

'And I lost without you, my love.'

'I've prayed for you every day and every night. I've spoken to you at your grave, wishing each time that you could answer back.'

'I wish I could be there by your side but I know that one day you will join me and I will no longer be alone.'

'Is it very lonely there?'

'Aye, my love, but don't worry for me. Time passes quickly. A day in your world is but a minute here. The hands of the clocks in heaven whizz round like the wings of a snipe fly. And I'm not on my own. There is a child by my side.'

'Is he with you? Oh, that's wonderful. Not a day goes by when I don't think of him. Not even an hour.'

'We are both waiting for you, my dear. Fear not. Death hath no dominion.'

The girl's eyes closed, then her body went rigid, before collapsing on the floor. She lay there with her arms by her side and her head resting on one cheek.

'Is she all right?'

'She'll come round. Best to leave her for a minute or two. It takes a great deal of strength. The effort required to connect the two worlds, the material and the spirit, takes a huge amount of energy. Sometimes she sleeps for days afterwards.'

'Oh, the poor thing. Will you take something for your trouble?'

'I wouldn't dream of it, madam. Our payment is your loving face when you spoke with your late husband. And our wages are your comfort.'

'I insist. Please.'

She took out her purse.

'Really, that's not necessary.'

'I'm afraid I won't take no for an answer. Please, it will make me happy.'

'If you insist, it will ensure my sister and I will be able to have a hot meal and somewhere to sleep. But only a shilling if you can spare it.'

She took out some coins.

'Here, have a shilling each. One for you, Obadiah, and one for your dear sister, Clarissa. Please, it's the least I can do.'

I pocketed the two shilling pieces.

'Thank you, that's very kind.'

I unclasped the watch chain from Emily's fist and handed it back to the woman. I helped fasten it around her neck. I walked her back to her husband's grave and bade her good-night. As I did I noticed the gravestone. Under the inscription of her dead husband was that of another: it was the inscription of her son who had died at just five years of age. Had Emily seen this? Was it a trick? But I'd heard the voice of Tom uttered from her lips. A ten-year-old girl was capable of many things, but not to change her voice entirely to that of a man's. It wasn't possible. Then there was my mother, whose words I'd heard tumble from Emily's tongue. That had to be real. My mother had spoken to me. I was sure of that.

As I was walking away, the woman said, 'She will be all right, won't she, your sister?'

I nodded solemnly. 'It's a gift from God,' I said. 'God will restore her.'

The woman smiled and thanked me again. I walked back to the tree. The girl had recovered her faculties.

'Did I do well?' she said.

'Yes, you did well. Come on,' I said. 'Let's eat.'

We walked back into the town along its crowded streets. We'd done it. We'd actually done it. It had taken five attempts and several patient hours but we had done it by hook or by crook. Down Fountain Street, we passed more gin barrows and harlots selling their flesh.

'Where's my money?' Emily said.

'How do you mean?'

'One shilling is mine.'

'I'm keeping it safe,' I said. 'Don't you trust me?'

'Do I fuck.'

We passed an open privy, where people were pissing and shitting in full view, then entered the largest alehouse we could find. Emily ordered hasty pudding and pease-kail, and I ordered roast beef, the first real meat I'd eaten in weeks. We sat by the fire and waited for our supper. The flames lit up Emily's face, making her skin glow and her eyes sparkle. We were both in an ebullient mood and we chatted about this and that as we waited for our grub. My mouth was watering with anticipation of the meat. I rubbed the coins in my breeches pocket. Two shillings was the equivalent of two days' labour. Not bad going for two minutes' work. On top of this, I still had pennies in my sack.

'That was good going back there,' I said as we tucked into our supper.

'All in a day's work,' she said as she heaped in spoonfuls of food. 'We'll do all right, me and you.' She smiled at me as she ate with her mouth wide open.

What a pig, I thought. But even pigs can raise a pretty profit.

'And tomorrow?' she said.

'Well, my feeling is that there's plenty of brass round these parts. Why don't we stay for a few days, make a few guineas so that when we get to Liverpool we'll be comfortable off.'

'Suits me. Can I get a new dress?'

'Well, let's see how rich we get. I don't see why not.'

'I liked the one that girl was wearing.'

'Which one?'

'Outside the milliner's shop.'

I tried to recollect. I saw in my mind the couple with the girl the same age as Emily and the same white-blonde hair.

'The blue one?'

'Yes, the blue one.'

'We'll see.'

'Don't be a cunt.'

'I said, we'll see.'

'And some boots?'

'That all depends on how lucky we get.'

'Oh, we'll get lucky,' she said, and stuffed some more food into her mouth. 'There's loads of folk round this town with grieving hearts. I can just tell. It's us doing them the favour, you know. They'd be lost without us.'

I watched her load up another fork. She was some girl, for sure. Had she really conjured the dead? I weighed it up. She'd just earned us an outstanding supper, so what the hell. And I wanted to believe. Not that my mother had died on the ship, but that I had a mother and I had spoken to her and that she was now in heaven watching over me.

I picked up my knife and fork and cut another slice of beef. It was still red in the middle with the blood of the beast, and I thought again about Dick Taylor's wound, pumping blood on the floor of the barn. Surely he had bled to death. No one could survive a bloodlet of that scale. After we had finished our food, I ordered some tea and some cordial for Emily. She started to cough. It was just a tickle at first, but then it built into a hacking cough. She took out a handkerchief and covered her mouth with it. I noticed that it was the white silk handkerchief the widow had used.

'Emily, where did you get that?'

She just shrugged.

'Listen to me – we need to keep a low profile. No filching fogles, or anything for that matter. Do you understand?'

She nodded.

'I'm not laiking about. They can hang you for that. No fucking stealing, do you hear?'

'Do you think we can get a pudding?' she said. 'I'm still hungry.'

In the Shadow of the Gallows

We lodged that night in the alehouse and the next day we breakfasted on boiled milk and oatmeal, sweetened with thick syrup. I was still smiling inwardly from yesterday's success. It was raining when we set out but soon cleared to a fine mist, then passing altogether, revealing a window of blue. In the town square there were pigeons feeding on the scraps of last night's supper. A man with no legs, perching on a short-wheeled cart, was making his way across the paving using his hands to propel his body. The pigeons scattered in his wake. The man grasped greedily for the crumbs they left behind. Manchester town was a place of contradiction and for every story of triumph there were two stories of despair. I tossed the man a coin.

We walked up Deansgate and across Market Place. Along Withy Grove and Shudehill until we climbed up out of the town to another burial ground. This one was about the same size as the first, but the graves were more ramshackle. The ones placed flat were in the shadow of a looming chapel. There were beech trees where rooks reeled and ragged, and beneath my feet my heel crunched on last year's husks. We walked over to the other side, where the headstones were planted. We noted the flowers placed by. There was a grave with the name Bartholomew; next to this someone had placed a glass of claret. I watched Emily scour the stones.

'Well?'

'I'm Arabella.'

We found a clump of trees and waited.

We encountered several grief-stricken victims during the course of the morning and once again we were met with various forms of rejection – suspicion, accusation, fear and indifference – before we struck gold once more. It was close to noon when we saw a frail old man approach. He wore a blue frock coat and a cocked hat with a wide brim. He stopped by a grave and laid down a wreath of white flowers. The mound was still fresh. I left Emily under the bough of a tree, picked up a bunch of red flowers from a grave nearby, and approached the man. He looked to be in his eighties. Beneath his coat he wore a black suit with a long blue kerchief wrapped around his neck, and an embroidered waistcoat. There were gold buckles on his shoes.

'Excuse me, sir. Could I trouble you for the time of day?'

He noticed me for the first time. He took out a gold watch from his waistcoat pocket and flipped the lid. He examined the face of the watch.

'It's half past the hour of eleven,' he said, tucking the fob back into his pocket.

'Is it really? Then I'm not late as I'd thought. You see,

I have a very important appointment but I had to come and see my mother first. Today is her birthday. She would have been forty years of age, if the Lord hadn't taken her from me.'

I thought about my own mother in heaven, but pushed the thought away.

'I'm sorry to hear that.'

'It was many years ago. Bless her soul. She's buried in yonder corner,' I said, pointing. 'I've never missed her birthday. I always bring her red flowers. Red was her favourite colour.'

I produced the flowers and held them out for the man to see.

The man was aloof at first and looked over my tattered surtout with disdain, but as I spoke of my own tragedy in more detail, he softened to my cause.

'I've just lost my last child. I had four but now they've all left me.'

We chatted for a while until I found a place to introduce the subject of Emily. The man was initially reluctant, but I assured him of the virtue of the endeavour as I had done with the woman yesterday. I ushered Emily over.

'My name is Bartholomew Stone and this is my stepsister, Arabella.'

'I had four daughters each as pretty as you, Arabella. And now I have none. Four of the sweetest creatures to bless this world have left me and gone to heaven. My wife died after giving birth to our youngest. My girls all died of the slow fever. 'Tis a cruel disease. The last one took months. She was delirious by the end. Kept calling me Tessa. Refused to wear clothes. The maids didn't know what to do or where to look. She died in my arms while I tried to feed her semolina and honey. Her last words were, "I prefer chicken." I died too in that moment. What you see before you is a walking shell. Life is a tedious, senseless business.'

'Indeed, it is a mystery at best. Only God understands our purpose.'

The man nodded sagely.

Emily carried out her work conjuring the man's wife. I watched again as her body, flaccid at first, became animated by the vigour of a restless spirit. Her eyelids flickered involuntarily and when they opened once more, her pale grey eyes were alive with a sleepless spectre from the hereafter.

The visitation moved the old man to tears. I pocketed our reward and we both stood and watched him depart, still trembling from the experience. The morning's work had been difficult, but our efforts had paid off. I reflected that we would have more luck if we appeared in our attire more respectable. When he had gone I turned to Emily and noticed that she was holding something in one hand.

'What's that?' I asked.

She unclenched her fist to reveal the old man's gold watch.

'You bloody fool, what did you steal that for?'

'Worth a few bob, that.'

I took the fob watch from her and examined it. The gold was polished and shiny and the casing was carved with an ornate pattern. I turned it over and there were three initials: 'E.B.T.'

'Look at this,' I said, holding it up so she could see. 'This mark will give the game away. A man like that, with so much wealth, he's no doubt very influential hereabouts. It's not worth it. If we get caught with this, we'll hang.'

'So what are you saying?'

'We have to give it him back.'

'He's not going to fall for that. He'll know we've stolen it.'

'Well, you managed to pilfer it off him under his nose, you can put it back under his nose too. We need to find him, quick, before he discovers the theft.'

We ran out of the burial ground and down the street but the man was nowhere to be found.

'Maybe he came by coach,' Emily said.

'I didn't see one parked outside.'

'You weren't looking for one.'

'Where do you think he's gone?'

'I've no idea.'

We carried on down the street, past houses and shops. But there was no sign of him.

'Perhaps he's gone for something to eat,' Emily said.

We searched some of the taverns, pie shops and cof-fee-houses. Nothing. We spent an hour or more looking for him, combing each street, checking in each shop. We wandered around the market. It amazed me how such a frail old man had managed to give us the slip. It was early afternoon, and we were about to give up, when we saw him outside a bookshop, leafing through a leather-bound tome.

'Now's our chance,' I said.

'He'll know the watch is missing by now,' Emily said.

'All right, I've got another plan.'

I went up to the man and tapped him on the shoulder. He turned with a start.

'Thank the Lord, we've found you,' I said. 'You see, my sister and I have been looking everywhere for you.'

'Oh, really?'

I took out the watch. 'It was after you'd gone that we spotted it by the side of your family grave.' I handed it over.

He took hold of the watch and examined it.

'I thought I'd lost it. A gift from my wife. The chain needed replacing. My own fault. I can't thank you enough. Here, let me give you something for your trouble.'

'I wouldn't dream of it,' I said. And refused the offer. He shook my hand and smiled.

'You are both good Christians.'

Later, when we were some distance from the man, I turned to Emily. 'What have I said about not stealing? It's not worth it. We need to keep as low as stoats. We're conspicuous enough as it is, without drawing more attention. So no more fucking stealing, right?'

'I suppose,' she said, grudgingly. 'Can we get that dress now?'

~

I took stock at breakfast the next morning. Yesterday had been productive and my pockets were heavy with gold and silver, but we'd also had a near miss. I'd had a hard word with Emily and I believed she had learned from her mistakes. The watch had been returned and our excuses had been accepted. I put the incident in perspective. Manchester was a big town. We weren't done with it yet. My plan was to have a leisurely breakfast, then get kitted out with some new garments, explore

127

some of the further-out places, and find some more stately graves to get to work on. There were bound to be several places of burial where the rich were entombed. It was just a case of wandering around and taking our chances. I was learning that it wasn't just worms who could feast on the remains of the dead. I went to look for the innkeeper. I wanted to ask him if we could arrange for a bath when we returned from our work. It had been many days since I had washed properly, and I reckoned we both probably stank like sewer rats. I couldn't find the man and asked his wife, who was standing at the sink in the kitchen, if she knew of his whereabouts.

'He's out back,' she said. 'Seeing to the horses. Got late guests last night, in a carriage.'

I went out to the stables, but before I had a chance to find the innkeeper, I heard voices coming from one of the outbuildings. One of them was familiar, and I felt a tightness grip me. I approached cautiously. Without looking behind the stable doors, I was close enough now to hear clearly the voices of two men alongside the innkeeper's. I couldn't be absolutely sure, so very tentatively I peeped through a hole in the wooden door. It was him: Dick Taylor. The man with one hand and his straw-haired companion. I didn't stop to listen, but ran back to where Emily was still eagerly stuffing her face. When she saw me she dropped the spoon.

'What's the matter? You look like you've just seen a ghost.'

I grabbed hold of her and lifted her out of her chair. I took her hand and yanked her from the room.

'What's wrong?'

'No time,' I said, and ran out of the tavern and down the street, pulling Emily along. 'This way.'

I turned off the main street and down an alley. Halfway down I turned off again. It was only after a good five minutes of running turn and turn-about that I stopped and let us get our breath.

'Are you going to tell me what's going on?' Emily said, panting.

'It's them. They're here.'

'Shit.'

'Dick and his mate.'

'How do you know?'

'I saw them in the stables. Talking to the innkeeper.'

'What did they say?'

'I didn't hear it. I ran as soon as I saw them.'

'What do you think he told them?'

'I don't know.'

'Do you think he said where we were?'

'I don't know. Come on, let's keep on going.'

We walked down another road. Then another street and through another alley. It was still early and there weren't that many people around. The cobbles were glistening from the evening's rain.

'We're fucked,' Emily said.

'No, we're not. Even if the owner ratted on us, they don't know where we've gone. Manchester's a big town. Tens of thousands of people. They'll not find us.'

'But what if they do?'

'They won't.'

I felt that we were far enough away now to be out of any immediate danger, but I walked at a pace nevertheless, without arousing suspicion, pulling Emily along with me. We

129

said no more about it and walked on in silence. We turned down Long Lane, where, despite the hour, already there was much activity. There was a fruit-seller on the street corner. I stopped and bought a few apples for the trip. I asked for directions to the canal.

The man pointed over in the distance. 'Head for Deansgate. Hit a left when you get there and follow the road straight down until you get to Castle Field. You'll see a brick mill by the quay. The duke's canal is further on.'

'And it goes to Liverpool?'

'Turn and turn-about, if that's where you're heading.'

I pocketed the apples and thanked the man. We made our way down Peter Street until we came to the junction at Deansgate. When we came to Bridgewater Street, I guessed that the canal must be close.

'How do you know about the canal?' she said.

'A man named Sticks, worked with him on the farm – the tall thin bloke, do you remember?'

'Not really.'

'I told you about him. He used to be a navvy. Sticks said that the man who built it was a duke and that this duke had travelled Europe as part of his education. And in France he had fallen in love with a lady of some standing. I can't remember her name now. Anyway, this lady had spurned him. Returning to England, licking his wounds, he vowed never to fall in love again, and instead devoted himself to industry. When he came back to England he was resolute. He'd seen a canal in France and decided he wanted to outdo the French.'

'So the canal was his revenge?' Emily said.

How many great things had been achieved, Cathy, because

a woman spurned a man? Perhaps in a peculiar way your cruelty would prove useful to me.

'I think my dad loved my mum,' Emily said. 'I'm sure he did. He said he only hit her because he loved her.'

'Well, don't ask me,' I said. 'I'm no expert.'

We came to a market square. As we did, a noisy procession of people blocked our way. There was no possibility that we could force a path through so we stopped and watched the procession. I kept my eye out for Dick and his mate. There was a cart of people. Men in gaudy attire and women in white with baskets of flowers and oranges. We watched the women throw the oranges to the crowd that had gathered around the procession. There were pedlars and tinkers. Ballad-singers and hawkers. And then I saw it, high above us – the gallows.

The men in the cart were the condemned and they had come to meet their end. By the gallows the hangman stood, biding his time. We waited in the shadows until the crowd thinned sufficiently for us to make our way. I observed Emily staring up at the wooden scaffold.

'Come on,' I said, 'let's get going.'

'He gave a speech, you know, before they put the noose around his neck.'

'Best not to think about it,' I said.

'It was a very cold day, not like today, and he was shivering from the cold. People said he was chicken, but it was freezing. I was cold myself even in my woollen shawl. I was with his friend Lizzy Lawrence. She was shivering too. There were icicles hanging from the boughs of the trees. It was unusually cold that day. They released him from his fetters and a pair of leg-irons. There was no one else to hang that morning so he was the star turn. He was alone on that platform, just him and the hangman. Then the priest came and they prayed together. They sang one of the psalms. It was so cold that his voice faltered. You could see his breath mist in front of his face. There was a huge crowd. He stood perched upon the gallows ladder. Then he turned to his audience and made his speech.'

Emily stared up at the wooden construction again. It looked like a giant pointing finger.

'And?'

'He said, "Good people, I forgive you all, as you should forgive me. There will be no peace in hell. I have done many bad things in my life and I will have plenty of time in an eternity of damnation to recall them. I've murdered men, women and children, and things much more wicked than that besides."'

'Did he really say that?'

'Lizzy said she thought he was drunk. He was slurring his words. I kept waiting for him to notice me in the crowd. To give me a wave. Or just to look at me.'

'And did he not?'

'There were so many people there. It couldn't have been easy.'

I looked over to the gallows once more, Cathy. The condemned men were at their stations now and the hangman was tightening the rope around the neck of the last one. I pulled Emily away.

'Come on, you don't need to see this.'

I took her by the hand and we wove through the throng, being jostled as we did so. It was not a pretty gathering and I was glad when we got to where it was thinning and were able to leave it behind. We soon came to the mill and the quay as the man had directed. I looked around to make sure we hadn't been followed. The coast was clear. By the quay there was a large flat barge loaded with coal. It was being pulled by a horse. A man jumped off the barge and tied a rope that was attached to it around a thick wooden post. The horse came to a standstill and bent down to chew the grass by its feet. We heard a cheer in the distance, emanating from the direction of the gallows, and I guessed the men had made the drop and were now dangling from a rope. The last dance of the damned.

I looked over to Emily. She had her face in her hands and her chest was heaving. I stopped for a minute to let her shake it out. I thought about what she must have seen. Her own father swinging by his neck. She tried to stifle her sobs, but I saw the wet drops fall from between her fingers onto the cobs below. I put my hand on her shoulder. She wrapped her arms around my waist and clung on, burying her face in my coat. Her body shook violently. I placed my hand on her head and stroked her hair. We stayed like that while it worked itself out of her. She pulled away. I wiped the wet from her cheeks.

'Are you all right?' I said.

She nodded.

'Let's go.'

A little further by the mill entrance were more boats. They contained a system of square boxes filled with coals. The boats were manoeuvred under a well, where they stopped and the rope fixed to the crane above was let down with hooks. At the end the boxes were fastened and then drawn up. The crane was powered by a waterwheel. Two men and a boy were employed in the unloading. They took no notice of us as we walked past them. I looked back one more time to make sure we were not being followed.

What I saw next was a scene of industry like no other. At the mouth of the canal was a door fastened on hinges at the bottom of the water, which stopped the water entering a trapdoor. Further on a large timber yard, well stowed with all sorts of wood and timbers for framing buildings and constructing boats, barges and all kinds of floating machines. Next to this was a stonemason's yard, where vast piles of stones lay, ready squared for loading onto barges. The barges here were drawn by mules, until they came to a tunnel. What we saw next, Cathy, was quite ingenious. The towpath ran out at the tunnel, and instead a boy led the mules the long way, over and around the tunnel. Here is the clever part: at the point where the barge entered the tunnel, the men onboard lay on their backs and used their legs to power the barge through its length, making the boat look like a giant scurrying insect. The engineer had left just the right distance from the barge top to the ceiling of the tunnel so that the men were able to 'walk' on the brick ceiling of the tunnel until they appeared out of the other end to be reacquainted with their mules. In this way they were able to power the boats at the same rate as we had observed them being pulled by mule. We stopped for a while observing the scene, neither Emily nor I saying a word. After we had got a good eyeful we carried on our way.

It was easy walking by the side of the canal. We just had to avoid the horses and mules that were pulling the barges, and the canal workers. Most of the barges were loaded with coal. There were a few passenger boats as well, and interspersed were other barges carrying a variety of goods. The canal itself was an impressive structure, Cathy. You would have been impressed by this feat of engineering. I remember you telling me about the pyramids of Egypt. You said that's where gypsies were from. You told me about these huge constructions built by the hands of hundreds of slaves. You showed me some drawings in one of Mr Earnshaw's books. You would be equally impressed by this canal though, I assure you. It was dug out of the earth, and completely level, so that the water didn't flow like a river but sat like the water in a bath. The canal itself snaked through the landscape, remaining level at all times. It had taken some toil to dig it out, no doubt. Although not the duke's toil, I suspect. Hundreds of men with pickaxe and spade. Sweat and blood. It had a peculiar smell. A metallic tang. The walls were constructed of large flat stones, with heavy top stones to finish the job.

'Here,' I said, and handed Emily one of the apples. I bit into the other one.

It was pleasant going on this towpath, no uneven tussock grass or boggy peat moor. The land was level and it was good to walk by the water, with the occasional flash of orange and bright blue of a kingfisher. We saw one dive for fish, then re-emerge, like a flame from a fire pit.

I tried again with Emily.

'We'll need lodgings when we get to Liverpool. We'll need money. We'll have to work the graves.'

She didn't respond.

'I've heard it's a very splendid town. More splendid even than Manchester. Have you ever been?'

She shook her head.

'We'll have to go to the docks.'

'Why?'

'The voice that spoke through you, my mother, she said that I came to England on a ship. Do you remember the voice?'

'No.'

I wondered whether I should get Emily to do her conjuring again. I needed more answers. But the experience had spooked me badly and in truth I was a little afraid of speaking with the dead. I was fearful that they would drag me across, into their world. And I wasn't ready to go there yet. Or that they would come across and possess me in this world, so that I would look like me but inside be the soul of another. And I hadn't yet worked out who I was.

'Do you remember? When you conjure the dead?'

'No. It's like going to sleep.'

Had I travelled on a ship? I tried to recollect. I used the constant river traffic and the water to trigger buried memories.

'I remember a dark confined space,' I said.

Could this have been on-board a ship? It wasn't clear in my mind. I just had a memory of the light from a small window and the sun pouring in. The heat on my skin. Motes of dust sparkling. My shirt wet with sweat.

I remember being under a table, or was it a chair? The room was full of men. But I could only see their feet and their legs. The air was filled with clatter. There was muck on the floor, mashed-up peas and orange peel. The man with the black teeth was reaching for me, with a knife in his other hand.

It was something of a shock to remember it so clearly. But at the same time I questioned these new memories. Had I really remembered that, or was it the voice that had come from Emily's mouth? I wasn't even convinced that the voice was that of my mother. It sounded older than I imagined her to be. But what age are the dead? And what do they sound like?

'Where were you?'

I couldn't recall anything else. There was nothing boat-like about the memory.

'I remember being asleep on the knee of a woman,' I said. 'Only I wasn't asleep. I was pretending to be asleep. People were talking about me. I remember opening one eye very slowly, leaving just a crack to peep from, and seeing a black cat staring back at me with pale green eyes. All around were shiny objects, reflecting and distorting the scene.'

But I couldn't remember a boat. Or even a deck. I remembered walking barefoot on a stone floor and stepping on a pin, but holding back a cry of pain. I remembered climbing up a wooden staircase and avoiding the third stair because I knew that it would creak. How old was I? I remembered watching a boy and girl play with a ball. It was a sunny day and they were catching the ball and running across a field. I remembered wanting to join in the game.

'I remember a boy throwing a ball into the tree and the ball getting stuck. It was a red ball.'

'Then what happened?'

'I don't remember. I don't remember being on a boat. Trees, fences, stone walls, high buildings. There were four-wheeled carts and horses. Men loading and offloading. There were ships of every size. Sails flapping in the wind. Rowing boats. Dogs. Fishing nets. I was taken to a room. About

137

six-foot square. The floor, ceiling and walls were all stone. There was an iron gate.'

'And?'

'I don't remember. I remember sleeping on the streets. I had nothing to eat. I had to fight the gulls for scraps. I had to chase the rats from the bins. That's when I must have come across Mr Earnshaw.'

'Your adopted father?'

'Yes. Or rather he came across me. He said he'd take me home with him. He said he'd look after me.'

'And did he?'

'He kept his promise. Things weren't so bad at first. His wife didn't like me. Mrs Earnshaw. She said she didn't trust me. Didn't know where I was from. But Mr Earnshaw persuaded her to look after me all the same. I remember one night, I couldn't sleep. I could hear raised voices in the kitchen. I crept from my sleeping place and put my ear to the door. It was Mr and Mrs Earnshaw. They were talking about me. "Why have you brought this filthy creature into my home?" "I felt sorry for him. He had no one." "You can't bring every waif and stray back with you. You silly man." I must have been a force of conflict between them, which they never truly reconciled. A few years after I arrived, Mrs Earnshaw got a fever. I used to watch Mr Earnshaw mop her brow. I'd fetch fresh water for him. He doted over her. Still, she never recovered from that fever. When she died Mr Earnshaw changed. He withdrew, became more distant. He'd spend hours in his study reading his books. Long into the night he'd sit, with just a candle for company. Or else he'd stay by the fire and stare into the flames. But he never neglected me. When Mr Earnshaw was around, he kept Hindley in check. He even sent him away so that he couldn't beat me. But when Mr Earnshaw died, it all changed again. Hindley came back and he seemed to blame me. Not just for being sent away, but for the death of his father. Somehow, in his warped mind, I was responsible.'

'This Hindley sounds like a right cock.'

After a time the barges thinned out and working men became scarcer. The sun rose high and I was grateful for such clement weather. There were two puttocks above us and I watched them soar upwards. Emily came out of herself properly and started to chat again beside me; her talk helped to pass the time.

'How did they know we had come to Manchester?'

'Who?'

'Those men. Dick Taylor and that other knob.'

'I don't know.'

'Someone must have told them.'

'How? We didn't tell anyone where we were going.'

'Well, how did they know then? They're not bright enough to work it out for themselves. Do you think it was that old woman we passed on the moor, the one with the stick?'

'I suspect they just guessed. Perhaps they'd tried other places first. They got lucky, that's all.'

'But they came to the inn where we were staying. A minute later we'd have been mincemeat.'

'Just a coincidence, I'm sure. Don't worry about it. They won't get lucky again.'

I wondered how many inns they'd tried. Was ours the first or had they tried a great many others?

'Are you sure?' Emily said.

'Of course.'

In attempting to convince Emily, I was in fact attempting to convince myself of this. In truth, Cathy, I was deeply perturbed to consider that the men had tracked us to the inn.

'There are as many people in Manchester as there are rats in the sewers. There are inns on every corner, gin bars in every cellar, a dark skin for every half a dozen pale skins. That will keep them busy for a while. They'll have travelled by horseback no doubt, so have that advantage. But we have the advantage of being only two in a world of millions. Like looking for a needle in a haystack.'

'But it's easy to find a needle in a haystack,' the girl said.

'How so?'

'You set fire to it, and all that is left is the needle.'

'Well, let them set fire to the whole of England, they'll still not find us.'

We came to an area with lots of boats toing and froing. You should have seen those boats go, Cathy. Faster than any horse and carriage, each one floating through the water like a swan. The surface of the water was a mirror of the sky, fringed with trees and green foliage. Occasionally we would come across a hump-backed bridge and the arch would complete itself in the glass of the canal, forming a perfect circle. There were herons perched on the edge of the bank, still as statues, their bills like spears waiting to stab a fish. Although there couldn't have been many fish in this water, I didn't think. But I was wrong. As I looked across the surface I saw that there were circles forming on the film of the water, as the fish came up for insects. Life seeps into the cracks everywhere you look.

'It's all right this, in't it?' Emily said.

'Yeah.'

'How far do you reckon?'

'I don't know, we just need to head west.'

'Does this canal go all the way?'

'As far as I know.'

'Never been here before, but I remember my dad talking about it. There was a load of blabber about whether they'd do it or not. It cost a lot of money.'

'Made a lot of money too, I expect. One thing you can be sure about, if some rich bastard is prepared to splash out, he's doing it because he knows he'll make a shitload of bunce.'

'My dad talked about working it.'

'Robbing?'

'He preferred to call it redistribution. He looked into it but decided it were too risky. Too many people about.'

There were still sections that were incomplete and navvies grafted on the banks either side, shifting the stones into place. Mostly Irish by the sound of it. The sky was as grey as ton slate and I wondered if it would rain again. My coat had only just got fully dry and I didn't fancy another soaking. The rain made the walking twice as hard. There was a mist over yonder but nothing significant. I recalled one time with you when we'd been up on Penistone Hill and a witch's mist had set in, thick white smoke, rolling and settling beneath our feet. It had looked like it was solid, like we could walk straight across it to Crow Hill. You'd told me the tale of King Arthur's father, Uther Pendragon, who had disguised himself as his enemy and slept with his enemy's wife at Tintagel. Where she had conceived of Arthur. How he had walked across the mists that Merlin had magicked into being.

Deceit and treachery never far away. I told Emily the tale to pass the time.

'My dad could work magic,' she said.

'Could he? What sort?'

'You name it. He could make things disappear off the face of the earth.'

'Really?'

'That's what the magistrate said.'

As we came out of Manchester there wasn't much to look at. The landscape was flat. By the side of the canal was bramble and blackberry. Linnets picked at the berries. Every now and again we would have to stop to make way for the horses pulling the boats. They were harnessed with thick ropes and they dragged the cargo along the length of the canal. The towpath was wide, but the horses were big, muscular beasts, bigger than the horses around Wuthering Heights. Occasionally we saw a boat being pulled by a pair of donkeys, and often, smaller boats being dragged by mules. The snaking of the canal, I found out later, was to avoid locks. Locks being one of the main reasons for the slowing of traffic. It made our journey more interesting as the path curved and our view in front continually changed. Some of the barge workers stared at us. I supposed we made an odd couple.

'How will you go about it?' Emily asked. 'Finding out who you are?'

I'd given this a great deal of thought, but knew not the first thing of how to go about tracing my roots.

'Go to the docks. Ask around. Do a bit of digging. Someone must know something.'

'You say that, William Lee, but it's been nine years. That's almost as long as I've been on this earth. A lot changes in nine years. There might be no one left with a memory for those days, for all you know. In any case, suppose you do find out, what will you do then?'

'I don't know. It's a hell of a thing. Finding out who you are, where you're from.'

The towpath ran out as we came to a sign: 'Throstle Nest Bridge'. We had to cross to pick up the towpath on the other side. Boats queued while the horses were transferred over. I wondered why they'd designed it this way. The next thing I saw were concentric circles forming on the surface of the water, spreading outwards and morphing into each other. Then I felt the cold drops of water on my neck.

'Oh fuck, it's raining again,' Emily said.

I looked up; the sky didn't appear too threatening and I hoped it would pass over.

'The one thing about my dad,' Emily said, 'he might have been a highwayman, but he never lied to me.'

'Well, you're lucky there,' I said.

'Why do you think he brought you back?' she asked. 'Mr Earnshaw, I mean.'

'That's one of the things I want to find out. It doesn't make a great deal of sense right now. But I intend to make some sense of it.'

Bright yellow lucifer grew tall along the towpath where the canal forked. One side going left, the other side right. We stopped.

'Which way?' Emily said.

The clouds were thickening and the rain was now siling. The film of the canal water was a chaos of creases. Everything was sopping. We looked for a passing boat to ask for directions, and as we waited we picked the plumpest blackberries from the nearby bush. After a short time, a boat approached. The bargeman told us to go right. We crossed over another bridge and joined the yonderly towpath. I still had a handful of blackberries. I ate them as I walked. They were sweet.

The canal straightened out for a time and the barges thinned by. There wasn't much to see. A crow. A wagtail. Trees. Grass. Canal. The plash of rain.

'This is boring,' Emily said.

'Can't win with you. One minute you're moaning because it's hard going. The next minute you're moaning because it's too easy.'

'I'm getting wet.'

'No kidding.'

'I'm fucking soaked.'

'Yep.'

'Tell me more about this Hindley,' she said.

I told her of another time when I had inadvertently saved his son's life. I don't know where you were, Cathy, probably at the Lintons' with your feet under their table.

'Hindley was drunk and carrying on,' I said. 'He was standing on the stairs and he held his son with one hand and a bottle of brandy with the other. He dangled Hareton over the balcony.'

'What was he trying to do?'

'I don't know. Perhaps in his drunken madness he thought his child would enjoy the excitement of being on the precipice. I happened to be walking past as he dropped the brat, either by accident or by design, I don't know which, but I remember catching it in my arms. It was instinct. I wish I hadn't done it. I wish I'd let it fall to the floor and dash its brains out. But it was good to see the brat scream when Hindley tried to make amends and stroke its cheek. It hated Hindley almost as much as I did. And it gave me solace to know that. Nelly told me later how Hindley had held a knife to her throat when he had caught her hiding the brat. He had grabbed it and threatened to break its neck. She had watched him carry the brat upstairs and hold it over the banister.'

'I'm glad that you saved the brat's life,' Emily said.

'Why do you say that?'

'Gives you something else to beat Hindley with.'

As we walked by the water, I thought about this. It made a great deal of sense.

We came across a flock of Jack Nicker. A dozen or so, feasting on thistle seeds. They flashed gold and red, the only colour for miles around. Everything else was grey and the falling rain was like lead pellets. All this time I kept my eye on the way we'd been, looking back furtively so as not to alarm Emily, but I made sure we were not followed.

'I've got seeds stuck between my teeth,' Emily said.

So had I. We stopped and I picked two stems of woody grass and fashioned them into toothpicks.

'I like crunching the seeds between my teeth,' Emily said. 'You get a sort of satisfaction, destroying things.'

'I suppose you do.'

A Game of Skittles

'I could murder a beer,' Emily said.

'I didn't know you drank.'

'I didn't. I've just started.'

We were standing by a bridge to the side of a tavern. We'd been walking all morning through braying rain. My surtout was clinging to my skin and the seams were rubbing the flesh raw.

'I suppose we could both do with a drink and something to eat,' I said.

Inside, the barman eyed us suspiciously. We must have been a sight to behold, Cathy. A barefoot girl in an oversized shirt, a ripped frock tied at the waist, and a dark-skinned gypsy in naught but a coat and breeches. Wet as water rats. He refused us custom at first but I managed to persuade him. I bought us some bread and cheese, a flagon of ale for the girl and some hot tea for myself. We sat on stools around a small table next to a group of navvies and bankers. They were drinking ale and smoking their clay pipes. I watched them chat and laugh. One was dark-skinned like me and it was good to be in the company of another. I earwigged as Emily supped. The dark-skinned one had been transporting goods on the coaching roads and was talking about how much safer it was on the canal.

'So we go to the docks and we make some enquiries, is that the plan?' Emily said.

'That's the start of it. What will you do?'

'I'll come with you.'

'You can't just follow me around all the time, you know.'

'Why not?'

'My long-term plans, they don't involve you.'

'What long-term plans?'

'To get an education. To get wealth. To get what's mine.'

'Well, I want an education too, you know. And I want wealth. I want what's mine.'

She started coughing from deep down in her lungs. I watched as she hacked and spluttered. I waited for the coughing fit to finish.

'You'll have to find your own way. I can't be responsible for you all the time. Besides, once I've got my wealth and my education, I'm going back.'

'To Wuthering Heights?'

'To Wuthering Heights.'

'What for?'

'Unfinished business.'

'Are you going to stick it to Hindley?'

'I've not decided yet.'

This was true. All I knew at this stage was that cunt was going to get it. And as for you, Cathy, I was still thinking on how best to teach you a lesson and make your life a misery.

'My dad would have the lot of them rounded up and shot like cattle. He wouldn't mess about. Your problem is you spend too long thinking about stuff instead of doing it. My dad used to say that there are two types of people: people who get stuff done and people who are cunts.'

Yes, I wanted to say, and look how he ended up. But I bit my tongue.

'What about the cake shop?'

'What about it?'

'Can we open a cake shop there?'

'Where?'

'Near Wuthering Heights.'

'There's no call for cake in those parts.'

'Everyone likes cake, in every part I've travelled, anyway, and I've been almost everywhere. You're not travelled like me, you don't know about these things. Don't take this the wrong way, but you're just a farm boy from the sticks. I've done this, done that. Been here, been there. It's time you took some advice from one who knows.'

I watched her stuff the last of the cheese into her mouth, followed by a heel of bread, then slurp the dregs of the ale. We got up and made our way back to the canal.

In the distance I could hear a cuckoo's hooting call. I remember Nelly one time saying that I was the cuckoo of the family and I'd asked you later why she'd said it. You told me that a female cuckoo lays its egg in another bird's nest and that bird brings up the infant cuckoo – and that's what Nelly meant. That I was a foreign infant, a parasite. But I found out later that when the infant cuckoo hatches, it pushes all the other eggs out. So in fact I wasn't a cuckoo at all. I was the one who had been pushed out of the nest, first by Hindley, then by you, Cathy. Or maybe that's what I should do. Go back to Wuthering Heights and kick you all out of the nest. I'd enjoy doing that. Be the cuckoo you all thought I was.

The rain had stopped and the sun was burning through the clouds. I took off my coat and carried it over my shoulder, hoping it would dry. As I walked I mused. We'd be in Liverpool soon. But would I find what I wanted to? I had no idea how I would go about it. Emily was right. What if I found out nothing? What then? I would still need to raise the capital for a decent education. How was I going to do that? It all felt out of my grasp. And yet what did I have? Only to go on with the plan. There was nothing else to keep me on this earth.

'This is boring,' Emily said again.

'You're boring.'

'Tell me a story.'

'I don't know any stories.'

'You must do.'

I thought back. I'd told her everything I knew. I shrugged.

'If my dad were here now, he'd tell a brilliant story.'

'Well, he's not.'

We walked in silence for a while, with the water to our right and bramble to our left. I tried a few attempts to get Emily to talk but she'd gone quiet again.

'Here, let's pick these,' I said.

We stopped. I picked some berries. Emily stared at her feet.

'They're good, try for yourself.'

I handed her a blackberry but she didn't respond.

'You were saying earlier on, about your dad. About him

149

thinking about working the towpaths. That he said it was too busy. Did you hear that man in the pub back there?'

'What man?'

'He was talking about how it was safe. Working the canals. He meant safe from thieves.'

'Maybe.'

'Well, it might be that your dad was right, that it's because there's too many people about, but I've been thinking, I mean, there's hardly anyone along this bit. So it can't be just that. It would be easy to come along on horseback and hold up one of the boats.'

'And steal what? A ton of coal?' Emily said.

She thought about it for a bit.

Then she said, 'Besides, it would be easy to duck inside. And a horse can't walk on water, so as long as the boat is in the middle of the canal, it's safe. I mean, even if they fired and shot the boatman, how could they get to his booty? There would be no sense to it.'

'That's a fair point,' I said. 'No good for your dad then.'

We came to an aqueduct. A stone bridge that allowed the canal to cross over an expanse of water beneath. As we walked along the narrow towpath, I looked down at the river below. The water was almost as still as the water in the canal. When we got to the other side of the bridge, I looked back at the aqueduct. The water was up to the brim of the bank.

'How come it doesn't overflow?' I said.

'I don't know.'

'I bet your dad would know.'

'He would,' she said. 'He'd definitely know.'

We rejoined the towpath, where two adult swans glided

through the water, followed by their young. The cygnets were almost as big as their parents, but their feathers were dull and grey and their beaks were black. I heard that swans mate for life, Cathy. The pen doesn't make a promise to the cob and then renege on that promise, when a poncier cob comes along. The pen stays true to her word. She doesn't betray her heart's desire, she knows what matters most.

As we approached a place signed Worsley, the water in the canal turned at first from brown-green, to russet, and then an umber colour, until eventually the water was bright orange.

'Why's it turned colour?' Emily said.

'I don't know.'

'Maybe someone spilt some paint.'

'I doubt it.'

'There were two men back there painting a fence.'

'They weren't painting it orange though, were they? Besides, did you see the size of the tin?'

She shrugged. She went quiet for a while.

'Why's the sky blue?' she asked.

'I don't know. You might as well ask why the grass is green. Or why a buttercup is yellow.'

'Don't you ever think about these questions?'

'I've got more important things to think about.'

'Like what?'

'Like where I'm going. Where I've been.'

'Well, I think about them. I asked my dad the same question. And he knew the answer.'

'And what did he say?'

'He said the sky was blue because God wanted it that colour.'

We came to the end of the canal. The waterway terminated by a dock. I looked up at the sun. We were heading north – in the wrong direction.

'What's the matter?'

'It can't be this way.'

There were barges parked up, being loaded with coal. The clock nearby was striking thirteen. I remembered Stick's words. I recounted the story to Emily.

'The flatmen were getting back late after their dinner break. They were down the pub, getting bevvied up.'

'Bevvied up?'

'That's what Sticks called having a beer. Anyway, they were having a beer and getting back late, so the duke had a special clock fitted, rang out thirteen times when it was one of the clock. Crafty sod, that duke.'

We asked another boatman. He told us that we needed to go back to the aqueduct. The water underneath the bridge was the Irwell. This was the waterway that would take us to Liverpool. I remembered Sticks's words again. I'd misunderstood what he'd meant. It was only three miles back the way we came, but I was getting tired, my legs and feet were aching, and the thought of retracing our steps made my heart sink. Nevertheless, we turned around and walked back the way we had come to the bridge.

'We've got to walk all the way back. Because of your mistake,' Emily said, shaking her head.

'I didn't see you correcting my error.'

'I'm not an expert on canals.'

'Neither am I.'

We got back to the bridge, then we dropped down onto a

path by the side of the huge expanse of water. As we headed west once more I could feel the sting of another blister, this time on the heel of the other foot. The Irwell was not like the Bridgewater. While the Bridgewater had room for two or three barges, this stretch of water could fit a full fleet and still have space either side.

We walked along its length, watching the barges and boats snake up and down, carrying their heavy loads. We saw a ship piled up with bales of raw cotton, no doubt destined for the Manchester mills we'd seen half-starved children pour out of. In the opposite direction, going towards Liverpool, we saw a ship loaded up with the finished cloths. There were boats carrying tobacco, sugar, tea and coffee. Spices from faraway countries. All kinds of finery. There were boats everywhere and men working the loads. There were ships powered by sails, but some were pulled by beast. We even saw a boat being dragged by a gang of men.

'Why don't we get a lift?' Emily said.

'Eh?'

'We've got money. We could offer one of the boatmen some bunce to take us to Liverpool.'

'We'll see,' I said. I was reluctant to get chatting with anyone for any length of time.

I thought about Mr Earnshaw. He had walked from Wuthering Heights to Liverpool, as we were doing now, and walked back again with me under his arm, carrying also a whip and a fiddle. He would have followed this route by the river, I imagined. What was Mr Earnshaw travelling to Liverpool for? We had never spoken about it. We had often spoken about my origins.

You kept changing your mind, Cathy. One of your theories was that I was the son of an Egyptian prince. Another, that I was the son of a Yemeni king. Yet another theory said I'd descended from a Moor of the Maghreb, and we imagined the regal legacy that was due to me. It seemed strange to me now that we had been so curious as to my paternal origins but never about the nature of your father's journey. He'd risked his life making it. The roads were filled with thieves and vagrants, waiting to stop a man and take his wealth. There were pickpockets and cutpurses who would think nothing of murdering a man for a few shillings.

An even bigger threat were press gangs. We had heard many horror stories of them grabbing wayfarers and drugging them, making them sign away their lives for the king's shilling. Then there were those who took the shilling willingly without being insensate with drink or drugs. In a country such as ours, which at least pretends to be free, it becomes a matter of no small surprise that so many thousands of men should deliberately renounce their privileges and voluntarily sell themselves to the most humiliating and degrading slavery, for the miserable pittance of sixpence a day.

Sticks had told me of those volunteers who had thought they would become soldiers and see the world, but had just ended up with a chest full of lead. He had told me also of the men who had been kidnapped. Grabbed from off the turnpike and tied to the carts. Within a day they were on a boat heading for America to fight the war of independence. Somewhat ironically. I kept my wits about me. I had escaped one form of slavery and was in no rush to volunteer for another. I had my own war to fight. I had my own independence to defend.

'My feet are killing me,' Emily said.

So were mine.

Emily had a cut on the sole of her right foot. She stopped and I examined it. By now I had a third blister to match the other two. We walked in silence, alone in our pain. The rain was braying again now, and I could feel the water dripping onto my head and down my spine. I tried to think warm thoughts. I pictured you naked: the skin which had never seen the sun was as white as milk, and you were lying across the purpling heather. I was on top of you, and inside you.

Emily scowled and dragged her feet. I resented her presence, she was an uninvited guest. At the same time I felt pity for her. She had nowhere to go, and no one to turn to. Like me she had nothing. We were united by our penury. We were wet and tired and our feet were sore. We stopped by the side of the path to rest. Emmets teemed beneath us. Dodging raindrops. Carrying leaves and other bits of vegetation. I took off my boots and examined my feet. One of the blisters had burst and the wound was bleeding. We were just past a place called Irlam, according to a sign. It was a grim place. Even the sycamore trees looked feeble and sickly. Not quite green enough. The rowan berries looked paler than they did in Yorkshire, more orange than red. Emily was looking up at the sky. The rain was easing off, and she was staring at a white disc, where the sun shone through the mist.

'Do you think God sees us?'

'Whether he does or he doesn't, makes not a blind bit of difference to me. Unless he throws down two lightning bolts, one for Hindley and one for Edgar, he can kiss my arse.'

155

'Do you think it is possible to get into heaven when you've done a bad thing?'

'Depends on how bad the bad thing is, I suppose.'

I thought about you, Cathy, saying that heaven was no place for us. You told me of that dream you had, where the angels threw us out in anger onto the middle of the heath on the top of Wuthering Heights.

'Because it wouldn't be fair, would it? If, on no account of your own doing, circumstances arranged themselves around you, and, you know, you ended up doing something really bad, that you didn't want to do, that you wouldn't have done, if things had worked out different. That wouldn't be fair, would it?'

'I don't suppose it would.'

I imagined she was thinking about her father but thought it best not to ask. I didn't care about damnation in eternity, as long as I could get even on earth.

We got talking to a boatman who was moored near where we were sitting. He was a big black man with skin so dark that I was as pale to him as Emily was to me. He had a huge bald head that looked like a giant lump of coal and shoulders like an ox. He was eating something from a small metal box perched on his knee. He asked us where we had been and where we were going. He told us he'd worked more on the canal than on the river.

'Used to haul coal by cart before that. In them days, you'd have to go back and forth with that cart all day to carry what I can now shift in a morning. Half the time you wouldn't make it. A wheel would break, you'd get stuck in mud. Robbers. This is loads better.'

'Can you give us a lift?' Emily asked.

'Shush,' I said. 'Sorry about my sister. She speaks out of turn.'

'I'd gladly give you a lift,' he said. 'Only, I'm stopping here till tomorrow. Got to pick up an order.'

We carried on our way. We walked another three or four miles. Our steps getting shorter, our pace slowing. The journey was catching up on us and I could feel every muscle ache. I looked back. Emily was behind me some way now. I stopped a while and waited for her to catch me up.

'I can't go on,' she said.

'Keep going.'

I slowed down to her pace and together we traipsed further on. I was barely aware of our surroundings, just the rubble and mud beneath our feet, but the next thing I saw was a cartwheel in our path. Too tired to walk around it, we stopped. I looked up and saw that it was attached to an open-backed cart with two horses reined to it. There were four men and they were standing around a sack that had fallen off and spilt grain. The man at the front was tall and stocky, with a large bulbous head and long scraggly hair. He scooped up the grain and loaded the sack. He hefted it onto the cart.

'Help us,' Emily said in a feeble voice.

The man stopped what he was doing. There was something shifty about his manner. I wanted to shush Emily but it was too late.

'Look at these two,' he said to his companion, a man with curly hair and a pointy nose. 'Reminds me of when we were in the army. That thirty-mile hike we did across Dartmoor. Do you remember?'

The pointy man laughed. 'I remember the sergeant shout-ing in our ears till they rang like bells.'

'I bet we looked like them.'

'We need a lift to Liverpool,' Emily said, in a firmer voice. 'Where are you heading?'

The bulbous man shrugged. He whispered to his close companion and gave the nod to the other two.

'We've got money,' I said. 'We'll pay you.'

'We are heading that way, as it happens. In't that right, Bert?' the bulbous man said to the pointy man. Bert nodded.

'What do you think, lads?'

The other two men mumbled something.

'How much have you got?' the pointy man asked.

'Enough,' I said.

'How much?'

I pulled out my bag of coins and opened it up.

The next moment the bulbous man was pointing a gun in my face.

'Hand it over.'

The barrel of the gun was staring down at me. I should have been afraid, or angry, but I felt nothing. I did as I was told.

'Fred, get that rope.'

There was another man now and another gun.

We were grabbed, jostled, tied to the cart and gagged. I tried to free myself, but it was no use. They put sack hoods over our heads. I could hear the men get onto the cart and gee on the horses. I could feel the cart move underneath us. Slow at first, then quickening.

'He'll fetch a shilling but she'll fetch more,' the bulbous

man said. 'I know a bloke who'll pay a pound for a young'un like that.'

'I know a fella who'll pay two pound,' another said.

There was laughing and more talking. I couldn't make out what they were saying. I tried to shift in my bindings but they were too tight. I tried to nudge closer to Emily but there was no give in the rope. The road was bumpy but as we travelled it got smoother. We journeyed on the smooth road for a long time, maybe half an hour, before the road got bumpier again. I had no idea where they were taking us or what they planned to do when they got to where they were going. I tried to halt my imagination from running wild.

Eventually the cart came to a stop and we were taken off the cart and bungled into a room. I sniffed the air. It was musty. I could feel the hard ground beneath my feet and the hands of the men, grabbing me and pulling me across. I could hear objects being moved. The sound of wood against stone. We were jostled about again. Put them there. Grab this. Hold that. Here, give me that. Pushed down. Held down. Our hoods were removed.

We were inside a shed of some sort. The room was lit by shafts of grey light that poured through gaps in the wooden slats. There were boxes and bags and some tools stacked against the wall. I looked over to Emily. Her eyes were wide with fright. Both our arms and legs were firmly bound with rope. Another length of rope tied each of us to the chairs we were sitting on.

'Wait here,' the bulbous man said, and he and the pointy man disappeared out the back way. The other two sat opposite us, pointing their guns at our heads. One wore a flat cap and the other had a red shirt with a rip in the sleeve. They each sat like that for some time without uttering a word. I could see Emily twist and turn her wrists every time the men looked away, trying to loosen the rope without success. I did the same.

After a while, the man in the flat cap said, 'How long are they going to be?'

'Don't know,' said the other one.

'I'm thirsty.'

'There's some ale in the kitchen.'

The man in the cap got up.

'You all right while I fetch it?'

The man in the red shirt nodded.

The man in the cap came back with a flagon of ale, took a sup, scrunched up his face, then passed it to his companion.

'I think it's on the turn.'

The man in the red shirt took a slug. He sloshed it around his mouth, then swallowed.

'It's all right. Better than nothing.'

'He'll probably bring some more.'

'Better had do.'

I looked around the room. There was a rake, a spade, a scythe and a number of other implements, including a mattock. I thought about the mattock. It was a short-handled one, fixed to the wall with two nails. The blade looked sharp. But it was no use to us. There wasn't much we could do tied up, and with guns in our faces. I glanced over to Emily and tried to give her a reassuring look.

'I need a piss,' said the man in the red shirt. He got up and wandered over to the corner of the room. He unfastened himself and pissed up the wall. I could smell the tang of his urine.

'Do it outside, you dirty bastard,' said the man in the cap.

'It's raining. Fuck that.'

The two men laughed. The man in the red shirt shuck himself dry and buttoned up his breeches. He went back to his chair, picked up his gun and sat back down.

An hour or two went by. The men finished off the flagon. They talked about inconsequential things. The man in the red shirt smoked a pipe. The other yawned and complained about having to wait so long. Eventually the bulbous man and the pointy man returned.

'Well?' said the man in the red shirt.

'He won't get here till tomorrow,' the pointy man said.

'Tomorrow?'

'Fuck that.'

'Let's have some fun.'

'No,' said the bulbous man. 'We'll get more for a filly than a mare.'

'Who's to say she is or isn't? He'll believe what we tell him. As long as we're careful not to mark her,' the pointy man said.

'I said no.'

'Come on. It's been a long day. We could all do with something to unwind.'

The bulbous man shrugged. 'Suppose it would be a shame to waste what we've got.'

'I'm going first,' said the pointy man.

'Fuck off. Why should you go first?'

'It was my idea.'

'It's my cart and my nags.'

'We'll toss for it.'

'Did you fetch some ale?'

'There's some on the cart. I'll get it later.'

The pointy man walked over to where Emily was tied. He took out a knife and cut through the rope that was holding her to the chair. He hoisted her over his shoulder; she strained her neck around, looking at me with terror-filled eyes, but there was nothing I could do. I pulled with all my might. I was fixed firmly to the spot. I could see her wriggle in her bindings. Her body jerked as she fought impotently against the rope. The man disappeared with her into another room.

'No marking. Do you hear me?'

'Wait for me.'

'And me.'

All four men disappeared.

I had to free myself somehow. I had to get to Emily. I studied every detail of the room. I looked at the mattock again. It was only a few feet away but that seemed like a long way from where I was sitting in my present state. But if I could shuffle across I might be able to rub the rope along the blade. I rocked quietly but the chair didn't move. I stretched my legs so that the tips of my toes made contact with the floor of the shed. I managed to move the chair only a fraction of an inch, but it was something. The effort strained my muscles but I persisted, until I'd managed to drag the chair several inches. I was still a long way from my target but I needed to rest. There was no time to rest though. I fought fatigue and the stabbing pain in my calf and thighs. I could feel muscle rip.

I could hear raised voices and laughter. I thought about Emily and the men.

I tried again. I managed another three or four inches before I needed to rest once more. Again, I fought the urge. Faster, come on, move. I was in agony with the effort but I carried on. Eventually I made it across to the mattock. I managed to nudge the chair around so that I could reach it. I rubbed the rope frantically against the blade, praying I wasn't too late. It was thick rope and it took a lot of effort but I got through the fibres enough and broke the chair free from the bindings. I turned around and, in a frenzied state, worked on the ropes around my wrists. It was slow going but eventually they came loose as well. I took the mattock to the ropes around my ankles. Eventually I was free. I picked up the mattock and stumbled over to the door where the men had disappeared.

It was a darkened corridor, with a dim grey light at the end. In the distance I could hear muffled voices. I hurried along the corridor as quietly as I could, until I came to an open door. I peered in. It was a kitchen, with a cooking range in one corner and pans hanging from the ceiling. There was a three-legged stool next to the range with a flintlock on top. In the middle of the room was a wooden table. The chairs had been pushed to the sides of the room, and one of them was knocked over, lying on its side. Emily was spread across the table, jerking and wriggling. Three men held her down. The pointy man was standing behind her. His belt was by his feet, coiled like an asp, and next to this a flagon. The man had his back to me, but I could tell that he was fumbling with the buttons on his breeches. The other three men were looking away from where I was standing.

'Thirsty work, this,' he said, and reached for the flagon.

I ran at the man as he raised the flagon to his lips and

launched the narrow end of the mattock into the back of his skull. I heard bone crunch. The man dropped the flagon and it shattered on the stone-flagged floor. He collapsed on his front, his arms splayed. The three others turned to look at me. Their expressions shifted from shock to anger. The bulbous man let go of Emily and looked over to the stool where the flintlock lay. He made a run for it. I intercepted his path, swinging the mattock around so that the sharp end embedded itself into the man's forehead. It stopped him in his tracks. He fell to his knees, a wedge-shaped gash bleeding where the mattock had chipped out a chunk of his skull.

The other two men were running at me. I lifted the mattock again, but as I swung it around, the one in the red shirt caught hold of my arm. As he did the capped man kicked me hard in my chest. I was thrown against the wall. The red shirt swung his fist and it connected with the side of my head. I dropped the mattock and fell to the floor. The man grabbed hold of the mattock and lifted it high, about to drop it down into my cranium. As he did, I heard a bang. The back of his head exploded. Blood and brain spattered the wall. The man dropped the mattock and crumpled onto the flags.

There was another bang. I looked and saw the capped man hold his chest. His hands were red. Emily was standing five or six feet away from him, clutching the flintlock, which was smoking. The man staggered towards her, muttering something. I picked up the mattock and finished him off.

The room was swaying. I looked about me. The flags and walls were decorated with spats of blood, brain and bone fragments. And acrid smoke hung in the air. I could smell blood and gunpowder. I dropped the tool and went over to where Emily was standing. I reached out for her, but she balled her fist and punched me in the gut. I let her go at me, punch after punch. In my gut. In my chest. I didn't fight back. I let her punch me until she had no energy to punch me any more.

I grabbed hold of her and held her tight. I could feel the strong rhythmic pulse of her heart beating beneath my own. 'I'm sorry,' I said. 'I'm sorry.' I stroked her hair.

'Let's get out of here,' she said, as I let go of her.

I nodded. The shots had been loud. There could be other men nearby. We had no time to waste. I went over to the sink and took a cloth. I hurriedly rubbed the gouts of blood from my face and surtout. I threw the cloth down and made my way to the doorway.

'Wait,' she said.

She went over to the corpse of the bulbous man and retrieved my purse from his pocket. She handed it to me. She spat on the man and kicked him in the face.

'Cunt.'

We ran out of the room, along the corridor and into the shed. We opened the shed door. The nags and the cart were outside.

'Let's take these,' Emily said.

'We can't.'

'Why not?'

'I've told you, we get caught for stealing a horse, it's a hanging offence.'

'And killing four men isn't?'

'A squire thinks more about his horse than he does a farm labourer.'

'We don't even know where we are.'

I looked around. We were on the grounds of a small farm. Stone walls marked out two fields. One with horses, the other barley. I looked to where the sun was whitening the clouds.

'This way.'

I led the way along a path that trailed to a gate, then along a cart road. We walked for miles along that road, then miles across country before we came to the Irwell once more. We were back near Barton Bridge and had to re-walk the last six or seven miles we'd gone before we were grabbed by the men. My feet were rubbing raw in my boots. We walked slowly, side by side. I wanted to say something to Emily to comfort her, but I didn't know what. Instead we walked on in silence. I knew what it was like to fear for your life. To have no one in the world. I knew what it was like to feel shame. To feel like dirt.

I'd had it bad. She'd had it worse. And I'd let her down. There was no conceivable way I could ditch her. No, I couldn't leave Emily now. I was sure of that.

Eventually the built-up walls by the side of the river started to fall away, and the locks that had been constructed along its length to stem the tide were running out. The banks giving way to salt marshes. We were in the mouth of an estuary. There were strange birds wading in the sand. Lanky-legged like heron and whaap, with long thin beaks, like woodcock and jack snipe. They prodded the sand, and turned stones with the ends of their bills. I could smell the salt in the air and knew that we couldn't be that far now from the coast. I had another blister forming behind the ball of my left foot. Emily was limping along behind me. I waited again for her to catch me up.

'We've not got long to go now,' I said.

I got no response. I carried on walking. My feet felt like they were on fire. Burning and throbbing. On and on we walked. The path beneath seemed to get harder with each step. The water to our right mocked us with its coolness. I looked back. No Emily. I stopped. About twenty yards down the path, Emily had collapsed by the side of the path. I tried to stand up straight. I traipsed back across to where she lay.

'Come on. It can't be far.'

Nothing.

I bent down and shook her gently.

'Come on, Emily. You've got this far. You can do it.'

'Can't.'

'Yes, you can.'

'Can't.'

I took her in my arms and carried her. The extra weight made my feet burn up even more. Each step was like being branded with a red-hot poker. I took one at a time. Each step another victory. The road seemed endless for the last hour of that journey. I was walking so slowly that a snail could have overtaken me should he have had the inclination. My thoughts were single words. Sand, stone, dirt, road. One foot. Then another. Keep going. Left. Right. Left. Right. I kept my eyes to the ground. Willing my feet to move. First one, then the next. Keep doing that. Till you get there. Every now and then I would look up. But mostly I looked down at the dirt road. The dust and the stones. My boots. Somehow, I became vaguely aware that we had reached a town by the coast.

The dockside was bustling but I was too tired and worn to take any notice of the bustle. I laid Emily on the grass, then rested a while. I bought us both a bowl of broth from a street vendor and collapsed by the stall near to Emily. There were merchants and dockers, sailors and pedlars. Kittiwakes careened in the breeze. Gulls gyred above luggers. I let the broth revive me, dispensing with the thible and supping straight from the lip of the bowl.

I walked over to the dockside, leaving Emily to rest. I saw an old man mending a fishing net.

'This is Liverpool, right?'

The man laughed. He attached more twine to the shuttle.

'Close.'

'This isn't Liverpool?'

'You're in Runcorn, mate. Liverpool is over yonder.'

He pointed east over the estuary with the shuttle.

'How do we get there?'

'Swim.'

'You're kidding.'

'Course I am.'

'Then how?'

'You can catch a ferry.'

I noticed that the accent of the people around me had changed. They had the same harsh nasal tones as Sticks. I made further enquiries. There was a ferry departing in ten minutes. A penny each. I went back to where Emily was slumped on the grass, too tired to spoon the broth into her mouth. It lay by her side untouched. I explained our error.

'We've got to catch a ferry.'

'I can't move another inch.'

I could see she was in no fit state. Instead, I took some broth on her spoon and held it to her lips.

'When I was young, younger than you are now, I caught a fever. Mrs Earnshaw had just died of a fever and there was talk that I'd go the same way. Mr Earnshaw was still deep in grief, so Nelly nursed me. Every day she would sit by my sleeping place and feed me broth. She'd tell me stories of when she was a girl and Mr Earnshaw was a young man. He was a bit of a one, according to Nelly. She called him a "rum'un", whatever that meant. She told me that Mrs Earnshaw didn't know the half of it. Said it was just as well she had died without knowing. Day after day she'd bring me broth, until I gained my strength. Cathy would come to see me too. She'd sit by my sleeping place and tell me stories. After a few weeks the fever broke and my brow began to cool. I was back on my feet shortly after that, but I don't think I'd be here today if Nelly hadn't taken pity on me.'

Emily nodded. I fed her all the broth, then left her once more while I found us digs for the night. I didn't stray far, while I made enquiries, making sure I had her in my sight all the time. When I returned for her shortly after, she'd already ligged. She was curled up on the grass, sucking the broth thible like a dummy.

~

I let Emily have a lie-in the next morning. I couldn't have shifted her if I'd wanted to. Eventually, after breakfasting on porridge and kippers, we set off for the dock. Emily came around as she scoffed her grub.

'Are you all right?' I said.

'Yeah.'

169

'Are you sure?'

She shrugged.

All that way. Afterwards. She hadn't said a word. I wondered if she blamed me. Perhaps we could have cadged a lift earlier. We could have paid a boatman. We had enough money. There had been plenty of opportunities. I should have known there was something suspect about the men. There was something conspiratorial from the outset. All that whispering. I should have trusted my instincts. I shouldn't have shown my hand. It was foolish getting my purse out like that. Letting them see the size and weight of it. I couldn't allow anything like that to happen again. I would have to be much wiser from now on. I looked over to Emily again. I had failed her. I wanted to say something else, something that would make it better. But what can you say, Cathy?

Eventually I took hold of her hand and said, 'I'm sorry.'

She just shrugged.

'Look, Emily, I promise you from now on, no matter what happens, I'll keep you safe from harm. I promise you that nothing bad will happen to you again.'

I looked her in the eye.

'You've got to believe me, Emily.'

I squeezed her hand gently.

At last she returned my gaze and nodded.

We made our way to the dockside and I paid the ferryman tuppence. The ferry was almost full, and there was an air of excitement as we cast off. The boat was powered by a large sail that one man trimmed while another took the tiller. We sailed across the choppy water, gulls gliding in our wake. We could make out Liverpool seafront from where we were sitting. Like Manchester, there were many tall buildings with domes and spires. There was a sea mist, making the scene ahead a magical one. The air was damp and tangy.

'It's like in a fairy tale,' Emily said. 'Where they go to a far-off land and everything is different.'

The sun glinted on the tips of the water like polished silver. Strange fish as big as pigs swam by the side of the vessel. They had skin instead of scales and noses like bottle tops. They leapt out of the waves and smiled at us.

'What are them?' Emily said.

I shrugged.

A man sitting close by leaned over to Emily. 'They're dolphins. That's what they are. It's a good sign, dolphins following us. It means we'll harbour safely.'

I'd heard of these mythical sea creatures, half-human, half-fish. I remember you telling me, Cathy, about sea monsters with eight arms and swords for mouths.

'Do you think we'll see a mermaid?' Emily said.

'I hope so,' I said.

'I don't. My dad said that mermaids bring bad luck. They look like angels but are really devils. What about dragons? Don't some of them live in the sea?'

'I suspect they do.'

I suspected no such thing, Cathy, but I was happy to see Emily revived somewhat from yesterday. She clung onto the side of the boat and leaned over.

'Not so close,' I said, pulling her back. 'You don't want to get eaten by a sea dragon.'

When we got to Liverpool docks it became obvious that Liverpool was very different from Runcorn. Where Runcorn had only one small dockside, Liverpool had several massive docks. Where Runcorn had a dozen boats, the waters of Liverpool were teeming with every type of vessel as far as the eye could see. Every colour, every shape, every size. Shallop, dory, skiff. Dogger, cutter, sloop.

I came across a shipyard with ships and boats in various stages of construction. Among them was a vast galleon that was only halfway built, so that I could see all the workings inside. There were cordoned-off areas that were clearly built for storage. Hundreds of them. The height of which was ten inches or so. I wondered what cargo the ship was built for.

We wandered around, examining the various places and buildings. The air was pungent with the stench of salt and fish. Gulls careened above us, screeching and diving. All around folk mulled. A cacophony of voices. We saw by the end dock the town's gaol, a dark foreboding building, like a haunted castle in one of your story books, Cathy. Next to this was Coat Yard. We made our way back to the main docks. There were lots of large ships moored up. There were sailors and merchants loitering around and further back there were whores plying for business. Some not much older than Emily.

A chill down my spine made me shiver but I wasn't cold. The docks were familiar to me. I remembered them. The memory was rising to the surface like something coming up to breathe. I'd stored it in a room in my mind and locked the door. But now, being here, looking at the square of water and the buildings surrounding it, standing on the waterfront, watching the ships, listening to the gulls, was the key to the lock. The door was opening. I was six years old. I was hungry and cold. My mother was dead. But I could speak my mother tongue and I could speak the language of this land. Some of the words came back to me. They formed in my mind but then evaporated. I tried to grab them. They were solid, they had their own taste and flavour, but then they were smoke. I felt dizzy with emotion. I steadied myself and clung onto the iron railing.

'What are you thinking about?' Emily asked.

I didn't say anything. I breathed in deep and closed my eyes. I saw an eye staring at me. The iris like a blazing fire.

'I like it here,' she said. 'It's even better than London.'

A dog came up to us, wagging its tail. Emily bent down and stroked it.

'I'd like a dog,' she said. 'Maybe we could get one.'

'I don't think so.'

'But when we get the shop we'll need a dog to guard the place at night. My dad would never let me have a dog. He said I was enough trouble, without another meddlesome creature. We could feed him the cake that was left over. Dogs like cake.'

'Talking of which,' I said, changing the subject, 'let's get some grub.'

Further back from the dockside, we found an alehouse called the Gallows Inn and I ordered us refreshment. We sat by the fireplace and watched a game of skittles. There were four men playing for pennies. Sailors. One of them was talking about their next voyage to Africa on a ship called *Destiny*. He'd never been before and the others were telling him of how dark-skinned the natives were, black as coal, and how the women went around bare-chested with everything on show, bubbies out. The man's eyes lit up and they joked around. The man lost his game and handed over his money

173

to the others. When he went to the bar, I followed him. He was rummaging around in his pockets. He turned to me.

'You know, I got paid yesterday, a week's wage, and it's almost all gone already. I just can't seem to keep hold of it.'

'Why don't I buy you a drink?' I said.

'Are you sure?'

'Of course. What will you have?'

I bought him a glass of brandy and handed it over.

He had thick, greasy brown hair and the hair from his chest was growing out of the top of his shirt and up his neck. He was stocky but a good few inches shorter than me.

'You're a sailor then?' he asked.

'Not me,' I said.

'Then what?'

'I'm a farm labourer.'

I thought back to the burial ground above Shudehill, and to a grand memorial with an eagle sculpture and gold lettering carved into the stone.

'The name's Isaac Addison.'

'Jack Bird,' he said. 'Nice to meet you, Isaac.'

We shook hands.

'Done farm labouring myself one time. Cutting the hay, baling it. Those bales don't half get scratchy.'

He laughed, showing off a row of black and crooked teeth.

'I'm no farmhand though. Ships are my thing. First voyage I went on, I got flogged for drunken behaviour. Said I'd never sail again. That was six years ago. My feet have hardly touched dry land since.'

He laughed, flashing those teeth again.

'You off on this next voyage then? *Destiny*, I think it's called.'

'Not me,' he said. 'I'm not part of the crew this time. Got in there too late. Captain's got his crew. I'm waiting on another ship. So what brings you to Liverpool? There's no farm labouring hereabouts.'

'Bit of unfinished business.'

'Oh, aye?'

'I'm trying to trace my roots.'

'Lots of roots round here. And there's them without roots.'

'I was found in the streets hereabouts when I was a boy. Taken to Yorkshire.'

'When was that?'

'I don't know exactly. About nine years ago.'

'The docks was busy in them days. Twice as busy as they are now.'

'Why's that?'

'This war has been bad for business the past few years. A big drop-off.'

I assumed he meant the war in America, but I didn't want to show my ignorance so I just nodded.

'Well, nice talking to you, Isaac. Best get back to my game.'

'You wouldn't know anyone who could help, would you?'

'Well, there's only one bloke I know been here nine years.'

'Who's that?'

'A man named Edward Cubbitt.'

'Who's he?'

'He's worked the docks longer than anyone I know. There isn't much he doesn't ken.'

'How would I find him?'

'He's not hard to find. Anyone will tell you. Looks after the South Dock. Used to be a sailor. And a privateer. Getting on a bit now. About my height, bald head, grey beard, big belly. Good luck. And thanks for the drink.'

He took his glass from the bar top and went back to his game of skittles.

Our plates arrived and Emily tucked in, not looking up or pausing for breath until her plate was empty. I'd seen dogs eat like that, back at Wuthering Heights. But never people. She used the last of her bread to mop up the gravy. Then, clasping the plate in both hands, she licked it clean.

'It's good stuff, that,' she said. 'That's what you want, good grub and good ale. Good grub and good ale keeps you out of mischief. That's what my dad used to say. Didn't keep him out of mischief though, did it?'

I looked around me at all the men in the inn, different heights, different builds, different-coloured skins. I felt detached from the scene, as though it were a dream. It felt so strange being back. I felt myself drift up to the ceiling, watching the scene from the corner of the room, looking down on me and Emily. Maybe it was the white walls or the sailors, or maybe the skittles, but I recollected an earlier time. A different pub or the same pub? I couldn't be certain. I tried to dig down in my mind. To get at the memory. Roaming streets. Lost. Hunger pangs. The smell of cooking. Entering an inn. Warmth and bustle. But nothing more would come. I couldn't rely on my brain. I would comb these streets and taverns until I got the picture as clear in my mind as a painting.

I thought back to Wuthering Heights, at how small the world was that we occupied. The moors had seemed vast but

I'd seen so much since I'd left that now it felt as though the moors were just the edge of another world.

A barmaid came over to our table and cleared our plates. I asked her if there was a room for hire for me and my sister. She said she'd enquire. She came back a few minutes later. They had a room we could have. She would make up the bed. Would we need a bath? I said we would and thanked her.

'You know when you were talking earlier about your mother, about her being a whore?' I asked.

'Only till she met my dad. She wasn't a proper whore.'

'And that she died in childbirth.'

'She did.'

'How do you know?'

'My father told me. He said she'd turned to whoring because she had no other way of earning a living. She was an orphan like you. As soon as she got with my father she gave up her trade. She was a good woman.'

'According to your father. Who was a highwayman.' I raised my eyebrows.

'At least I know who my mother was. Maybe yours was a whore too. At least my mother didn't die a whore.'

'My mother was no whore.'

'How do you know? You don't know anything. You don't even know your own mother's name.'

I could feel my blood boil but I reined in my wrath, Cathy. I tried to focus on the game of skittles through a fog of pipe smoke. I watched the light flit on the tops of the pins.

'When did you first know you could do it?' I said at last.

'Do what?'

'Get dead people to speak through you.'

Emily stared into the empty pit of the fireplace.

'I found my father in the kitchen one day on his own. He was sitting on the floor, drinking brandy and crying. I was probably no more than five years old.'

'What was he crying about?'

'He was crying over my mother. He said he missed her. He said they'd argued before she died. She was pregnant and she said she didn't want me because she didn't want a child of hers to have a thief for a father. He stormed off and when he came back half-cut, I was born, and she was dead. He said he just wished he'd been able to tell her how much he loved her. He said if there was a spell to bring her back to life, even for one moment, he would pay anything to get it. I just remember being overtaken by this feeling. Everything in the room was swimming. Then I became aware of another world behind this one. It was like this other world was trying to break through. I could feel myself sinking into its dark waters. I was helpless, unable to stop it. I don't remember what happened next. I just remember waking up. I was on the floor with a banging headache. My throat was so dry I couldn't swallow. My ears were ringing and I had pins and needles in the tips of my fingers. My dad was stood over me. He was smiling. He picked me up in his arms and kissed me on the forehead. He stroked my hair and said he'd spoken to her. We were always close, but after that he never left my side. That's when I started working for him.'

Emily told me of another robbery.

'This one wasn't on the highway, but in a home. We broke into this house of a nobleman. Got over a thousand pound in gold and silver. My dad tied them up in their beds. It took my dad a while to get them to confess. The money was where they said it was. There was a packet of gold lace too. That was valued at eighteen hundred pound.'

She stopped and stared into the fireplace.

'It was his last job,' she said.

'How do you mean?'

'He was going to give it up. He had enough money to quit. He had a friend who was setting up a business, needed a partner. If he hadn't got caught, things would have been very different. If only that servant hadn't come in. If only he'd left us to it.'

'What happened?'

'What do you think? He got a good crack to shut him up. And the rest. It was his own fault.'

She went quiet and stared into the fireplace again.

'Come on,' I said. 'Let's get a bath and lig down for the night.'

I bathed first, the privilege of age. Emily had to bathe in my water. She complained initially but then stripped off and plunged into the grey soup. I got into bed first, Emily joined me shortly after.

'I didn't tell you, did I?' I said.

'Tell me what?'

'When we were in the bar earlier. I met a man who gave us a lead.'

'What lead is this?'

'He said to look out for a man called Edward Cubbitt, works the South Dock.'

'Well, it's a start,' she said, settling into the covers and putting her head on the pillow. 'Tell me a story.'

'I think we've had enough stories for one day. Let's get some sleep. I need you to be fresh for the morning.'

I thought she might complain but she was snoring in no time. I couldn't sleep with her racket. I thought about poking her in the ribs, telling her to shut it, but she looked so angelic in the moonlight with her head on the white pillow, her eyes closed, and her white-blonde hair splayed around her. I lay back and wondered about Edward Cubbitt.

Jonas Bold

The shrieking of gulls above the Gallows, the clatter and clammer of industry, were our alarm call the next day, and after breakfast we set off for the docks again. There were several large docks, rectangular in shape with high stone walls and a sloping wall at one end. People everywhere, fetching and flitting. We weaved through the crowd and walked past the King's Dock, Salthouse Dock, George's Dock, up Chapel Street. There were goods sheds, tobacco warehouses, spirit vaults, breweries, inns and taverns. The air was rich with sharp and strong aromas. The stench of things baking, boiling and burning. Mashing, malting and milling. Sweet yeast and bitter hop. We took a walk around the town to familiarise ourselves with its layout. The Exchange Building was the first thing to grab my attention. It was very grand with a domed tower and a spire that reached up to the heavens. There were many stone pillars and archways and a fine bell tower. There was a notice attached to the wall:

To be sold by auction at George's Coffee-House, betwixt the hours of six and eight o'clock, a very fine negro girl about eight years of age, very healthy and has been some time from the coast. Also, one stout young negro fellow, about twenty years of age.

Human flesh being sold openly in the street, among market stalls and butchers' shops. Another chattel being flogged for bunce. We walked up Paradise Street and watched the whores on the corner. Some approached us and asked for business. Then along Bold Street, past the almshouse. We wandered down Brownlow Hill Lane, past the poorhouse and the house of correction. Rivulets of piss and heaps of shit. The crowds thinned, and their voices dimmed. Gulls and pigeons gathered on the ledges of tall buildings. They shuffled and huddled. We walked past the bowling green and the Methodist meeting house. There were cooperages, block-and-spar-makers' shops, waterworks, drinking fountains that we made use of, sheds and boat-building yards. But above all there were burial grounds.

'When I see a grave I see a wage,' I said.

'Eh?'

'We need to get to work.'

We walked up Renshaw Street and Berry Street, along Great George's Street, until we came to St James's church. We examined the graveyard. It was vast, a tall stone wall enclosing it with lush ivy growing up one side. The church cast some of it in shadow, but further out the graves were clean and ordered and glistened in the sun. There were many fine ornate tombstones, with elaborate carvings and fanciful headstones. A Cupid plucking a bow and an angel clasping its hands. Its wings proud. A sculpture of a man and woman embracing. Seraphim and cherubim. A stone carved Jesus. A marble Madonna and a piping girl. It was clear that the dead buried here had been of moneyed stock.

We studied the names on the graves. From one stone slab I took Jeremiah, and from another, Nelson. I saw Emily do the same and we agreed on our monikers.

We waited under some trees for our first customer. We experienced further disappointment as we had in Manchester, and the same accusations, suspicions and indifference. The first looked disdainfully at our tattered apparel and refused to converse, the second was a pious man who accused us of witchcraft. The third listened to our tale but refused us, saying he'd rather not meddle in demonology. The fourth just shook her head and said not even the dead could console her.

Many hours passed before our first success. A young man, in a fancy yellow frock coat and a brown tricorne. The silver buckles on his shoes shone brightly in the sun as he approached a grave and stood close by. We waited for the right moment, then I initiated conversation. It was his mother who had died and I told him that mine had just passed over too. I shared his grief. He explained that his mother had perished giving birth to his half-sister. She had married a second time when his father had died of consumption.

'There was hardly anything left of him towards the end,' the young man said. 'The strangest thing was his fingers. Like drumsticks. His nails were as shiny as polished pearl, with thick ridges running down them. I remember my mother taking his hands in hers, examining them as though they were another man's. Then kissing them before weeping silently so as not to excite him. She mourned him for three years before my stepfather came into her life. A horologist from Hartlepool. My mother was from Abergavenny. They were both so happy when she became round with child. She gave birth to my half-sister on St David's Day. They were attending church that morning when her waters broke. She died clutching the red dragon on the flag my stepfather had laid out over her bed. For one to die so young on the festival of one who died so old . . . He was a hundred years old when he died, St David.'

'A cruel irony,' I said, 'but that was just how our mother died. In bed with her loved ones around her.'

We got talking and with some skill I was able to turn the conversation around so that when Emily appeared he was glad to make her acquaintance.

'My name is Jeremiah Nelson,' I said. 'And this is my half-sister, Constance Nelson.'

He introduced himself as Emmerson Pitt and we talked more of our respective deceased. It turned out that we had a great deal in common. I watched Emmerson as he was drawn into our net and judged when the time was ripe to reel him in.

Emily found it difficult at first to summon his mother's spirit but Emmerson was patient. Eventually, where blackbirds and throstles sang, the grave fell silent, and I saw once more the dead take possession of her body.

We left the graveyard, with ten new shillings still hot from the man's pocket. It seemed that they paid well, these Liverpool people. We walked around Toxteth Park and along Parliament Street. There were so many fine houses of great dimensions. And like Manchester town, there was wealth and poverty cheek by jowl. To an even greater extent, in fact. For every fancy man in a top hat and a silk coat, there was a barefoot beggar in a doorway asking for change. For every silver-tipped stick there was a crooked crutch. There were black faces everywhere – some of them too begged on the street. I gave the first some money, but turned the rest down. I may have been like them at one time, but I had no intention of ever going back there. The tower was on our right-hand side; its castellated turrets and loopholes were an impressive sight. Directly in front was St Nicholas's church, and another opportunity to make some money.

The building was opulent, with complicated tracery of flowers decorating the east and west windows. The gable was decorated with two ogee-headed niches. There was a fearsome dragon and a beast with a lion's head and a goat's body. There was a stone cross at the apex. Above the doorway was a carved text: *Laudate Dominum.*

This time our customer was an older man, whose son had travelled with the Royal Navy and had been assistant to the ship's surgeon when it was attacked by a Spanish fleet.

'He was fettered on the poop,' the old man explained. 'Exposed to the enemy's shot. The doctor accused him of being a spy. He was going his rounds among the sick when he was taken prisoner. Carried to the poop by the master-at-arms, then loaded with irons and stapled to the deck. He was accused of conspiring against the captain's life. My lad. How ridiculous. He was exposed to the worst conditions. The scorching heat of the sun and the unwholesome damp of the night. But they never brought him to trial. My lad. He owed his misfortune entirely to the hatred of the doctor. And there he stayed till the ship engaged with a frigate, a man-of-war with a hundred and twenty guns. Dashed to pieces by the enemy's fire. He received a great shot in his belly, which tore out his entrails. My lad. The truth came out at his funeral. The doctor was tried and sentenced. But that didn't bring my boy back, did it?'

I consoled the man. I told him about my brother, who by coincidence had also had an untimely death in the cruel Atlantic Sea. The victim of French privateers.

I paused to recollect the tombstones we had taken our new names from.

'I'm Nathaniel Newton,' I said. 'And this is my cousin, Florence Mackshane.'

The spiritual possession of Emily's body was a particularly fervid process on this occasion. And the man shrieked when she shook so violently. I had to hold him steady when his son's eyes shone from Emily's sockets. Afterwards, Emily was deeply fatigued. We sat down for a while to allow her to recover.

My pockets now were heavy with gold, silver and copper. We walked back out to the gates of the church. A crowd had gathered and we jostled our way to the front to get a better view. We saw a bear chained to a post by its neck and four or five large, fearsome dogs attacking it. One grabbed the bear by its throat. The bear fought back, lashing out. It managed to claw the dog's head, tearing the skin and exposing the skull beneath. The dog ran back to its owner and was replaced by another, even bigger and more savage. There was biting and clawing, the baring of teeth, growling and roaring. One dog was tossed into the air by the huge fist of the beast and it tumbled into the crowd, before recovering, getting back onto its feet, then showing its teeth again and running at the bear once more. The bear was now cut in several places and bleeding. There was blood and slaver everywhere. There was a large riotous crowd and much money changing hands. I had no interest in watching the suffering of this beast. My entertainment was watching the suffering of those who deserved it. I didn't believe, as Joseph had tried to teach, that killing was a sin. Only the unjust deaths of the innocent offended God. The guilty had it coming. Unjust suffering was a divine crime. But to kill those who needed to be killed, God looked down with approving eyes. For hadn't God given Samson the strength to slay an entire army with only the jawbone of a donkey? And wasn't it better in God's eyes to slay that army than to slay the innocent donkey? And wasn't Saul rejected by God when he killed all the men, women and children, as instructed, but not the king?

We walked past the town hall and the spire of St George's church rising above the Goree Warehouses. I gave Emily a look.

'Have you regained your strength sufficiently?'

She nodded.

'We can rest some more if you like?'

'I'm fine.'

'This connection you make, between the material and the spiritual, is it harmful?'

'How do you mean?'

'Can the dead take over? Is there a danger that your own spirit will be cast out?'

'I've heard that happen. To some. But it's not like that

with me. Although I can't hear them, I can feel them moving around in my body and I can push them out if I like with the force of my will.'

We had to wait over an hour for our next target, with two more rejections and yet more accusations of evil-doing, but it proved to be worth our patience. Another rich young man with a tragic tale to tell. This one had travelled many miles to Liverpool town, to seek his fortune. As I had also, it turned out. He had fallen in love here with a merchant's daughter, as had I. He'd got married but lost his newlywed on the moor.

'It was the Bowland Fells. Our honeymoon. We stayed at the Three Fishes. We set off the next morning with a picnic packed, just the two of us. We had scones and clotted cream and strawberries. We walked along the Hodder over Cromwell's Bridge. We found a lovely sheltered spot just below Ward's Stone. I laid a blanket out and we put out cuts of cold meat and bread. There was cheese and apples and a bottle of brandy the ostler of the inn had sold us. We got talking about the future. I wanted to purchase a lurcher but she was afraid of dogs. She'd been bitten by a Bedlington terrier when she was an infant. It was a silly quarrel. She got up to stretch her legs. I stayed where I was, refusing to budge, cogitating over our heated words. The wind picked up. Black clouds descended. I rose from my stupor and called out her name, but the wind stole my words. I wandered about the moors looking for her, searching every clough and crag. When I eventually came across her, it was her body in a ditch. She had fallen from the top of a rock and smashed her skull on the stones below.'

Heavier still with our riches, I suggested we find somewhere to eat and drink. It was now past midday and I didn't want to push Emily any further. We passed the fish market on James Street, but the stench enticed neither me nor the girl. We walked up High Street, past a shoe warehouse.

'Come with me,' I said.

Inside there were shelves of every type of shoe and boot. I'd decided that we both needed a more respectable appearance in order to continue to extract money from the rich. The cobbler led us to the back of the shop, where there was a seated area. I let Emily go first. The cobbler measured her foot and then brought three pairs for her to try before she was satisfied. I paid for a fine pair of brown leather boots with laces. I looked at my own footwear. The stitching had come away at the toe, and the sole and the upper had parted company. I purchased a new pair to replace them. The cobbler, eyeing the gold sovereigns, said he could make them from scratch, made to measure. Fit like a glove. But I didn't want to splash out that much just yet. I promised myself that one day I would have boots specially made to my requirements, but for now we would make do with what we had bought.

We stopped outside a butcher's shop. In the window was a pig's head and a hock of oxen hanging from a hook, as well as rows of sausages and cuts of other meats. Rib, rump and chop. Next to these were some sumptuous-looking pies.

'What do you think?'

'I'll have two.'

I bought us two pies each and we sat on a bench and ate them. There was a coaching office across the street with a notice outside its window: 'Liverpool to London in three days' was its boast.

'Why don't we go there?' Emily said. 'There'll be tons of graves.'

'This number we're working, it's not something we can do indefinitely,' I said.

'Why not?'

'Because it's something that people get wise to.'

'It's not a trick, you know.'

'I know it's not. But all the same.'

She shook her head and bit into the second pie.

'What I mean is, Emily, word gets round. You've seen the reaction we've got from most people. They think we are in league with the devil. People in London will have the same hostility. Me and you, we're too conspicuous. We can do a few more, no doubt, but at some point soon we'll need to get proper work.'

'Fuck that,' Emily said, stuffing her face with piecrust. 'I like things just as they are, thank you very much.'

An old man in rags was holding his ass by a rope rein. It was loaded with red pots of various sizes and types. He tried to sell them to those who passed him without success. He approached us but Emily told him to do one.

'Do you want to end up like him?' she asked.

There were men in felt hats with gold braid and women in bell-shaped bonnets. Carriages, coaches, carts loaded up with barrels. After we had eaten we made our way back to the docks. We went past the Custom House by the Old Dock, between Cooper's Row and Hanover Street. There we met some dockers, loading up a ship with sacks and crates. I got talking to one of the older blokes, a blackamoor with a thick neck and hair as black and wild as my own.

'I'll tell you how it is, right. Edward Cubbitt's already set sail. Went a few days back. I loaded up the boat with crates of gin and bales of cotton and this and that.'

'Where was he heading?'

'He was heading for the west coast of Africa.'

'When's he due back then?'

'Not for weeks yet, pal. I'll tell you how it is, could be months. What's to get back for? Hassle from the wife and this and that.'

'What's your name?'

'Enoch's the name, Enoch Cotton.'

I recalled a crypt and a Celtic cross.

'My name's Robert Dyer. Folk call me Bobby. Do you need any spare hands?'

He stopped what he was doing and sized me up.

'You're a big, strapping lad. Could probably find some work for you hereabouts. Why don't you come back tomorrow when I've had a word with the gaffer?'

There was nothing much to do with our day. We were still full from the pies and we'd walked around the town enough to get familiar. We hung out around the docks, watching the men load up and load off. Hogsheads of tobacco, hogsheads of sugar, puncheons of rum. Loading up, loading off. We watched the cranes and ropes. I learned much from just sitting and watching and listening to the men as they worked. I reckoned I could take to this work. It wasn't that far from farm work: physically demanding but not difficult to learn.

Pipes of old Madeira, bags of pimento, bags of ginger, tanned hides, casks of tortoiseshells, casks of indigo. I tried to imagine all the places the cargo had come from. Had some of it come from the land where I was born? I wondered. The bank sloped down to the river, where there were several large sailing ships and, around these, smaller vessels. A large schooner laden with tobacco, another with spermaceti and candles. A third piled with coffee and molasses. Clothing and bedding being loaded onto a frigate. A shallop laden with ivory. A brig loaded with chests of soap, fruit, wine, tar, hemp, iron and oil. There was a rhythm to the work that I found hypnotic. The workers were always accompanied by the gulls, as bold as brass, waiting for their chance to pilfer food. Occasionally, they would get so close to a docker that he would shoo it away, or kick it with the toe of his boot, but on the whole, the men were remarkably tolerant of these scavengers, the way a horse is with an errant fly. I even saw some of the men encourage the birds, by tossing crust and crumbs in their direction.

Bales of muslin and white bafts, tons of saltpetre, bags of sago, billets of ebony, ankers of cochineal, bales of chocolate, chests of vanello. In the distance, almost on the horizon, an impressive twenty-eight-gun ship, her topsails set. She flew a red ensign at the stern and a long pennant from her main mast. There was a female figurehead at the bow. Next to her a three-mast ship with yellow ensign and blue pennant, beneath them a rowing boat with eight men aboard. We watched a shrimper with his net and basket, a dog and small boy by the water's edge.

'There's a lot of stuff about,' Emily said.

'Indeed there is.'

'I've never seen so many items.'

'Me neither.'

'I don't know what half of it is. What's cochineal for?'

'I don't know – isn't it for dying clothes?'

'What about vanello?'

I shrugged.

'Why don't we nick some of it?'

'What for?'

'It must be worth a fortune.'

'And if we get caught?'

'We won't get caught.'

'It's not worth it.'

As tempting as it was, it would have been madness to have stolen any of the goods. There were too many people about and I didn't want to attract the wrong attention. We had plenty of money, a place to stay. We just had to act the part we were playing until we could find out some more information. I couldn't wait for this Edward Cubbitt to come back from his voyage. I went over to where Enoch was smoking his pipe between loads.

'What's there to do round here when you're done with grafting?'

He sucked on his pipe and blew out a plume of smoke.

'There's bull-baiting, cock-fighting, dog-fighting, drinking, carding, whoring, a bit of pugilism. This and that. Whatever takes your fancy, pal.'

'I'm thinking of my sister here.'

'Why don't you take her round the market?'

'What's there for a girl?'

'There's jugglers, magicians, ballad singers, Punch and Judy. There used to be bathers on the beach up there. That was popular for a time.'

'But not now?'

'No, they don't come any more.'

'Why's that?'

'Afraid of the press gangs.'

We wandered around the market and up the main shopping street. Emily stopped outside a dress shop. In the window was a dress like the one we'd seen on the girl in Manchester, pale blue with white frills around the collar. I opened the door and we went inside. I explained to the shopkeeper that my sister wanted the dress in the window. Emily tried it on. It was too big for her. Would she try another? No, she wanted this one. The man tutted but made some alterations until it fitted her perfectly. She looked at herself in the full-length mirror and beamed all over.

'It's the finest thing I've ever seen,' she said.

It gave her an innocence that fitted with her age but not her temperament. She tried one on in green striped dimity too. I told the man that we'd take both of them and I paid him. Further up the street we found a tailor's and I bought a whole new outfit: new coat, new shirt, waistcoat and breeches. I examined myself in the looking glass. How easy to pass for a gentleman, I thought. What would you think of me, Cathy, as good as Edgar now? Not too degrading for you?

In the square we sat down while Emily watched a Punch and Judy show. I thought she was a bit old for kids' stuff but I didn't say anything. When Punch beat his wife over the head repeatedly with a massive stick, Emily fell about laughing. A girl was walking around with a hat and I threw in some money.

Another girl was standing by the entrance of a striped

tent, shouting: 'Ha'penny for the next show, maggot man the human maggot, cowface and the screaming freak.' Emily tugged at my sleeve and we paid ha'penny each to gain entrance. Inside the tent, our eyes adjusted to the dark. There was a small crowd standing around a raised stage. On a broad plinth was a man with no arms or legs, wriggling up and down. The skin on his stomach and chest was hard and calloused, like the skin on the heel of a foot. We walked over to another stage to see cowface, a man with no nose, just a big hole in the middle, which joined with his mouth. He didn't much look like a cow. There was a woman in a cage with an elongated head like a batten. Her tongue was so long that it hung from her mouth like a neckerchief. A man in a brightly coloured waistcoat poked her with a stick and she screamed.

Back at the Gallows, I bought us both pewter tankards and we found a free table close to where three men were playing cards. The ale was sour but it was a refreshment of sorts. I was getting used to its bitter brew, but only as a means of quenching my thirst. A man was standing by the fireplace, his head on the mantel. He was insensible with beer. I watched him roll his temple on the stone ledge and groan. I saw him drool onto the floor. How I despised him. How I despised people. They were weak. They were fools.

As I raised my tankard to my lips I noticed that it had a glass bottom.

'Weird,' I said, holding mine up so the light shone through it.

'It's so you can see if you've been conscripted. If there's a shilling in it you can refuse the drink,' Emily said. 'That's what my dad said, anyway, but I never really believed him. I mean, why would they bother? If the navy want to conscript, they can do it by force.'

She had a point.

The man leaning his head on the mantle groaned again. I turned to the players' table and watched the men sport. It was a game I wasn't familiar with. I asked one of them what the game was and he said it was called gleek. I studied it closely. The men exchanged cards, with a view to gaining a flush. This was the 'gleek' the game got its name from, and consisted of three of a kind or mournival, which was four of a kind. This was followed by a round of trick-play. Different cards were attributed different points, so that an ace was worth fifteen but a king only three. The cards were given names, such as tib, tom and tumbler. There were four parts to the game: the draw, where players bid for the right to draw card replacements in the hope of improving their hand; vying the ruff, where the players vie as to who has the best ruff; gleeks and mournivals; and finally tricks. There were twelve different tricks played.

Lots of money changed hands as the men played and I became fascinated by it. I watched game after game until I felt as though I was beginning to understand it.

'See, Emily,' I said, 'the dealer deals twelve cards each face down, in three batches of four.'

'I know how to play it,' she said. 'I used to play it all the time with my father. If the turn-up is a tiddy the dealer receives fourpence from each player. He gets fivepence for a towser and sixpence for a tumbler. That's where he went wrong.' She pointed to the loser, when he lost sixpence. 'He shouldn't have vied the ruff.'

The man who seemed to be doing most of the winning came over to our table.

'You both seem keen,' he said. 'Do you want a game?'

'Not just now,' I said. 'But thanks – another time, I'm sure.'

When the men had finished and returned the deck to the innkeeper I requested it for our use. I played Emily several games, she coming out the winner in each instance. It hurt my pride to lose to so young a player, but it was a necessary pain. It was made worse by her continual gloating every time she won. Still, we carried on playing. I was determined to improve my luck. When Emily pocketed the deck at the end of our game, this time I turned a blind eye.

~

The next day we found a cemetery on the east side of town. Despite our improved attire we still suffered the usual rejections, but we did manage to persuade a dapper fellow by the name of Mr Jeffrey.

I cast my mind back to a crumbling headstone in Manchester, its markings weathered by a century of age, and introduced myself as Abel Adams. Emily was my adopted sister, Mabel.

'Abel and Mabel Adams. Your parents clearly had a sense of humour.' The man smiled.

'Indeed they did, sir.'

He allowed Emily to summon his loved one, his dear wife who had passed away not two months since. But here our luck was to run out.

'It's me, my love. How I've missed you.'

'Do my ears deceive me?' He staggered backwards, almost falling over. I rescued him from falling.

'It is she,' I said. 'My sister is no longer here.'

'Remarkable. I have thought of nothing else and no one, since you departed,' he said.

'Oh, my sweetness. How I love you still.'

'I have prayed to God to look after you.'

'God is protecting me here. Do not fear. But it gets lonely without you.'

'I can't sleep in our bed by myself. The bed feels too big without your warmth.'

'Oh, Jeffrey, my one sweet love.'

'What did she say?' he said, turning to me. 'My name is Thomas, not Jeffrey. Jeffrey is my family name. My wife never called me Jeffrey in her life. What cheap trick is this?'

'I'm sorry, sir, sometimes the dead are changed in death. It can be terrible hard to confront a loved one in such a changed state. Such a shock to the system.'

'Nonsense. You are both nothing but confidence tricksters. I don't believe a word. I'll have you arrested. I'll report you to the beadle. Exploiting people in this manner. It's a disgrace!'

I tried to calm the man down, but he just became more agitated. He started shouting at the top of his voice. 'Police! Over here! Police!'

I grabbed hold of Emily and we ran down the path and out of the walled garden. We sprinted up the street, making our way across the town. We ducked into a doorway to catch our breath.

'It's a trick, isn't it? You lying bitch!'

'It doesn't work every time,' Emily said, holding her sides.

'You must think I'm stupid.'

'It's you. It's your fault. Putting me under pressure.'

I'd been well and truly duped, Cathy, by this wily infant.

'Well, that's the end of that,' I said. 'And we'll have to keep our heads down.'

We looked about us. The coast seemed to be clear. We carried on our way. Protected by the crowd. As we walked I reflected. Inwardly I was deeply agitated. I clung onto the possibility that in fact Emily had been possessed by my mother – that she had been honest in saying it didn't work every time. But the more I thought it through, the more I was convinced of the falseness of her spiritual possession.

'Tell the truth,' I said. 'It's a trick, isn't it?'

'I suppose.'

'I knew it!'

'No, you didn't. I had you hook, line and sinker.'

'You little devil. It's a bloody good trick though.'

I laughed bitterly. Inside my mind was a muddle.

'You did have me fooled. You're right.'

I shook my head.

'Anyway, what are we going to do now? That was our only means of income.'

'It's not the end of the world,' Emily said. 'We've plenty of money still.'

I tried to rationalise my emotions. It was time to find some work on the docks, in any case. And I put this proposition to Emily.

'What for?'

'It's the perfect place to snoop about. If Edward Cubbitt

is nowhere to be found, no matter, there are plenty of other people in this town.'

As we walked down Chapel Street I reflected more on Emily's trick. So, my mother hadn't spoken through Emily. She hadn't died on a ship after all. But perhaps she had died in some other way. Maybe she was here in Liverpool. She could even be working on the docks for all I knew. My mind raced with the possibility. There was a chance, albeit a slim one, that I would be united with her again. I wouldn't give up. I was more determined than ever to find the truth, regardless of the cost.

We found Enoch Cotton by the largest of the three cranes, hauling a barrel with the windlass.

'Well,' I said, 'any luck with the gaffer?'

'My word, you've smartened yourselves up,' he said, looking us over. 'As it happens, there are a couple of vacancies. We need a dock hand. What's your name again?'

'Bobby.'

'And your sister?'

'April.'

'Well, I tell you how it is, right, you see that office up them steps?'

I nodded.

'That's the gaffer's headquarters. His name is Pierce Hardwar. You go up to his office and say I sent you.'

~

The office was at the top of the stairs. I took Emily with me. The door was closed so I knocked twice. I heard a voice from inside beckon us in. I explained that Enoch had sent us.

'Brother and sister, eh? You don't look much like blood.'

'I'm adopted,' I said. 'April's parents took me in.'

'A sooty, eh. Well, I don't mind that. Got lots of sooties on my books. Lascars, niggers, Turks. Good workers. Plenty of strength and stamina.'

'What about my sister – do you have work for her?'

He turned to Emily. 'I dare say we can find something for a pretty little girl to do.'

He smiled a crooked smile and peered over his spectacles, the way a crow eyes a caterpillar.

'What sort of labour are you used to then?' He leered at Emily.

'I've done all sorts in my time,' she said. 'Farm work, mine work, and the like.'

'You can work for me,' he said. 'I've spare.'

We were taken on that morning and set to work. My job was as a dock hand, loading and unloading cargo mainly. Shifting and lugging. Emily's work was less defined. Gofer and sweeper-upper. The wages were poor, Emily's not being enough to even feed herself; the object, however, was not to become rich, but to gain knowledge. I wanted to find out more about dock life, to discover who, if anyone, knew Mr Earnshaw. My plan was to find out who I was. I worked alongside Enoch, soon becoming tired of his conversation.

'I'll tell you how it is – my wife, she's not too good. She's taken to her bed. Can't get out. Doctors don't know what it is. She's a mystery to every physician in the land. Lucky my two daughters are old enough to look after themselves. I'm not kiddin', I don't know what I'd do without them. They cook the evening meal, do all the cleaning and the laundry, this and that.'

'Is that so?'

We were unloading a medium-sized dragoon by the name of *Lord Rochester.*

'That's how it is. I come home from here and there's generally a hot meal waiting for me. Been married to the wife now fourteen year. Oldest girl is fifteen, youngest is thirteen. They're young women, you know what I mean. Got boys sniffing round them like dogs round a bitch in heat. I'll tell you how it is. I'm not kiddin', if I find out they've done something, I'll knock 'em into next week.'

Most of the time I was able to ignore what he was saying. It wasn't conversation. He didn't ask me any questions. All I had to do was nod from time to time. I got the impression that whether I had been there or not, he would have nattered on regardless. He would have talked to a gull or even a barrel.

'Don't say much, do you? I like that. I'm not one for idle chit-chat either. Some folk don't know when to shut up, I'm not kiddin'.'

I helped him hook a box of indigo to the rope of the crane.

'How well do you know Edward Cubbitt?'

'As well as any do round here. Worked these docks over eight year now. Edward's one of the oldest workers. Must be in his fifties. Thought he'd given up his sea legs. Plenty of life in the old dog yet, eh. What did you say you wanted him for, any road?'

'I want to talk to him.'

'Be careful with that,' he said as I dropped the rope and the block swung towards him, nearly missing the side of his head. 'Crack someone's skull, one of these,' he said, taking hold of the block so that it stopped swinging. 'What do you want to talk to him about, any road?'

'A Mr Earnshaw.'

'Never heard of him.'

'You won't have. He came here nine years ago. He found me on the street. Brought me to his home. Brought me up as one of his own. He died a few years ago.'

'Well, there's plenty of other blokes go back that far. You could start with the gaffer, old Mr Hardwar, goes back at least twenty year. There's Jack Lancaster too, works in the Customs House, goes back twenty year an' all. I'll tell you how it is, there's no shortage of old-timers here. As for strange men and orphan boys, there's plenty of them too.'

After the shift had finished, I waited for Emily to return from an errand, delivering a note to someone at George's Dock, then we walked over to the Customs House. Enoch had given me a good description of Jack Lancaster. Tall man with a stoop and a mop of curly blond hair. In his forties. We went over to the Harbour Board offices and to the Customs House. The office door was open. I peered in and saw a man by the description Enoch had provided sitting behind a table. We waited by the harbour for him to finish work. Near to these buildings was a big slate with the names of ships coming into the docks: the *St Inez*, the *Carnatic*, the *Fortune*, the *Lottery*, the *Enterprise*; next to these, the time of the tide, what time they were coming in, and what dock the ship was going to.

Eventually the gentleman who fitted the description of Jack Lancaster left the building and locked the door behind him. The rest of the workers had already gone home, or gone to one of the many alehouses thereabouts. He walked slowly and we were careful to keep our distance as we followed him up the lane. We saw, on the corner of Dexter Street and St James Place, a number of small children huddled together on the step of a public house. They were barefooted and had scarcely enough clothing to cover their nakedness. They were weeping. None of the passers-by took notice. We watched as this Jack Lancaster approached the children. He dug deep into his pockets and poured pennies into their hands. So grateful were they that they commenced weeping again, but this time tears of joy. So this Jack Lancaster was a bit of a soft touch. Good.

We carried on up the street with the silhouette of Jack Lancaster in the distance. We speeded up, closing the gap but careful to retain enough space between us so as not to arouse suspicion. Eventually we saw him enter a tavern. A few moments later we were outside ourselves.

'All right,' I said, 'let's each play our parts. Leave all the talking to me.'

Inside it was dark, there being only one small window at the far side of the bar. There was a billiard table that had two gentlemen around it, playing a game. I saw Jack Lancaster at the bar counter ordering a drink. He sat down in the corner with his tankard. We got served and walked over to his table.

'Mind if we join you?'

'Do I know you?'

'I'm Robert Dyer, and this is my sister, April. We work in the Old Dock. Just started today, as it happens. I recognised your face just now. You work thereabouts too, don't you?'

We sat down at his table. He looked perturbed.

'I'm waiting for a friend,' he said. 'I'm not being rude but that seat is taken.'

'Don't worry,' Emily said, 'we're not stopping.'

'Yes,' I said, 'should your friend arrive, we'll gladly exchange seats. Anyway, like I was saying, I wouldn't bother you, it's just you looked familiar and with us just starting work . . . We're new to the area.'

'We don't know anyone,' Emily said.

'I do work near the Old Dock, as a matter of fact. The Customs House,' he said.

'Oh, right, yes. That must be where I've seen you. Seems like a good place to work.'

'It's not bad. Not as good as it used to be, back in the day.'

He took out a tin of snuff and pinched some onto the back of his hand. He snorted two lines, one up each nostril.

'Do either of you partake?'

'Not for me, thanks. Nor my sister. You worked there a long time then?'

'Twenty year.'

'Perhaps you can help us,' I said.

'In what way?'

'We're trying to trace someone. Our father. He's gone missing. He came here nine years ago and we wondered if he'd been seen since.'

Jack Lancaster laughed. 'Nine year, you must be joking. I can't remember what I did last week, let alone a man from nine year back.'

'He was called Mr Earnshaw.'

'Nope, name doesn't ring a bell.'

He shook his head vigorously. He looked furtively around the room. I described his appearance.

'I can think of half a dozen chaps look like that,' he said.

He scratched the end of his nose.

'He was from Yorkshire. Near a place called Keighley.'

'People from all four corners of the world come to Liverpool. There's nothing remarkable about that.'

He scanned the room again and fiddled with his collar.

'I miss my dad,' Emily said. 'If I could just see him one more time.'

She looked at the man with doleful eyes.

'I'm sorry. I can't help. Lots of men come and go. Then there's men like me that stick around. I sometimes think I should have moved on when I had the chance. It's too late for me now.'

'Please help us,' Emily whispered. She looked up at Jack mournfully.

'I've told you. I don't know your father.'

Emily's bottom lip trembled. Her eyes welled up. She held onto Jack's sleeve. Jack looked around awkwardly. The clock on the wall ticked. Emily tightened her grip and tears rolled down her cheeks.

'Please, sir,' she pleaded.

Jack looked around the room cautiously, then, shuffling up closer, he said in a low voice, 'Listen, there was a man by the name of Mr Earnshaw back in the day.'

'Where was he from?'

'I suppose he could have been from Yorkshire. He had some business arrangement with Jonas Bold.'

'Who's he?'

'Who's Jonas Bold?!' The man looked scared for a moment. He glanced around the room again. 'A very powerful man. Even got a bloody street named after him. Owns half the town. And then some. Owns an iron foundry, a sugar refinery, two distilleries. Lots of fingers in lots of pies. Bit of a do-gooder these days. He set up a dispensary a few years ago to provide free medicines for the poor. Never stops nattering on about it. Gets on your nerves. There's them that do good and them that like to be seen to be doing good.'

'And where might we find him?'

'Search me. He doesn't live in the town these days. He's got a big estate in the country. I see him from time to time in his coach, pulled by four white thoroughbreds, bloody show-off. He has a lot of business interests abroad, and down south. He's here, there and everywhere.'

'What does he look like?'

'Big fat fucker in a powdered wig. I mean, who wears wigs these days?'

We thanked the man and made to leave.

'Listen,' he said, in an even lower voice than before, 'don't you ever mention my name alongside the name of Jonas Bold or Mr Earnshaw. Is that clear?'

I nodded. We made our way back to the other side of town.

'Well, that's something,' I said.

'Something's better than nothing, that's what my dad used to say, except when it's trouble. Then nothing's better than something.'

I thought about this Jonas Bold. What hold did he have on this town for men like Lancaster to be so circumspect? And what business had he with Mr Earnshaw that had to be kept so silent?

It was still light and there were plenty of people about town.

'Let's have a wander,' Emily said. 'My father always had a walk before and after supper. He said the walk before was to work up an appetite, and the walk after was to walk the meal off. I never understood that. You'd think working the roads all day would give you an appetite.'

'Maybe he just liked walking.'

'He preferred drinking and carding. And whoring.'

We strolled past St James's church, where the stones were carved with grotesque gargoyles and where there were men congregated, talking away, children running around and people sitting on the doorstep. There was a quarry close to the church between Parliament Street and Duke Street from which stone was obtained, I presumed, for the public buildings that were all around us. There were faced blocks piled high at one end, but the workers had finished and their tools had been tidied away. I thought about our own quarry, Cathy, near Penistone Crag, where Joseph and I had spent many a day breaking stone while you were convalescing at the Lintons', growing accustomed to all the trappings of wealth. I broke stone until my hands throbbed and I couldn't make a fist. All the time wishing that I could break the heads of Hindley and Edgar. A task I would never tire of. As you were softening with privilege and pamper, I was turning blisters into burrs. I wondered what you were doing now. Were you with him drinking wine? Were you in his arms? Perhaps by now you were married. Maybe even fecund with his child. I shuddered at the thought of such a grotesque spectacle.

Opposite the quarry was an artificial hill called St James's Mount. There was a sizeable garden and a walk called Mount Zion, where the wealthiest residents promenaded.

'Let's sit down for a minute,' Emily said.

We sat and watched the display. Emily smirked at the sight of these fops. There were old men wearing elaborate embroidered frock coats, decorated silk fabrics, lilac with silver and diamond-stitched patterns, buttons of silver, green and white spangles. The young men wore coats cut at the back to resemble a swallow's tail. Pink, light blue, lavender suits, ruffles of lace, spots, stripes and chevrons, braided seams.

'Look at this one,' Emily said, nudging me.

Walking towards us was a man in his early twenties wearing a coat and vest imitating the stripes of a zebra.

'He looks a cunt,' Emily said.

There was another, about the same age, with a coat decorated with the spots of a leopard. We sat and watched as they paraded along the garden walk. Short waistcoats and tight-fitting breeches. Round hats with wide uncocked brims. Gold-banded and tasselled. Shoes with decorative chains, hung with enamel plaques and cameos, so that they jangled as they walked. Two watch chains either side of their waists, curls plastered to their foreheads.

The women were just as preposterously attired. The older wore boned stays and hooped petticoats. The younger, softer-lined bustles, making them resemble downy pigeons. Robings and petticoats covered in flowers. Puffed pleats. Chintz and printed cotton. Neckerchiefs fluffed up so high that their noses were scarce visible and their nosegays like large shrubs. Their hairstyles were just as ridiculous, so high on their heads that they exceeded the length of the face, covered with feathers of all colours, or else a frizz of curls and loose ringlets. Enormous hats covered with ribbons, tulle and roses. Was this how ridiculous you had become, Cathy, in your new vain world?

Emily and I watched with some amusement. She pointed and sniggered at such vanity and pomp. I pictured you, Cathy, all trussed up in these latest fashions. I could just see you and Edgar arm in arm, looking like a peacock and a puffed-up pigeon, wandering around the garden. But in truth, this ostentatious display eclipsed even Edgar's pomposity. I envied the rich their wealth and power, but not their diversions, which seemed beyond frivolous to me. I vowed that no matter how rich I became, I would not succumb to such narcissism and self-regard.

'Why do they want to look like cunts?' Emily said.

As we sat there watching these primped-up prats, I thought over my plans. I was resolved to stay in Liverpool town till I discovered something of Mr Earnshaw's business. No matter how long it took. I was determined to learn what I could of my origins. Whether my mother was alive or dead. I had to know the truth.

'My dad liked his clobber but he didn't overdo it. He said there was a fine line between looking stylish and looking like a cunt. This lot remind me of some of the people we robbed. You don't feel so bad about it when they look like that,' she said, pointing to a woman dressed in a gown with silver buttons, her hair stuck on top of her head like a loaf of bread, red ribbons dangling down.

'They sort of deserve it, really. They are asking for a bullet dressed in that garb. My dad said that when folk have more money than sense, it's for those with more sense than money. Called it the fair distribution of wealth and wick.'

Pierce Hardwar

For the next week or so I spent the days working on the docks with Enoch Cotton lugging and slogging. With my ears still ringing with his yacking, I spent my evenings following up leads. I had names and I went looking for their faces. I wandered each street and lurked in every alley. I went from tavern to inn and every social gathering. I passed tenements teeming with sailors and victuallers. Thirsty men looking for drink to guzzle and a hole to poke. Dockers singing shanties and rigging for a cruise. The streets swarmed with strumpets pursued by wanton privateers. I saw men stripped to the waist fighting in the streets for a farthing. I watched games of ring-taw and able-whacket, barley-break and hot cockle. But away from the mirth and the merriment, the docks at night were an eerie place. There were fogle-filchers and cutpurses on every corner. Their faces looked ghostly in the light of the street lamps and their voices echoed over the muted waves. The sound of water lapping at the dockside took on a sinister insistence without the screaming of the gulls and the cacophony of industry. Everywhere the streets were filled with shadows, dark corners and unfriendly whispers.

One night we were sitting by the South Dock after another lead that had sounded promising had turned out to be a dead end, when Emily said, 'So what are you going to do now, William Lee? You can't just hang around here all the time, hoping that something will come good. It won't.'

'I've made a decision,' I said.

'What?'

'Despite my better judgement, I'm going to approach Mr Hardwar.'

'He won't listen to you. He won't even give you the time of day.'

'Well, maybe not. But I've got to give it a try, Emily.'

'I don't like him.'

'Who does?'

'He gives me the creeps. You know what he said to me the other day? He said he'd give me a shilling if I stopped behind one night when everyone had gone and come up to his office.'

'What for?'

'What do you think?'

'Dirty bastard. What did you say?'

'I said I wasn't that type of girl.'

'What did he say?'

'He offered me two shilling.'

This only confirmed my feelings. I had already heard rumours from Enoch and from other dockworkers that Hardwar had an unhealthy interest in young girls. I had kept a close eye on him.

'Look, despite what we both feel about him, he could be useful. He knows things and I've got nothing to lose.'

So I bided my time, waiting for the right opportunity to come along. Then one evening in the third week of employment, I found myself working late, with everyone else, barring Mr Hardwar, having gone home.

I told Emily to meet me back at the Gallows. I waited until my work was finished and the old dock was entirely deserted, then I climbed the wooden stairs and approached Pierce Hardwar's office. His door was open. He was at his desk, quill in hand, scribbling away in a red ledger. He didn't see me so I knocked on the open door to get his attention.

'Excuse me, sir, sorry to bother you at this late hour.'

'What is it?' he said without looking up.

'I've finished my work, sir. I'm done for the day.'

'Very well. Off you go then.'

'Have you much work yourself, sir? You seem to keep such long hours.'

'Work's the only salvation. Keeps you on the straight and narrow. God made the world in six days. Deadlines are lifelines.'

'I'm told he rested on the seventh, sir.'

'Who told you that?'

'It's written in the scripture, is it not?'

'Don't believe everything you read.'

'Have you been here a long time?' I asked.

He looked up from his work and glared at me.

'That's none of your business. Who do you think you are, coming up here, poking your nose in?'

'Sorry, sir, I was just interested.'

'Well, don't be. Now go and close the door behind you.'

'Very well, sir. It's just, I've got something that might interest you.'

'I doubt that.'

'Please, hear me out, sir. I promise you I won't waste your time.'

He dipped the quill in the ink pot and wrote something in one of the columns, then he put the quill down.

'This'd better be good.'

'My sister, sir. If you were interested to have some private time with her, I could arrange it.'

He peered over his glasses at me and raised his eyebrows.

'How much?'

'Nothing. Well, not money in any case.'

He narrowed his eyes and puckered his lips. He regarded me with suspicion.

'Then what?'

'Answers. To questions. I'd like five minutes of your time for half an hour of my sister's company. That's all.'

He scowled and twiddled with his sideburns, but then he nodded and relaxed his glower.

'Very well.'

He picked up a sandglass that was by an ink pot.

'When this is through, so are you.'

He turned it over so that the grains of sand began to fall like water.

'You've got five minutes, starting from now.'

'How long have you worked here?'

'Eighteen years. Give or take.'

'Are you a native of this town then?'

'Yes, born just a mile from this very spot. I've got Liverpool in my bones, you might say.'

'I've roots here myself, I'm told.'

'Your accent's a Yorkshire one, is it not? One of the wapentakes of the West Ridings, I'd wager.'

'It is, sir, but my father had business here. Perhaps you knew him.'

'Perhaps. I've known many a tyke and tinker.'

'His name was Mr Earnshaw.'

He leaned across the ledger, his eyes reaching into mine as though into a darkened room. He lowered his glasses and twiddled with one of his sideburns once more. He gave me a crooked smile.

'Nope. No one I know.'

'He was an associate of Jonas Bold. Have you heard of him?'

'Of course. He owns half this town. Everyone knows Jonas. I don't have anything to do with him personally. I've no time for the frivolity of society.'

The sand was almost through. More like one minute than five, I thought. I'd been short-changed.

'I'm very eager, sir, to learn of my origins. It's every man's right to know his roots.'

'Nonsense. A man has no more rights than is accorded to him by his station.'

'But even a tree knows where it's planted, sir.'

'I'll tell you what your origins are, same as any man's. You're the son of Adam. Even you are one of God's children.'

'But, sir. A little knowledge is all I ask.'

The sand had ceased to flow. The grains were spent. My minute was over. Mr Hardwar eyed the glass. He picked up his quill again and dipped it in the pot of ink by the side of the ledger.

'Time's up. Good day to you,' he said and commenced scribbling in the book once more.

'But, sir, perhaps if I described in detail this Mr Earnshaw. Some nine years past now he was here.'

He looked up briefly. 'Seek not wisdom when it brings no profit. I'll talk to you later about our arrangement.'

A drop of ink dripped onto the page of the ledger.

'Now look what you've made me do.'

He dabbed at it with a blotter.

'But—'

'No buts. Send me your sister. If she pleases me, we will see if I can stir a memory or two.'

Defeated, I went back to my room in the Gallows. Emily had already bathed and changed for supper.

'What kept you?'

I explained my meeting.

'You did what?!'

'Don't worry, I've no intention of keeping my side of the bargain.'

'That doesn't matter to men like Hardwar, you fool – a deal is a deal.'

She tried to stifle a cough. But the more she did the more the coughing built, until she was hacking away violently. I waited for her to stop.

'Look, I'll make sure he doesn't touch you.'

'And how will you do that? You've offered me. To bargain with that freak. And for what? He didn't give you anything. How many people have you approached now?'

I tried to tot up the tally in my head but I'd lost count.

'How could you, William? How could you? After . . .'

Her words dried up and she stared down at the floor.

How could I, Cathy? After what had happened. After what I'd promised. That I would keep her safe. But I meant it. I wouldn't let that man anywhere near her.

'I'm really sorry, Emily. But I promise you, under no circumstances will I allow anything bad to happen to you.'

She shook her head. 'This isn't working, William. And now you spring this on me. Well, you can stuff it. I'm not going back there after what you've done.'

'Well, we can't work the graves. You put an end to that, you pillock.'

'So this is my fault? Don't think so. Using me like that. I'm not a bloody brood pullet.'

'Look, I'm sorry. I had to use something. I'll get you out of it.'

'How? He's a powerful man.'

'Listen, here's the deal. I'll tell him you're laid up with a fever, all right? I've still got three or four leads to follow up. It won't take me more than a day or two. Give me to the end of the week and whether I'm any further on or not, we'll quit there and then, move to the next town and go back to the burial grounds. How does that sound?'

'Do you promise?'

'I promise you, Emily. On my life. I won't let anything happen to you.'

I made the sign of the cross.

Emily was quiet over supper. I tried to engage her in conversation. What was the soup like? Was the chicken cooked sufficiently? Were the carrots tender enough? Did she want afters? But she didn't respond. I knew inside that I'd let her down. I'd gone too far. I'd crossed the line, but I was determined to rectify my error. I watched her push her food around the plate. I ordered treacle pudding but even this didn't bring her out of her mood. Did she want custard with it? I ordered custard in any case. She left the bowl alone. The custard cooled and a thick skin formed.

I felt deflated too, not just with Emily's mood, but also with my lack of progress. I couldn't flog a dead horse for ever. All I had now was Jonas Bold and he was proving to be very elusive. Everyone knew him but no one seemed to want to talk about him. The rich man who got richer, then disappeared. Some use money to pursue fame, others to buy their anonymity.

~

The next day I went to Hardwar's office and told him about Emily. He didn't believe me but I assured him she'd be up on her feet in a few days, and that she would keep to our side of the bargain. He put down the book he was reading and folded his arms.

'She'd better do,' he said. 'And near on the port quarter. What sort of ailment is it?'

'Fever, sir.'

'Best thing to break a fever is hard graft. Does she say her prayers?'

'She's burning up, can't get out of bed. This day or two.'

'Feed her good broth morn, noon and aft. Make her pray dawn and dusk.'

'Yes, sir.'

'As soon as she's on her feet, tell her to report to me. With interest.'

'Interest? How do you mean?'

'My time is valuable. You waste my time, it costs you. I'll want the full hour when next I see her. And listen to me, sooty. No funny business. If I get wind of anything, if you're not being straight with me—'

'But I am, sir. I gave you my word.'

'Sooty words measure less than those of a gentleman. I'll take your word, but you look after your sister. Make sure she's fit for fettling. Here, while you're standing there taking up space, give me a hand with this.'

He stood up and walked over to the window.

'It's a two-man job, is this.'

He reached for a set of ladders and placed them under some bookshelves.

'Hold them steady.'

It looked more like a one-man job to me but I held them firm while he climbed the steps and reached for a book on the top shelf.

'I used to have a head for heights, you know, but not these days. It was a ladder such as this that Jacob saw the angels ascending. Come the day, I'll need Jesus himself to fix them to the gates.'

He climbed back down, holding a blue leather-bound volume. He took the ladders slowly and seemed relieved when he was at the bottom.

'Here, take this.'

He handed me the book, eyeing me in a curious way, as though he recognised something in me.

'You've a good, strong frame, I'll grant you that.'

'How do you mean?'

'Nothing, only if you take a mettled stallion with a thick cresty neck and you breed it with a docile filly you get a beast that is both strong and compliant.'

'I don't follow you, sir.'

'I had a fall, you know. Some years back. Took the wind out of my sails.'

He pointed over to his desk.

'Put the book there.'

I carried it to the desk and plonked it down.

'Right, I've got work to do, and you're in the way. Off you go and next time I see you I'll expect to see your sister too. And think on, prayers and broth. A sufficient quantity of each.'

~

I spent the rest of the week following up the few leads I had left and trying to get more information on Jonas Bold, but I managed to discover absolutely nothing and all my leads were duff ones. My method was sound – to ply them with drink first, loosen their tongue – but no matter how loose they became, once the name of Bold was muttered, they'd clam up again.

By Friday evening, with Emily still off work, and me no nearer my end, I resolved to cut my losses and do as I'd promised Emily. I was disheartened to admit defeat but I was not going to disappoint her again. We would move on to the next town. We would take up grave graft once more.

I'd been talking to Enoch about work further afield and he'd told me there was plenty in a port called Lancaster, north of Liverpool town. There was work on the dock there, and there were graves. It was far enough away for us to start afresh. I had failed to find out who I was and was resigned that perhaps I never would.

It was late and the warehouse contained only me and Pierce Hardwar. I went to his office again. I made sure I had my knife to hand. I was going to get what I was owed. I knocked on the door and he bade me enter. He was sitting behind his desk, working by the light of a lantern, which illuminated the gold brocade on his yellow waistcoat and the two watch chains that hung either side. He wore a white shirt with the sleeves rolled, and a yellow neck scarf. His jacket was draped over the back of his chair.

He looked over his spectacles and nodded, folding his arms as though they were the wings of an insect. The light from the lantern sparkled on the gold rims of his glasses.

'Well? Where is she?'

'She's not coming, sir.'

'What?'

'And I've finished, sir.'

'But we had a deal. You gave me your word.'

'No, I mean, I've finished for good.'

He shook his head to and fro, and peered over his spectacles again.

'You're quitting?'

'Yes.'

'What about the girl?'

'Forget about her. The deal is off.'

'The deal is off? Ha! You don't get to break my deals. That's not how it works.'

He unclasped his folded arms and began to tap on the table with his index finger.

'I'm telling you, it's not happening.'

Pointing his bony finger at me, he said, 'Now listen, I say what you can do and what you can't do.'

'I don't wish to cause trouble, sir, but I've other business I've been called to, an urgent matter.'

'The only excuse I accept for not turning up for work is a funeral, your own funeral. What business could be more urgent than my business?'

His finger was wagging now, erratically.

'I'm afraid I'm not at liberty to say, sir. It's a private matter. Now, if you'd just settle up—'

'Not at liberty?! A private matter?! A fucking sooty coming in here, shouting the odds like he's boss and I'm the lackey. And then expects me to give him money. You've got a fucking cheek, haven't you?'

'I'm sorry, sir.'

I shrugged but stayed my ground.

'That's me done.'

He stood up from behind his desk.

'I'll say when we're done, boy, not some fucking sooty half-breed. Do you hear me?'

'I'll be needing my wages before I go. Four and thrup-pence.'

He was about to say something but was lost for words. His cheeks had purpled with rage.

'You'll pay me what I'm owed,' I told him. 'I've earned that money fair and square.'

'Wha . . . ?! Who do you . . . ?! Get out of my office. Now!'

I saw Hindley with his whip. Boot. Club. Kicking me in my guts. Laughing in my face. I reached for my knife and brandished it. I edged closer to his desk.

'I want that money and I'm not leaving till I get it.'

Quick as an eel, Hardwar yanked open the top drawer of his desk and reached in. He pulled out a flintlock. He pointed it in my face.

'Sit down.'

I felt my heart quicken but I held my resolve.

'Take it easy, Mr Hardwar. There's no need for your finger to be on that trigger.'

'Sit the fuck down. Now.'

He had a frenzied look in his eye.

'I'll do as you ask, sir, but please, lower your aim.'

I took my seat at the other side of the desk.

'You think I wouldn't shoot you?'

'I don't know.'

'I've shot men before. I've shot plenty. No one leaves my charge without my say-so. *I* say when someone comes and someone goes. *Me.* I've got the law on my side. The judge of this town is an old friend of mine. I dined with him only last week. All I have to say is that you came to rob me. Shooting a man in self-defence is no crime. Especially a sooty.'

I could see the murderous intent in his eye but I tried to retain my composure. He moved around his desk, keeping the gun aimed at my head.

'Put the knife down.'

I dropped it onto the floor.

He placed the cold metal of the barrel against my forehead. I closed my eyes.

'You asked for this, nigger.'

I felt no fear as I waited for my end. I thought only of the warm place waiting to receive me. So I would beat Hindley to hell after all. The thought saddened me. Would I meet my mother there?

'Say your prayers, you miserable son of a whore.'

I heard the click of the trigger but no explosion. I opened my eyes. The flint hadn't sparked. Hardwar looked aghast.

Without even thinking, I snatched the pistol from his grip and smashed him in the face with it. He went down. I picked up my knife and held it close to his throat.

'Get up.'

He struggled to his feet.

'Sit back where you were.'

He stumbled over to his chair and collapsed into it, a line of blood visible at the point where the gun had connected.

'Now you're going to talk. You're going to give me answers. Or I'll slit your throat.'

'What is it you want to know?'

'You just called me a son of a whore. Why did you call me that?'

At first he didn't say anything. He held a handkerchief to

the cut on his forehead and shook his head from side to side. I took a step towards him.

'It's nothing,' he said hurriedly. 'Just an expression.'

'You know something. You're hiding something. I can tell. I'll give you one last chance to talk. That stuff the other day about horse breeding. And now this. Why son of a whore?'

He twiddled nervously with one of his sideburns and cleared his throat.

'I knew your Mr Earnshaw.'

'How do you mean?'

'I knew him quite well, as it happens. It's not the first time your Mr Earnshaw visited Liverpool.'

'How do you know?' I asked.

Hardwar hesitated and I moved the knife a little closer to his pallid face.

'He was here nine years ago or thereabouts, to collect you, as you know, but also the year before that, and the year before that again.'

'Why?'

'His business goes back as long as my tenure here, to before you were born. He was once quite the visitor of this town, I'll have you know. Couldn't stay away.'

'How come you by your information?'

'I know Jonas Bold.'

I sat down in my chair but made sure he could see the knife gripped in my hand.

'Go on.'

'Do you mind if I smoke?'

'Go ahead.'

He took out his pipe with shaking fingers. He reached for

a still from a vase and held it to a lighted candle, then he used the still to light the tobacco.

'He used to be a merchant, like many men round here. A very wealthy one. Your Mr Earnshaw invested some money in a business proposition that Mr Jonas Bold was raising finances for.'

He blew out a plume of smoke and squirmed in his chair.

'And what was this business venture?'

'The purchase of a certain fleet. The purchase of its crew, cargo and captain.'

'And what was the ship for?'

'On its outward journey, the transportation of gin and cotton, as well as a variety of worsted goods. To the west coast of Africa. On its middle passage, the transportation of negroes to the West Indies. To be bartered for sugar and rum, for transportation and sale to the motherland.'

'And Mr Earnshaw was aware of this?'

'He was.'

Hardwar rocked in his chair and sniffed.

'What was the ship called?'

'The ship they called *Harmony*.'

'And on its homeward-bound journey?'

'It was carrying not just rum and sugar on its cargo. As was usual.'

'What then?'

'A very small selection of negresses.'

'To what end?'

'They were the choicest negresses, you understand, carefully selected. No common-or-garden sooties. Most agreeable and pleasing to the eye. Hand-picked by the discerning eye of Jonas Bold himself. Tried and tested.'

'They were sold into prostitution? And Mr Earnshaw knew this?'

'He did. He made a special attachment to one of the negresses. Your mother.'

My brain reeled. My mother. Mr Earnshaw. Special attachment. I didn't want to put the pieces together.

'Are you . . . are you saying that Mr Earnshaw is my father by blood?'

'That is the case, yes.'

I tried to let the news sink in. My head was whirling. The room was swaying. I saw Mr Earnshaw at the dock, taking me by the hand, telling me he'd look after me. I saw him in his chair, by the fireplace, his blistered feet in a bowl of hot water, telling Hindley to treat me like a brother. I saw Mrs Earnshaw, confused. 'Why have you brought an orphan back? Why would you bring him all this way? You're going soft.' I saw her scratching her head. I saw Nelly feeding me broth, me in bed with fever. 'Oh yes, he was a rum'un, was Mr Earnshaw, back in the day. He got up to stuff. No one knows the half of it.'

'And why did he return? Why come back seven years after the transaction to collect me?'

'He was being blackmailed.'

'How do you know?'

'I was the one who was blackmailing him.'

'Why?'

'Because I could. And I needed the money.'

It all made sense, Cathy. The fiddle, the whip, they were guilt presents. He knew he'd done wrong. To carry me and those gifts, for three days over barren moorland and treacherous coach lanes, no one in their right mind would do that, unless they had to, to reconcile their conscience. My father, who I'd only ever known as a benign figure, a protector, a saviour, was cast in a new light. I saw the full picture. I saw the reason for his kindness, Cathy, and it was his conscience. It was his guilt. He'd kept the secret from Mrs Earnshaw, I had no doubt of that, and from all of us, all those years, carrying it inside his heart like a black lead weight.

'I want you to know, he wasn't a cruel man, just a weak one. Plucky, certainly, but fond with it. My reasons for black-mailing him were not personal. I did not set out to hurt him. I just saw an open purse. I quite liked the fellow. He did me no injury.'

My father. He was talking about my father. I could hardly comprehend.

'What about my mother?'

He twiddled with his sideburns.

'She died a few years after you were born.'

'How?'

'Took her own life. As many do. She was buried in an unmarked grave.'

Dead. She was dead. The chance of being united with her in this world, snatched from my grasp.

'How did she kill herself?'

'She fell into a complete state of stupefaction. Took to her master's loft. Stretched out on the bare boards and refused all sustenance. It was a tragedy. To see such a fine negress wither away like that. I'll never forget her face, all hollowed out. We tried to revive her but it was no use. Eventually she starved to death above Bold's parlour.'

I couldn't take it in. I breathed deeply and clung onto the arms of the chair.

'What was she called?'

'Lilith. They called her Lilly for short.'

'I meant her African name.'

'I've no idea. I doubt you'll ever find out. There were no records, other than what she raised at the marketplace.'

'What part of Africa was she from?'

'I bought her from a bazaar in Banjul.'

'You bought her?'

'Yes, along with others. Mainly male negroes. A few children too.'

'Where's Banjul?'

'Gambia. Where the Gambia river meets the ocean. No papers came with her. No one spoke her language. We called her Negro Number Twenty-nine. She was a slave in Africa. Born a slave, no doubt. Buying her and shipping her to Barbados was a kindness.'

'How do you make that out?'

'There's a lot of talk these days about abolishing the trade. Lot of stuff and nonsense. If you were to abolish the trade now what would happen? I'll tell you what would happen: you would be abandoning the negroes to a wretched situation.'

He was becoming more confident now. He was warming to his theme.

'Niggers are natural thieves. And cannibals. Slavery stops thievery, slavery stops cannibalism. Slavery on the plantations brings happiness to the slaves. Niggers are an inferior race, incapable of living as free men, or free women. People talk about them being packed as close as books upon a shelf, or like herrings in a barrel, but in reality, the voyage from Africa to the West Indies is one of the happiest periods of a negro's life. You mark my words.'

He smiled his crooked smile and took a puff of his pipe. It had gone out. He took out the tobacco tin and prised it open. I thought about the half-built galleon in the dock the day we arrived. The tiny compartments, not even a foot in height. Hundreds of them. They were not being built for indigo or sugar, but for human cargo.

He emptied the bowl of the pipe with the old tobacco, scraped the bowl, and filled it with the new stuff. He tamped it down with his thumb. I pictured him with my mother. His bony fingers on her skin. His insect arms around her.

I leapt up and over to where he was sitting and held the knife at his throat. He dropped his pipe.

'Wha . . . ?!' he spluttered.

'Did you ever touch her?'

'Many men enjoyed your mother. On many occasions. She was a comely wench.'

I pressed the blade to his flesh.

'Did you? Tell me the truth.'

'I . . . there were so many back then. It's hard to remember. One nigger is much like the next. I may have entertained myself. But no more than the next man. I assure you of that. I was never greedy. Rest assured, your mother died young, but she didn't die in vain. She brought great pleasure to many a lusty gentleman.'

Hardwar laughed and tried to supress it but he couldn't

help himself. For two years I'd watched Mrs Earnshaw dote on you, Cathy, and dote on Hindley. I'd wanted to know why my mother had abandoned me. There had to be a reason but how could she do it? And I'd been jealous of you both. Now I saw the reason and I tried to shove the image out of my head. I could feel the heat rise again and the spiralling upwards. The room blurred in front of me. I gasped for breath. Motes of dust that had been floating in the light froze. I wasn't aware a clock had been ticking but I was now aware that the ticking had stopped. I could feel a vein pulse in my neck as though it was about to burst. I clutched the knife and thrust the blade into Hardwar's mouth and out of his cheek.

He fell to the floor. I jumped on top of him and pulled the knife out of his mouth. I used it to skewer an eyeball. I plucked the jelly from the end of the blade and tore off his breeches. He was too shocked to scream.

I grabbed his genitals. His gonads were as warm and soft as a chicken's gizzard.

He cried out, spluttering on the blood that was streaming from his mouth and eye socket.

'Please, please, don't! I've money. Plenty. Take it all. You . . . you don't need to do this.'

'Where does Jonas Bold live?'

'I . . . I don't know.'

I held the knife under his ball sack.

'I'll give you one more chance. If you don't tell me the address of Jonas Bold, I'll cut out your pisser and shove it down your gullet.'

'A village.'

'Where?'

'North-east.'

'How far?'

'About seven or eight miles.'

'What's the village called?'

'Kirby. An estate just outside the village, near a wood. It's a walled garden.'

'Does it have a name?'

'Bold Hall. You'll see the name on the iron gate at the front. He preaches at the chapel on a Sunday.'

A man of the cloth.

'And that's where my mother died?'

'Yes, above Bold's parlour.'

With one deft slice I cut off his penis and ball sack and he screamed out in agony. Blood gushed from the gaping hole. I stuffed the bleeding genitals down his throat so that his screaming desisted.

I wiped the blood from my hands on his waistcoat and untied the silk scarf from around his neck. I fastened it tight over his bleeding mouth. I stabbed him in his thigh, in his shoulder, in his gut. Blood oozed from the wounds and dripped onto the floor. I cut out his remaining eyelid so that he could get a better view with his one eye. He peered through a curtain of blood that siled either side.

Once I'd got started, I couldn't stop, Cathy. I cut his ears off, his nose. Blood ran in rivulets down his face and neck. Blood soaked into the yellow silk scarf and into his white collar. Blood trickled onto his gold waistcoat. I slit open his stomach and pulled out the entrails. Blood bubbled and glugged from the slit. His one eye watched me all the time, wide open. I stood over him, panting with the effort of the work, getting my breath back. His insides were a steaming heap of stinking offal. Blood gushed from the wounds. Blood seeped into the cracks of the floorboards. Blood ran in rivers along the wooden grains. I felt cleansed by the act of butchery, as though I was washing something deep inside my soul.

I was in a state of reverie. All I could see was red and black.

I snapped back into the room. Had anyone heard his scream? I had to act quickly.

My heart was pummelling against the cage of my ribs. I furtled through his drawers and found guineas and gold sovereigns. I stuffed them into my pockets, cleaning my knife on his coat. I found a spare shirt in a wooden trunk, ripped my bloodstained garment off and wiped the blood from my face and hands with it. I stuffed it behind the trunk. I buttoned up Hardwar's shirt, then I walked out of his office, leaving him to bleed to death.

When I got back to the Gallows, Emily had bathed and was sitting on the bed, combing her hair. She looked at me in shock and said, 'What happened to you?'

'We need to go.'

'What's that in your hair?'

She walked over to where I was standing.

'Is it blood?'

'We need to go.'

'And your fingernails. What's that under them?'

'We need to go now.'

'Go where?'

233

'Away from here.'

'What've you done now, William Lee?'

'Never mind. Get your stuff.'

I put together the few possessions I had and stuffed them into the bag. I looked around the room. I tried to think straight. We'd have to find somewhere safe to sleep. That was the first priority. An inn or a tavern was no good. News would soon spread. We'd be the talk of the town in no time. We had money now, plenty of it, but it wouldn't be safe to be seen spending it. We were easy to recognise, a dark-skinned man with a white-blonde girl. We would have to find somewhere to hide out until I thought of the next move. We'd need blankets. I stripped the bed, folded some up and stuffed them into the bag. I looked out of the window. It was dark but not late enough for people to be in their beds. We needed empty streets.

'Change of plan. We wait here. We eat. When folk are asleep, we go.'

'Go where? What have you done?'

'I had a little business with Mr Hardwar.'

'And?'

I told her what Hardwar had said about my mother. I told her about Jonas Bold. That he was the man responsible for my mother's death.

'So what did you do?'

'Mr Hardwar is dead now, I suspect.'

'You killed him?'

'I left him to bleed to death. It won't take long. There wasn't much blood left after I'd done my business with him.'

'Cunt deserved all he got,' Emily said, packing the bag with

234

her things. 'I'll go downstairs and get the maid to make you up a hot bath and order some supper for our room.'

While she did this I stripped. I took off my breeches and washed them in the bowl. Using the soap to scrub off the gouts of blood. I watched the water turn pink, then red. I made sure my boots were clean also.

'So what are we going to do now?'

I went to the window and looked out over the town. All was black. The rooks were ready roosted. It was almost time. I was shaking but I felt nothing.

Emily began to pace the room.

'All right, here's what we do. We know where this Jonas lives now, thanks to Hardwar. Good of him, that. But it's too soon to make a move. We need to think it through. We need to hide out somewhere until we've got it straightened out. I don't know where. Away from the town. Away from people. We need to think about how we're going to hook Jonas. It's going to have to be good. We need to find out more about him. The streets will be quiet now. We'll head out towards this Kirby place Hardwar talked about. We'll find somewhere along the way. We'll need these as well as the others you packed.'

She crawled under the bed, pulling out two extra blankets. She rolled them up.

'It's warm this time of year, we can sleep rough. I've slept under the stars with my father loads of times. We can forage and hunt. There's plenty of food if you know what you're looking for. Are you listening to me? William?'

'Yes, I'm listening.'

She sat on the end of the bed.

'Well, you've got what you wanted, William Lee. You've found out who you are. I expect you're still taking it all in. You poor thing. My dad used to always say, "Be careful what you wish for, Emily, because you might just get it." It can be a terrible thing, the truth. Nobody really wants it. Last of all, those who seek it.'

Penny Buns and Jew's Ears

We watched the gloaming spread its shade until the sky was dark and sparkling. We left the Gallows and headed out of town towards the north-east. It was a clear evening and the sky was the colour of spilt ink. Emily led the way along a packhorse trail.

'That's the North Star, right?' she said, pointing to the heavens.

I nodded.

We were carrying the blankets and a bag. I followed in Emily's footsteps, still taking it all in. I pictured my mother. Alone. Confused. Desperate. Not speaking the language of her persecutors. Being passed from one man to the next. Starving herself to death. I wondered how Hardwar had been sure that I was the seed of Mr Earnshaw, when my mother must have been meat for so many. Perhaps Jonas Bold would know. I was barely aware of our surroundings as we traipsed across meadow, mire and moor.

'We need to get far enough away,' Emily said, 'so that they

won't find us when they come looking. And they will come, you can be sure of that.'

I thought about the trail of people that were after us: Hardwar's associates, the man we tricked in the graveyard, Dick and his companion. We were building up an army against us.

'We need to be ready for them. Word will get out soon enough. They've probably already started the search.'

We climbed up and into a dense forest. We clambered in the mirk, with just a sliver of moon and a few silver stars to guide us over bracken and bramble. We stumbled at various points, but the earth was soft and we came to no harm. Eventually we arrived at a clearing that was deep enough into the forest to offer us sufficient protection. We lay down where the ground was yielding and Emily wrapped the blankets about us.

'This will do for tonight,' she said. 'In the morning we'll scout round for somewhere better.'

Emily wanted me to tell her the details of what I'd heard. I told her the gist of it but skipped over the rest. I felt nothing. My violent frenzy had left me hollow.

'I saw my dad kill this bloke once. He kept killing him but he wouldn't die. My dad had his hands round the man's throat, and he was squeezing the life out of him. The man had a neck like a tree trunk. No matter how hard my dad tried he couldn't squeeze the life out. My dad was so close to the man. They were staring into each other's eyes. It was intense.'

Had my mother tried to keep me with her? Had she pro-tected me? Hidden me away? Had the men wrenched me from her arms? Did she plead for mercy? Had she cried herself to sleep? I closed my eyes and tried to picture her. Alone. Confused. Desperate. I kept going over it in my mind. She would have fought the men. She would have fought with all her strength. They would have beaten her. Kicked her, whipped her. Tortured her. Used her. Then I tried to rid my mind of the images that came rushing in.

~

In the morning we searched the forest. We found a clearing deep in the trees and set about making a shelter. I found a fairly straight, young tree and chopped off the branches. Then I used the axe and hacked away at the base of the trunk until I was able to snap it. I found two trees that were close together with branches at a similar height and suspended the felled trunk horizontally across the trees so that the branches cradled it. While I was doing this Emily went off to collect firewood.

Then I cut down lots of leafy branches and draped them over the felled trunk on both sides until there was an A-framed shelter big enough for the two of us to sleep side by side. I collected some more lengths, which I wove in horizontally so that there was a strong cover on both sides. It took several hours and by the time I'd finished Emily had collected a big pile of firewood. The weather was still clement, but all the same, it was good to have a roof over our heads and a means to stay warm.

'We've got nothing to make snares out of,' Emily said. 'We could dig a hole along a rabbit track and cover it with bracken. If it's deep enough the rabbit won't be able to get out. There's only really two ways into the clearing. The bushes are too thick roundabouts. Why don't we block one

239

of the entrances off, then dig a pit along the path of the other entrance and conceal it? A giant rabbit trap, only for people, so that if someone does sneak up on us, they'll fall into it. We've no spade, but we can use our hands and your axe. It's better than nothing. William, are you listening? I know what you're thinking about, you know. But it won't do any good. Do you think your mother would want you to go to pieces? No, that way they win. You owe it to your mum to see this through, so come on, snap out of it. We'll need to eat something first. And I don't much fancy munching on bracken. Let's have a look around.'

Emily had lied to me. But I wasn't angry with her. She'd lied to save her own skin. As anyone would do in her situation. Besides, she'd been right about one thing – my mother was dead and there was nothing I could do to bring her back. The only thing was to get the man responsible. I'd dispatched Mr Hardwar. Now I had to dispatch Mr Bold.

We spent the morning getting to know the lay of the land. The forest was dense, dark and impenetrable in places. Further on there was a steep clough, with a beck at its base. A felled birch made a bridge over the wider part. We found sorrel and berries. We dug a rabbit trap and a bigger pit for anyone trying to sneak up on us. We blocked the way of the other entrance with layers of thorny branches. We built a fire and found a piece of flint. I used the knife to spark it off. It wouldn't light at first and I had to peel the bark off the silver birch trees for tinder. Eventually a spark took. We sat around the flames and ate the small amount of foraged food.

'This Jonas Bold, preaches in Kirby?'

'That's what Hardwar said.'

'Well, let's take him at his word. He's hardly likely to lie with a knife under his balls. So this Jonas is a religious man. We can use that. And elderly, I'd imagine,' Emily said.

'He set up a hospital to help the poor.'

'Good, that's another weakness. I reckon what we do is wait until Sunday. Go to the chapel there and watch him at work. We need to get as much on him as we can. I'm sorry about what happened, William. I really am. This is the only way we can make it good.'

Part of me wanted to just find him and kill him. But I knew that Emily was right. We had to take our time. We had to do this properly. I needed to be sure Mr Earnshaw was my father and Bold was probably the only man on earth who could confirm this.

We dug some more rabbit traps and drank water from the beck. We played cards by the fire. Later we checked on the traps but they were empty. We searched some more and found a warren.

'We could dig them out,' Emily said.

'They'll just run off.'

'Well, let's dig some more traps, closer to the warren.'

The earth was soft near the warren holes and came away in damp clumps in our hands. We dug three more traps and covered them with bracken. We went back to the fire and the cards. We added wood so that the fire stayed at a constant size. Some of the wood was rotten and burned through quickly. Some of it was damp and hissed and whistled as it heated up. Other timbers made a cracking sound as the flames ripped them apart. We checked on the traps every few hours. Nothing. That night we went to bed hungry.

The next day we had no better luck. One of the traps had been disturbed but the hole mustn't have been deep enough because there was no rabbit inside and claw marks where it had climbed out.

'We need to dig them deeper,' Emily said.

We modified three or four of the best-placed traps and waited. But when we checked there was still nothing. We saw two roe deer: a doe and a buck. But we didn't have a hope in hell of catching them. They were too quick. They flashed their white rumps as they leapt into the dark. We collected more leaves and berries. But we went to bed hungry again that night. In the morning we checked the traps once more.

'This is ridiculous,' Emily said. 'We can't live like this.'

We were half-starved by now. Crippled with hunger pangs.

'I'll go back,' I said.

'What do you mean?'

'To Liverpool. I'll get us some food. I'll go at night so I won't be seen.'

'I don't like the sound of that,' Emily said.

'It'll be all right.'

'I'll come with you,' she said.

'No. No way. That's asking for trouble. Look, we can't go on like this. We'll be dead by the end of the week.'

Reluctantly Emily agreed. So that was the plan. I would go back to Liverpool town in the dead of night. I built the fire up and made sure there was plenty of good dry wood. I left Emily guarding it with instructions to keep it going for when I got back. I walked through the dense forest, over moor and meadow, back into the town carrying the bag. I proceeded very cautiously, making sure to stick close to the edges, ensuring no one could see me. Not that there was anyone around at first. My dark skin was, for once, an advantage. I came across a tavern on the north side of town. The dimpled windows were steamed up and the orange glow of candles flickered along the glass. I went around the back and peered into the kitchen window. The cook was clearing up for the night and putting away some utensils. I watched her cleaning plates and cutlery, washing them, then drying them before putting the plates away in a cupboard and the cutlery in a drawer. She wiped the damp from her hands on the sides of her apron.

When she had finished, she blew out the tallow candles and extinguished the lanterns and then left the room. I waited for a minute or so, then tried the back door. It was open. I sneaked in and crept across the room. It was hard to see what I was doing, with just a little moonlight to guide me, but eventually I fumbled over some matches and a striker and lit a lantern. I had my bag with me. I found a bottle of brandy, some bread, some cheese and some cuts of meat. I found some apples and some tea. I also found a pan. I put all these things into my bag, along with some knives, spoons and forks, two bowls, two plates and two earthenware tankards. I found a reel of brass wire and a pat of butter. My bag was full. I blew out the lantern and took that as well. Finally, I pocketed the matches and the striker, and then sneaked back out again.

I wandered back along a different street. As I came to the end and was about to turn up the lane, my eye was caught by a notice nailed to a fence. I stopped to examine it. Along the top of the notice it said: 'WANTED'. Underneath there were two drawings. One of a dark-skinned man and the other of a pale-skinned girl. Beneath this it read: 'Hath robbed and murdered. 50 GUINEAS REWARD. Come forward with any information leading to arrest.'

I felt an ice chill travel up my spine.

Several hours later I returned to our camp. It was raining now and I expected to find Emily lying down in the shelter fast asleep, but she was huddled by the fire in the mouth of the shelter, prodding it with a stick.

'You were ages,' she said. 'How did you get on?'

I emptied the bag and shared out our rations across the two plates, then poured a measure of brandy into each of the earthen tankards. Emily devoured first the meat, then the cheese, then the apple slices and finally the bread and butter. She slurped down the brandy in two or three gulps.

'You did well, William Lee,' she said, wiping her mouth with the back of her hand. 'You did really well. And you're sure no one spotted you?'

'There was a notice nailed to a fence,' I said.

'What sort of notice?'

I told her about what I had discovered.

'That didn't take them long.'

We sat and watched the flames die down to glowing embers. After a while, Emily said, 'So what do we do?'

'I've been thinking,' I said. 'The best thing is to hide out here for a few days. No more night raids. It's a risk we don't need to take.'

Emily nodded. 'We've got a pan now and some wire to make snares. There's plenty for us to eat round here. The snares will make it easier to catch a rabbit.'

'There's bear leek, dandelion and sorrel leaves, berries, seeds, nuts, plenty of good mushroom picking. This wood is a larder. And we've got it to ourselves.'

'Have you ever skinned a rabbit?' she said. 'It was something my dad enjoyed doing, so I never got a chance.'

'It's not difficult,' I said. 'I'll teach you.'

The next day we went back to the warren and placed some snares in strategic places, using sharpened sticks to stake them around the holes. We collected mushrooms and bear leek. I showed Emily which mushrooms were edible and which were poisonous. After a few hours we had a pan full of penny buns, blue-gilled blewits, horse mushrooms, blushers, yellow caps and Jew's ears.

'Why are they called Jew's ears?' Emily said.

'It's short for Judas's ear. After he betrayed Jesus he hanged himself from an elder tree. They cut his ears off and stuck them to the tree as a warning to other traitors.'

'You know your scripture, don't you?'

'So would you if you were brought up in the same house as Joseph.'

We filled the pan with a sufficient amount of water from the beck. We went back to where we'd placed the snares. We checked them one after the other, but no luck.

'We've just got to be patient,' I said.

'Yeah, that or starve,' Emily said.

We went to all of the traps throughout the day at regular intervals until at last we struck lucky. A rabbit was caught by its back leg and it was jerking and kicking. I took hold of it and wrung its neck.

'Watch how I do it,' I said.

I started at the back end, pushing the bone of one of its back legs through the fur. I did the same with the other back leg and pulled the fur free of the bones. I yanked the fur coat entirely free of the body, cutting the last of it off with my knife. Then I held the rabbit by the back legs and sliced down from nave to chop. I pulled out its guts and slopped them onto the floor. I thought about Hardwar's guts. I thought about Hardwar's blood. I thought about Hardwar's one eye staring at me. Still I felt nothing. We took the dead flesh back to camp.

We cut the meat into chunks and chucked them in the pot with the mushrooms and bear leek. I placed the pan in the middle of the fire and we watched as the water came to the boil. Emily added a splash of brandy to the pot. She sat over it, using one of the spoons to stir as the mixture thickened. When the stew was ready, I added a bit of salt and poured it into two bowls. It was actually rather good. The meat was succulent.

'Do you think we can live like this?' she said.

'Well, for now. I don't see why not.'

'Let's think about what we know about this Jonas,' Emily said. 'We know that he's made a lot of money from slaves and probably from other investments. We know that he's done a lot for the poor. We know that he's found God. In other words, he's a bit of a cunt.'

'We don't know anything about him really,' I said.

'So on Sunday we walk to Kirby. We find the chapel. We find Jonas Bold. What we do with him when we find him—'

'If we find him.'

'What we do is nothing. We bide our time. We don't act

in haste. I know your feelings are strong, William, but you've got to temper them.'

She looked to me for reassurance. I nodded.

'Good,' Emily said, shovelling in some more of the stew. 'These are a bit weird,' she said, picking out a Jew's ear. 'I keep thinking I'm eating human meat. My dad told me about a famine. Happened about two hundred years ago. He told me that's why they brought the Poor Laws in. They used to hang you for begging in those days. The first time you got caught you got bored through the ear. But the second time was neck time. Anyway, during this famine, things got so desperate that they used to play a game of straws. You'd each pull a straw and if you pulled the shortest one you were that day's dinner. They ate unwanted babies. So, you know, thinking about it, these are not so bad.'

She took the Jew's ear between her teeth and bit it in two.

After she had emptied her bowl she scraped what was left from the pan, scoffing every last remnant. I poured us a nip of brandy each and handed her a tankard. I raised mine aloft and made a toast.

'Well,' I said, 'here's to whatever comes next.'

'Here's to that,' she said. 'As long as it doesn't involve eating babies.'

I saw the naked flesh of an infant. And blood. I saw my mother clutching me to her chest. I was no bigger than a kittlin. The men were all around, trying to grab me from her arms. They say a mother will fight to the death to save her young. But they were stronger than her, and there was an army of them.

Humility, Cleanliness and Pure Thinking

At first, sleeping beneath the trees was discomforting. No stars and no moonlight penetrated the forest's canopy and it had a blackness that was complete and absolute. The forest in daylight was a place of intrigue – the green light filtering through the leaves had a warmth and a beauty – but by night it took on a different shape. It thickened around us. Bats would drop from the boughs, their tattered wings like ashes. The darkness took on a depth and a weight, and it started to press down on us and creep over us. We would hear unfamiliar noises and imagined men coming to get us. We would see their eyes in the distance, cold and penetrating. But they would turn out to be the eyes of owls or the eyes of badgers. We would hear the call of the nightjar and we couldn't be certain if it was in our heads or out there somewhere. It sounded like someone tiptoeing towards us. It sounded like someone tapping at a window. It sounded like someone scratching on a skull. We would go to sleep and dream. We would wake up in the black, and it felt like we were at the bottom of the ocean. We would hear gnats whine. Sometimes a fox sounds like a child screaming. And you don't know where you are. Who you are. And you don't know if you are awake or asleep. The hand that grabs you by the throat. The rancid breath on your neck. And you have to pinch your skin to know what's real. We would wake in the morning and see a silver trail over our bodies where snails and slugs had crawled. Spiders would weave threads through our hair. Ants would crawl up our legs. Earwigs would seek refuge in warm orifices. Some nights I would wake to the sound of Emily crying out in her sleep and I'd hold her and rock her until she fell back to sleep again.

After a few days and nights we began to get used to the darkness. If not entirely ever settled there. I'd slept under the stars before but there was just something about this wood. It was holding something back. Some terrible secret. Something buried. Something hidden. I was thinking about my mother, and the terrible secret the world had kept from me. Perhaps all dark places had their secrets. Emily continued to have nightmares and I continued to provide what insufficient solace I could.

～

On the next Sunday morning, just before dawn, when the light was an amber glow through the gaps in the trees, and the magpies made their mechanical rattle, we set off in a north-easterly direction. The trees thinned out and the bracken fell away and our view opened onto a moor. The moor dropped down onto farmland. We trekked across fields until we saw the spire of a chapel in the distance.

We came to a dirt track, which led to a stone bridge over a beck and a coaching road that took us past a tanning yard into the heart of the village. There was a sign announcing that we were in Kirby. It wasn't a very expansive place. A butcher's, a grocer's, a blacksmith's, plenty of cottages. Horses and sheep grazed on the green. There was a watering trough and a pillory. The pillory was a hinged wooden frame erected on a post. The post was on a stone platform and there was an old man with his head and hands poking out of the device. But it was too early for people so there was no crowd gathered to taunt him. His hair and face were covered in dried remnants of whatever rotten food he'd been pelted with the day before. We walked close by but he didn't look up. I thought for a moment he might be dead but as we got nearer to him I could hear his low moaning. He smelled of the toilet.

We made our way to the chapel. It was a small stone building with large stained-glass windows and a rounded tower. It was still too soon for Sunday service so we sat and waited in the burial ground among the resting dead. Rooks were waking up, mice were bedding down, rabbits scratched for roots. At last the villagers, dressed in their Sunday best, started to congregate outside the gates. There were children playing and much chatter among the adults. A man in a smock and cloth cap, who I assumed was the sexton, opened first the gate, then the door of the chapel, and the flock entered.

The air was cool and musty inside, and people spoke in hushed tones. The sun poured through a stained-glass window, projecting red, yellow, blue and green light into the room. In one pane of the window was a picture of Adam and Eve being tempted with an apple, next to this a picture of Moses holding a stone tablet and a staff. Further on was Jesus on the cross with blood pouring from his wounds. On the other side of the room was another brightly coloured pane, this time of a woman in a blue shroud, holding up the naked baby Jesus for all to see. She had a blue and yellow halo around her head. I thought about my own mother and her plight. I wondered if she'd ever held me up to the world so hopefully. In my mind's eye I saw men wrench the baby from her arms. I saw my mother fight with them. I saw them beat her into the ground. Tearing at her clothes. Holding her down.

We found an empty pew at the back. Motes of dust seemed to float up to the source of light. Eventually a portly man in a powdered wig, matching the description of Jonas Bold that Jack Lancaster had provided, mounted the pulpit. He was an elderly man, probably in his seventies. His gait was crooked and his movements slow and stiff. He was dressed in simple attire. The audience went quiet. Jonas turned the pages of a large bible that was open on a wooden lectern and addressed the crowd. He began his sermon.

'Good morning to you all,' he said.

The crowd answered him.

'Let us cleanse ourselves from all filthiness of the flesh and spirit, perfecting holiness in the fear of God. Receive us, Lord. Pacify us, oh God! So that we have wronged no man, we have corrupted no man, we have defrauded no man. I speak all of this to you not to condemn you but to uplift you. To witness your clean hearts to our Lord. Great therefore is my boldness of speech towards you, as our gracious Father glories in your sinless state. I am filled with comfort. I am exceedingly joyful in all our tribulation.'

I'd heard the bombast of base fustian many times before from both Joseph and the preacher in Keighley. I'd heard that the preacher in Keighley frequented the brothel there. It seemed to me that the more a man pleaded his innocence and virtue, the bigger a cunt he was. Emily gave me a look and rolled her eyes.

'I want to talk to you today about godliness and wickedness. As you know, I am a wealthy man. I have spent many years accumulating my wealth. I own an iron foundry, a sugar refinery, two distilleries. I own several large ocean vessels as well as a plantation abroad. But these riches do not bring me closer to God. For in truth you cannot serve both the Lord and Mammon also. I mean to do some good with my money. To this end, as many of you good people know already, I have set up a dispensary in Liverpool town to give free medical treatment and medicine to the poor. It has been there nearly two years now and many a sick man and woman has passed through its gates, healed by the physicians within. The physicians carry out God's work, for did not Jesus himself make the blind man see? And did not Jesus himself cure the leper and the lame?'

There were cheers from the congregation. Mr Bold held up his hands. The congregation became quiet again.

'This is not what I want to talk to you about today. What I want to talk to you about today are the Christian virtues that I hold closest to my heart: humility, cleanliness and pure thinking. Know that you are here to serve God. Know that filthiness of the flesh and spirit offendeth the Lord. Know that to be pure of thought is to be closest to God. For what is wealth and power without godliness? By all means go out and seek your fortune, become fabulously wealthy as I have become, but never forget, if you do not have God in your heart, your wealth hath no value in the eyes of the Lord.'

On and on he preached until his words blurred in my ears and his vision faded from my mind. This was my mother's killer. And worse. This dumpy frail old man with a daft wig on. Where was God's great vengeance and furious anger? Here we were in His house, with this poisonous dwarf, the destroyer of my mother, standing under His roof. My God had abandoned me.

I looked up at the crucified Christ, and imagined Jonas Bold nailed to that cross instead, wearing a crown of thorns instead of a periwig. With blood dripping down his fat face and pouring from the wounds in his hands and feet.

The congregation stood and sang a hymn. We waited for Mr Bold outside the chapel as the congregation thinned out. Some stayed and chatted, others hurried on their way. We saw Mr Bold leave the chapel by the back door and make his way to the burial ground. He walked with a cane in one hand. His gait was unsteady. We followed some distance behind, making sure we weren't spotted. He approached a grave. He stood over it and made the sign of the cross on his breast. He spoke to the grave but we were too far away to hear the words. After he had gone we went to the grave where he had stood. It said: 'Here lyeth Annabel Bold.' From the date on the tombstone, I was able to work out that she was only forty when she died and had only gone recently to the grave. Just three months under the earth. The grave was not ostentatious, as others were around it, but rather plain. This surprised me from one so wealthy, but it was clear that Jonas had loved her dearly and that he was still in the midst of his grief. We stood over the grave in silence.

'What are you thinking?' Emily said.

'The same thing as you,' I said.

When we got back to the forest we checked the snares and gathered some greens. We built up the fire for the pot. Emily was unusually quiet.

'I've been doing a bit of thinking,' she said after a time. 'I've changed my mind.'

'About what?' I said.

'We only get one chance with Bold. If we meet him at the grave next Sunday and he turns us down, where do we go from there? Have you thought about that? We know from experience that most people don't go for it. Some fear us, others are hostile. What's to say Jonas won't reject us in some way also? Then we're screwed.'

'But he's a religious man. He's lost his love. He is still fresh in grief. He's the perfect target,' I said.

'He is also pious. He will see the trick as devilry. We can't risk it. We know something about the man. We know he has wealth. We know he has been a powerful figure. We know his wife has recently died. He talked about humility and cleanliness and pure thinking. His past rests heavily on his head. He carries guilt on his back.'

'So what then?' I said.

'My dad used to do something he called catting. You ever come across it?'

I shook my head.

'It's where you copy your victim. You dress like them, you talk like them, you act like them, you even think like them. You be them. My dad was really good at it. He was an expert mimic. People like people who are like them.'

'I don't get you.'

'We make you in Jonas's image. We dress you like him, we make you sound like him. We make you be like him in every way we can. You strike up a friendship with him. We take it slowly, over time.'

'What for? I just want to make him pay for what he did to my mother.'

'Then you're missing the point and you're missing a trick. You've talked before about wanting to get an education. Well, you can't do that without a lot of money. This Jonas can give you what you want. If you play it straight.'

She was right again. His head on a pike was not enough. I could have his wealth as well. His wealth was mine in any case. For hadn't he made his money by breaking the will of my mother and others like her?

'But I can't talk like him. There's no way I can do that.'

'Yes, you can. I can teach you. How do you think I learned to do different voices? From my dad. Anyone can learn. It's just practice.'

I agreed to give it a go and that evening, after we had suppered, Emily gave me my first lesson.

'We are going to say some tongue twisters to get you

started,' she said. 'Say with me, "Round the rugged rocks the ragged rascal ran".'

'What for?'

'Just say it.'

I did as I was told. Emily made me repeat the phrase, lengthening the first 'a' in rascal.

'Your "a" is a flat "a". But posh people lengthen it to "aaaa".'

The next phrase was even stranger. Emily kept stopping me and getting me to repeat certain words.

'Slow it down. We've got to get rid of these flat sounds. They're a proper giveaway.'

It was hard going at first and my mouth resisted these foreign imposters, but with practice it became easier. Like new shoe leather around feet, the shape of my mouth began to form around these unaccustomed sounds. All week we practised until Emily said it would do.

'We'll have to do something about your appearance. We can get away with your clothes as they are simple and una-dorned like the clothes of Mr Bold, but you need to be clean-shaven, and your hair needs to be neater.'

'But we haven't got a razor. How do I shave without a razor?'

'All right, scrap that. I can use the knife to cut your hair and beard. As long as it's neat, that's the main thing.'

I sat down and let Emily cut my locks and trim my beard. The knife was sharp but still it took her a long time – standing back and circling around me, making a range of dissatisfied tuts – before she was happy with the result. Clumps of black locks fell all around me.

'I think that will do,' she said, standing back from her

work. 'Go and have a look in the beck and let me know what you think.'

I walked over to where the water was deep and still and examined my reflection. My hair was short and neat, and my beard had been trimmed so that it followed my jawline. The effect was to civilise me to some end.

'What do you think?' Emily said when I returned.

I nodded. 'It will do.'

'Another thing to remember,' she said. 'When you talk to him, let him take the lead. He's got to think that this is his idea. He's got to think he's the one making the moves. You take your cue from him.'

'But I'm still not sure what we're doing?'

'We're getting under his skin.'

'So we can get his wealth?'

'Correct.'

'But how?'

'That's what we're going to find out.'

~

The following Sunday we returned to the village. We both attended the service but agreed to split up afterwards. I waited close to the grave of Annabel Bold, concealed by a holly bush, and bided my time. I watched Jonas approach his wife's grave. He stood there in silence for a while. He muttered some words I couldn't hear. Then I watched him shuffle off and sit on a bench further on. It was then I decided to do as we'd agreed. I walked across to where he was sitting.

'Good day to you, sir.'

He looked up and wished me good day, not really taking that much notice.

'Forgive me for intruding but I've just attended your service and I wanted to say how moved I was by your words.'

'God's words, not mine.'

'I was travelling through and was in need of communion with the holy scripture.'

'A need we all have hour by hour in our daily lives,' he said.

'May I sit beside you while I rest a moment?'

He moved the cloth of his coat so that I could join him on the bench. I copied his posture, crossing my legs and clutching the other arm of the bench, mirroring his position.

'I've travelled many a mile.'

'To attend my sermon?'

'I am a lay preacher, sir, only recently accredited.'

'You have the same right to preach as the next man.'

'I am an itinerant preacher, you see. I travel from town to town to spread the word of the Lord.'

'Bless you, for that is a noble pursuit.'

'In truth, I have little experience so far. I came here today to see you teach the word of God. A holy man of some standing recommended you to me. Your sermon inspired me.'

'It is God's words that inspired you. I am merely his receptacle.'

'I have had much need of God.'

'Aye.'

'I am recently bereaved. And my grief feels like a fortress wall around me.'

'And I too. My dear Annie. I come here often and ask her for forgiveness. She's buried just there,' he said, pointing to her grave. 'God bless her soul.'

'My sister and I have recently lost both our parents. My father was a baker. There was a fire. He hadn't put out the fire in the oven. My parents' bedroom was directly beneath the bakery. My sister and I had a room further away. The Lord works in mysterious ways.'

'So he does. So he does. I'm very sorry for your loss.'

'Thank you, sir. It's been hard, especially for my sister, who is much younger than I. And much in need of divine comfort. Many a morning I have woken, to find her drenched in her own tears.'

'The poor thing. It must be hard for one so young. Well, I must get back home. I have the Lord's work to do. Will I see you again?'

'I am in the area for a time. I have some business hereabouts to attend to. So I expect you will.'

I recalled the shady corner of a churchyard, a flower-strewn shrine and the name inscribed thereon.

'My name is Adam Watkin.'

'Pleased to make your acquaintance. My name is Jonas Bold.'

We shook hands.

'Come next Sunday, Adam. I'd like to see you again.'

'I'd like that.'

Jonas got to his feet and took hold of his silver-tipped cane. I could see now that he was really quite infirm. He had to get up from the seat in various stages. First shuffling to the edge of the bench, then using the arm of the bench to lever himself up.

'Here, let me help you.'

I stood up and offered him my hand.

'Thank you.'

He took hold and I brought him to his feet. I watched him hobble back down the path.

Emily and I purchased a few provisions in the village, mostly edible ones, but I also bought a bar of soap. Perhaps Bold's sermon had rubbed off on me. He had spoken again about cleanliness. In any case, neither of us had bathed for a week now and the stench was starting to offend my nostrils. More importantly, I didn't want to offend the nostrils of Jonas Bold. We loaded up the bag and made our way across country, back to the forest. As we walked back I told Emily about my conversation with Jonas Bold.

'I think that went as well as to be expected,' she said. 'You didn't rush it. Good. It's important for us to gain his trust. We need to let him take the lead. We need him to be curious about us. It's good that you gave yourself the name Adam. Clever thinking. It will plant a seed. It's the subtle things. Somewhere in his head now he will think of you as God's first son.'

In fact, I'd thought of no such thing. The name had just caught my eye, that was all. I wondered again about my mother. About the name she had given me when I had come out of her belly. The name she had given me when she had washed the grease from my body. The name she had given me when she had pressed my lips to her teat. Mr Earnshaw had called me Heathcliff after his lost son. And I now realised why, Cathy. I was his lost son. I was your half-brother.

'We'll go back next Sunday,' Emily said.

'I'll introduce you to him. It will help our cause.'

'Do you think so?'

'Definitely. That we are both orphans. With you being so young.'

'In which case I'll need to have a new name too. When did his wife die?'

'June, according to her epitaph.'

'Very well. June Watkin it is.'

We found a decent-sized plunge pool, where the river gathered, and I stripped off. The pool was in the shadows of a rocky crevice; a waterfall frothed over the precipice and tumbled into the black water. Flies buzzed and martins skimmed the surface. I dived in first. The water's coldness took my breath away and tightened my chest, but as I swam, the heat soon returned.

'Jump in,' I said. 'It's lovely.'

'Fuck that,' Emily said.

She stood and watched me splash about. Then she took off her boots and dipped a toe in.

'It's freezing.'

'Don't be soft.'

She took off her dress, took a deep breath, then lowered herself in. She faffed about for a bit, clinging to an overhanging branch and kicking water into foam.

'Can't you swim?'

'No.'

'I'll teach you.'

I tried to teach her crawl but she couldn't get the rhythm right, so then I tried to teach her breast stroke but she soon tired of the lesson and we settled on a sort of doggy paddle. I remembered the time you taught me to swim, down at

Devil's Beck. You'd laughed at my attempts at first, but I soon overtook you, diving the depths, pulling you under. Letting my hands slide over your naked skin. Feeling the coarse hair between your legs. The animal part of you.

We bathed and I scrubbed our clothes clean. I hung them from the branches of a tree to dry. I looked at Emily's wound. It was almost healed. We checked the snares but none of them gave us a reward. And we ate just greens and what berries were left. We'd foraged most of what there was. The next day we set up some more snares but there was only wire left for another two. We talked about our new identities, Adam and June. Our parents had been poor but of good stock and breeding. Through tireless charitable labour they had raised some money for an orphanage. But not enough. Our father had gone to sleep one night and God had visited him in his dreams and told him what he was destined to do.

We checked the snares over the course of the day, but none yielded. When there were still no rabbits the day after that I turned to Emily and said, 'There's only one thing for it.'

'What's that?' Emily said.

'I'm going to go back to Liverpool tonight and see what I can get.'

'It's not worth the risk,' Emily said. 'We can buy some supplies from the village. It's not much further.'

'We need to keep hold of the money we've got. It will be fine. There's no danger there now, as long as I go on my own, like I did last time.'

'If you're sure.'

In truth, I fancied a change of diet. I also anticipated the excitement of another trip. And so that evening I left Emily guarding the fire and I made the journey again. I found a sizeable domestic dwelling of a wealthy family and broke into their pantry. I filled my bag with cuts of meat, strings of sausages, a cabbage, carrots, potatoes and cake. I found a bottle of wine also. I was making my way back when I came across a tavern with people spilling out. I heard raised voices and when I got closer I could see that two men were questioning some of the drinkers, who were sitting at a bench, supping ale and sucking pipes. Even from this distance, in the near-dark, just a dim light from the lantern close by, I recognised the men. It was Dick Taylor and his yellow-haired companion.

Yellow-head was clutching a creased sheet of paper. It was the drawing of me and Emily, and he was pointing at it. There were men standing about, in conversation with them. I strained to hear what they were saying, but there was a door between me and the men.

I darted into a doorway as quick as a hare. Luckily the men hadn't seen me. How had they tracked us down? Had the wanted notice spread beyond Liverpool town, perhaps as far as Manchester? I crouched there and waited, feeling the vein pulse in my neck, until the men had finished their inquisition with the revellers and were walking off in the opposite direction. When I was certain that the coast was clear, I hurriedly made my way back to camp.

I let Emily feast on our midnight picnic before I broke the bad news.

'I saw them.'

'Who?'

'The farmer's son, Dick Taylor, with his companion.'

'Where?'

'This evening, outside a tavern. They were questioning some of the customers.'

She bit into one of the cakes. I passed her the wine bottle.

'And you're sure it was them?'

'They had the wanted notice with them.'

'How did they know to come to Liverpool?'

'I don't know. Maybe they've put up notices there? Maybe we've made the papers?'

She uncorked the bottle and took a swig before saying, 'What are we going to do?'

'Nothing. They won't find us here.'

'You said that before. You said they wouldn't follow us to Manchester. But they followed us to Manchester. You said they wouldn't follow us to Liverpool but now they've followed us to Liverpool. Now you're saying they won't follow us here. One thing we know about them, they're persistent. They are never going to stop looking until they find us.'

'So what do you suggest?'

'I don't say this lightly, and if there was any other solution to the problem I'd be happy to go along with it. But there's only one way out of this. You need to dispatch them before they dispatch us. You need to go back there and kill them, William Lee. Like my dad used to say, it's kill or be killed.'

She was right, of course, once again. While they were waltzing and gavotting, we could never truly be free. The only solution was to end their lives. Something I should have done that night, when I had the chance.

'It's too late tonight, Emily. They'll be in bed now at their lodgings.'

'Tomorrow night, then.'

'Yes, all right, tomorrow night.'

She passed back the wine. I uncorked it and glugged it down. I would go back. I would do what had to be done. I would grab the adder by its tail and snap it like a stick.

The Man with One Hand

The next night it was raining rope and bucket. We watched it sluice and sile between the trees and heavy drops pearl on the underside of the leaves. We saw slugs climb down from their hiding holes. The moon and stars were concealed behind clouds and I took this to be a good omen. Darkness was my companion and ally. I sharpened both the blade of the knife and the bit of the axe until they could cut through the hairs on the back of my hand without pulling. Then I said goodnight to Emily.

'Don't wait up for me. Get some sleep.'

I kissed her on the forehead. She put her arms around me and wouldn't let go. 'Be careful,' she whispered in my ear. I left her, with a blanket wrapped around her shoulders, sitting by the fire.

By the time I got to town, my hair was dripping wet and my shirt was clinging to my skin. The sky was black and the streets were shadowed between the faint orange glow of the lamps. The rain came in pencils of silver, puddling between the cobbles. I went from street to street and from tavern to tavern, ducking in doorways at the first sign of any passer-by. I saw the wanted notices nailed to fence and door. Someone had been busy. The rain made the ink blur, so that our faces looked as though they were melting.

I approached the first tavern and very cautiously peered through the window. The room was busy with revellers of every description. I quickly scanned the room. I couldn't be sure but it didn't look as though the two men were there. I must have done a dozen inns in this way before I struck lucky. As I peered through the dimpled window of the Black Bull, there they were, standing to the side of the bar. A tall man with blond hair and a dark-haired man with a red skeletal face and one hand.

I found a doorway close by and waited. An hour or so passed as I stood in the shadows, wet and shivering. Eventually the inn door opened and the men left, making their way up Dale Street, their gait loose with ale. I noticed that Dick's gait in particular was lopsided and I wondered if that was down to drink or having a stump instead of a hand. I stayed as close as I could while remaining inconspicuous, until the men came to a coaching house with a stables at the back. They went inside. I waited another hour in my hiding place, watching raindrops plash up puddles and gloss the cobs, before going around the back of the building. I climbed over the wall, then up onto the roof, until I came to a window that I thought was big enough for me to climb through. I took out my knife and wedged it between window and sill, forcing the latch and opening it.

I climbed inside and found that I was at one end of the landing corridor. There were doors to each side. I walked slowly and quietly along the corridor, checking each floorboard, before lowering my weight onto it, until I came to the first of these doors. As gently as I could muster, I lifted the latch and nudged the door open just a fraction. I waited and listened. All I could hear were the heavy breaths of someone deep in sleep. I opened the door enough to place my head inside. I stared into the gloom. I could hardly make anything out. It was almost completely dark. I opened the door wider, so that the faint light from the corridor illuminated the room just enough for me to make out a dark rectangle that was less dark than its surroundings. This was a bed and I approached it cautiously. I tiptoed very slowly across the room, until I got close enough to the sleeper to see the long hair of a woman splayed on the pillow. Her cheek kissed the patterned cotton, a hand tucked neatly under her head. I retreated, closing the door silently behind me.

I did the same in the next room and the next after that. It was only when I got to the bed in the fourth room that I recognised the supine figure within. Like before, I started with the door slightly ajar, then slowly placed my head into the room, widening the gap. Then, and only when I could hear the heavy breaths of sleep, did I make my way to the dark rectangle at the other side of the room. As I got closer I could just make out the straw-like thatch of hair and the long thin neck. For a moment it looked like a mop, not a man.

I stood close by before very slowly closing the gap between me and the bed, but as I did I stepped on a creaking floorboard. I froze. The sleeping figure stirred. He mumbled something but he didn't wake. His lips parted and a trail of silver mucus dribbled down his cheek. I thought about a slug and how it spills itself over every surface. I stood over the man. He was the companion of Dick Taylor. I took out my knife and with my free hand I covered his mouth. He woke immediately and his open eyes bulged with fear as he saw me and the glinting blade. He struggled beneath my grip. Sleep had made him weak, but his fear was strengthening him. I bore down heavy upon him, shifting all my weight. He wriggled beneath me like a jack pike. Nevertheless, I held my grip and fixed his head to the pillow with one hand, while with the other, I slit his throat. He convulsed beneath my grip. Blood spurted from the wound. His whole body juddered up. I pressed myself against his chest. I gripped him harder and held him down as his body spasmed beneath me. Blood gushed like a foss, until at last his struggle ceased and he returned to sleep once more – only this time the sleep of eternity.

I wiped my hands and the blade of the knife on the bed sheets and tiptoed out of the room. The next two rooms were empty, but the seventh room held the object of my wrath, wrapped snug in blankets like a loaf. I made my way to his bed and took out my knife once more. Once again I stood over the sleeping figure, waiting for my moment. He lay on his side, with his handless arm on top of the cover and the other underneath. I looked at the stump. The skin had grown over the severed bone and there was a ridge of ragged flesh where the flaps of skin had been roughly stitched together. It looked like something that had been plucked ready for the pot. The vein on his neck was a pulsating worm. His mouth was closed and he breathed out of his nose. His face in profile was all bone. His cheek and jaw jutting out of his skin and the bony ridges of his forehead seemed almost naked. I watched the muscles in his nostrils expand and contract. I listened to him breathe. In. Out. In. Out. The air was sweet and warm with liquor. Then I gagged him as I had done his companion, but as I held him down, his eyes opened and his one hand appeared from under the covers, holding a pistol. Before I had time to thrust my knife into his flesh, a loud shot rang out. The man had pressed the trigger, but the bullet had missed me. The stench of gunpowder was a hot sting at the back of my nose.

I leapt off the bed and ran out of the room. I sped along the landing and reached the open window at the other end. Before climbing out, I turned to look down the corridor, and running towards me, with a look of malevolence, was one-handed Dick, in his nightshirt, clutching the pistol. I leapt out of the window and onto the wall. I jumped off the wall onto the other side of the stables as a second shot rang out. I felt the bullet part my hair. I ran up the road, splashing through the puddles between the cobbles, not stopping to look back, until I got to the outskirts of town. I leaned against a post, panting like a dog. I could taste the acrid, sour flavour of the gunpowder. My heart was beating painfully hard in my chest. I listened to the night. There was nothing. The evening was silent, hushed with secrets. As I made my way back to the forest, I considered how close I'd come to my end. I'd actually felt the heat of the bullet as it skimmed the hair on my head.

~

'Do you want the good news or the bad news?'

To my surprise, Emily was still up, despite the fact that it was nearly dawn.

'You've ballsed it up, haven't you?' she said.

'The blonde one, his companion – he's dead.'

'So that means Dick isn't dead, right?'

I explained the turn of events.

She shook her head and bit her nails.

'Shit, that's worse than if you hadn't killed either. He'll be after us with even more vigour than before.'

Then she started a coughing fit that lasted over a minute. I thought about my namesake, the real William Lee, and determined to take her to a physician as soon as we were in a position to do so.

'We'll have to stay put here now,' she said, recovering from her fit. 'No more trips into town. From now on Liverpool is out of bounds. It sounds like the whole place is plastered with our faces. Come on, let's get some sleep. You must be exhausted. We can check the snares when we wake up. You sure no one saw you heading back, William?'

'I'm sure.'

~

We spent the next few days close to our shelter. I blocked the other entrance even more thoroughly with thick gorse and hawthorn. I wove the branches together so they wouldn't yield. I dug the mantrap deeper and covered it with fresh fern leaves. We only ventured further afield to gather mushrooms, bathe, collect water or check the snares. One day we went onto the neighbouring moor. Hidden in the low, dense foliage thereabouts, we found the dark blue fruits of the bilberry. It took hours to gather enough for a meal, but the effort was worth it. The berries were succulent.

'We could do with getting hold of a newspaper. See exactly what they are saying about us. Do you think the papers will reach as far as Kirby?'

'It's too small a village. None of the shops sell papers. I think we're safe for now,' I said.

'You hope.'

'We need to move fast on Jonas.'

'Part of me thinks you should go back there and finish the job,' she said. 'I hate loose threads. They usually end up getting snagged on something.'

'I will do it if you think it's best.'

'No, it's too risky. He almost killed you last time. He's got a gun. You've got a knife. Gun beats knife almost every game. The only time a knife beats a gun is when the gun misfires. That's why my dad always carried two pistols. Double trouble, he called it. I remember one time, we held up this chaise. There was a driver with a man and woman in the back. My dad pointed the gun at the open window. He took out a sack and said, "Put everything you've got in there". He made them get out of the chaise and stand by the side. The driver had to stand next to them. My dad dismounted. He went up to the woman and pointed the gun in her face. The woman started to take off her jewellery. She was shaking as she unlatched her necklace and pulled a ring off her finger. She tried another ring but it wouldn't loosen. My dad threatened to chop her finger off, but she spat on it and managed to ease it away. My dad made her pass the sack to the driver, who took out some coins from his pockets. Then it was the man's turn. The man unbuttoned his watch chain from his waistcoat and put the watch and chain in the sack. He threw his purse in too. Then he rummaged in his coat. He held the sack up so we couldn't see what he was doing. When he went to pass the sack back to my dad, the man lunged at him with a dagger. Almost got my dad in the neck, he was that quick. My dad fired his pistol, but it was a misfire. The man smiled and lunged again but my dad already had his second pistol cocked and the bullet exploded in the man's face. He fell to the floor. The woman screamed, so my dad punched her. He took the dagger and stabbed the driver in the face. Then in his heart. Then in his kidneys. The man fell to the floor. He kept stabbing the man even though he was dead. In his back. In his leg. Then he started on the woman. She was lying on the floor, bleeding to death. Blood was pissing from her neck where my dad had drawn the blade. She tried to stop the flow with her hands. Blood spurting through the gaps in her fingers. She was wearing a beautiful blue dress. She was so pretty. Her skin was like milk. Staring at me with pleading eyes. Choking on her own blood. I wanted my dad to finish her off. Put her out of her misery. But he just left her there, gagging on her own blood. I remember the stench. It was shit. The woman had soiled herself.'

Emily looked down at her clenched fist. She seemed confused, as though she had forgotten what she was supposed to be doing. She unfurled her fingers. The berries were crushed and her hand stained with the juice. I wondered whether I should say anything or put my arm, around her. Or something. But I didn't know what to do, so I just stood there staring at her stained hand.

'That man shouldn't have got his dagger out,' I said at last.

Emily nodded. 'Stupid bastard. Stupid fucking bastard. It was the man's fault. His fault that woman had to die. What was my dad supposed to do? What would you do if someone came at you with a dagger? He had no choice.'

I was going to say something else, but I thought better of it. The woman was unarmed but maybe she would have squealed at a later date. I suppose it was too big a risk.

'He had no choice,' I said.

I knelt down and collected more berries.

~

When Sunday came again we headed out for the seven-mile walk to Kirby village. We had a good look, a round to see if there were notices nailed about, but there was nothing. News had not spread this far.

After the service we crouched in the holly bush close to the grave of Jonas's wife. After some time, Jonas appeared and stood over the grave. He was holding a bunch of yellow flowers and he placed them on the ground next to the tomb-stone. I didn't wait any longer. I crept out of my hiding place and went up to him.

'Good afternoon, sir. I hope I didn't startle you.'

He turned to me rather nonchalantly. 'Ah, Adam, isn't it? How nice to see you. Will you sit for a minute?'

We went to the same bench we'd sat on before.

'I was just spending some time with Annie,' he said. 'It was nice, just me and her. I had such a warm feeling just then, as though she were reaching up from the grave, and putting her arms around me. I brought her marigolds. Her favourite. I've prayed for you,' Jonas said. 'You and your sister have both been in my prayers this week. I've asked Annie to look out for you.'

'Thank you,' I said. 'I brought June to see your sermon today. She was deeply moved.'

'Your sister? You did? Where is she?'

'She's waiting for me over yonder,' I said, pointing to where she was standing.

'Bring her out. Don't keep her hidden away. What's wrong with you?'

I got up and returned a moment later with Emily.

'This is my younger sister, June.'

Jonas looked puzzled.

'I know we don't look alike. I was adopted, you see, by the kindness of June's mother and father. They were good Christian folk, very involved with the church. They set up a charity to raise money for an orphanage, and I was the first who was brought into their care. They never got to see the orphanage. They died before sufficient funds were raised.'

'Pleased to meet you, June,' Jonas said. 'Such a beautiful name. But my poor Annie died in June just as her favourite flowers were being born. Your parents sound like people after my own heart.'

'You would have liked them, sir. They served the Lord much as you do.'

'How sad for you to lose such benefactors.'

'I still have my brother.'

'How do you both survive? Did they leave you any money?'

'Sadly not,' I said.

'Not a penny?'

'They gave their own wealth, what little they had, to the trust set up to build the orphanage. As God intended.'

'Well, I must say, you both look a bit undernourished. Are you eating properly?'

'When we can.'

'And when did you last eat?'

Emily and I gave each other a look. By now we had an understanding between us. We both knew how to play the game.

'Let me see . . . When was it?'

'I can't remember if it was Thursday or Wednesday,' she said, twisting her head in contemplation. 'I lose track of the days.'

'By Jove, that's ages ago.'

'We find that our hunger diminishes after a time,' I said.

Jonas Bold's eyes widened in disbelief. He shook his head. He sat ruminating for a minute. We let the silence spill around us. Emily gave me a look but I raised my eyebrows to indicate for us to wait. Half the game is knowing when not to speak.

'Whenever my conscience troubles me, I ask myself one question – what would Annie do? Help me to my feet,' Jonas said, holding out his hand.

'Why certainly, sir.'

I took hold of his hand and supported him as he lifted his great weight. I passed him his walking cane.

'I'd like you both to come to my house for something to eat.'

'We wouldn't dream of putting you out like that, sir,' I said.

'You've far more important things to be doing,' Emily said.

'Nonsense. I insist. I won't be able to sleep tonight if I don't fill both your bellies. Besides, it's what Annie would do.'

'Well, if you won't take no for an answer, sir,' I said.

'That's very kind of you, sir,' Emily said.

'Would you both please accompany me back to my home? I've a coach at the front of the chapel waiting for us.'

'Yes,' I said, 'we would be happy to.'

We followed Jonas to where there was a splendid blue-and-gold carriage, with four white thoroughbreds harnessed. Jonas spoke to the coachman and we all climbed in. The interior was plush, cushioned with blue velvet and lined with gold brocade. The coachman cracked the whip and we set off down the lane, with thick blackthorn hedges on either side. We rode on past dry-stone walls, fields of turnips, fields of sheep, until we turned off the road and onto a less defined track that climbed up towards a wooded area and a walled estate. The coachman dismounted at the golden gates, inscribed with the words 'Bold Hall', and swung them open. He climbed back into position and drove the carriage through a copse, eventually reaching the front of a massive estate house with a grand white-pillared entrance.

'Is this your house, sir?' Emily said.

Jonas nodded.

'It's awful big, sir. I've never seen a house so big.'

The huge doors opened and a servant walked over to the carriage. He unlatched the door and helped Jonas climb down. Jonas passed the man his coat and cane. We followed Jonas into a marbled hallway with many large and magnificent pillars, walled with marble in front of a semicircle around a flight of steps up to the salon door. The gallery ran around these pillars. The salon itself was more of a gallery and one of the finest things I'd ever seen. It was hung with crimson material.

Emily went up to the material and stroked it.

'That's caffoy, from India. The very best,' Jonas said.

He seemed pleased with himself.

'It was at great expense I had the cloth shipped over. But it put such a smile on Annie's face. Her eyes sparkled like opals.'

He led the way into the next room. We were in a drawing room also hung with crimson caffoy, with agate tables beautiful beyond description. The light from the window made the gilding shine. I thought about you, Cathy, and what you would make of this opulence. Then we entered the landscape room, which was a dressing room to the state bedchamber, hung with crimson damask and French tapestry. Another flight of steps brought us down to the kitchens. Jonas asked the servant to prepare afternoon tea in the parlour and then he continued his tour of the house. The library was dark oak-panelled, with red leather-upholstered chairs. The walls were filled with shelves containing great volumes of literature. At one end there was a carved picture. It was a crest with a griffin in the middle, with a medieval knight's helmet above it. To the sides were obelisks with lanterns on top.

'Those are the lamps of King Solomon,' Jonas said. 'I chose the griffin because it is part eagle and part lion. Therefore, it is both far-sighted and strong. A griffin can sense gold. I have been, throughout my life, a consummate money-maker. A griffin mates for life, even if his partner dies, then he remains alone. The griffin knows that one day he will see his partner again in the life eternal.'

He led us into the dining room, which was also wood-panelled and painted duck-egg blue, with gold rails and frames, lavishly carved with curlicues and leaf motifs. He'd made money all right. Off the blood and broken backs of others. It was our time now to take that money from him. It would not be on the premises though. Men like Jonas had their wealth secreted and secured. I was sure of that.

Although the room was filled with thick rugs, ornaments and pictures, a long polished table dominated the space. Behind this was a grand fireplace and above it, a painting that was much larger than any other in the room. It was a portrait of a fair-haired woman, dressed in an ivory-coloured sack-back gown, with a matching lace choker and yellow flowers in her hair. Her skin was so white that it looked as though it had never seen the light of day. Jonas stood beneath her.

'This is my Annie,' he said, looking up at the picture. 'I had this painted just months before she died. You'd never guess by looking at the picture that she was gravely ill at the time. I wanted to capture her radiant beauty and godliness before the illness tainted her. It took hours to capture the image. I hired Henry Walton, one of the finest portrait painters in the land. My Annie sat as still as a statue, with a serene expression on her face, even though she was in constant pain. So selfless and so brave. I placed the flowers in her hair myself. Marigolds. My love's hair was as radiant as the marigold. They were her favourite flower.'

He turned to Emily. 'I was telling your brother, when she died, the next day, marigolds appeared at her window. Until she came into my life I was a sinner. I was a wrongdoer who thought only to line his own pocket. Sweet Annie shone light on my transgressive way of life and I learned the true meaning of God's love.'

'The love of money is the root of all evil,' I said. 'So sayeth the Lord.'

Jonas nodded gravely. 'Timothy, chapter six, verse ten. Some people, eager for money, have wandered from the faith and pierced themselves with many griefs. I was one of these.'

I studied my surroundings. We were in the midst of an opulence that made Thrushcross Grange seem more like Wuthering Heights by comparison. But there were no locked rooms or any sign of a safe. We were led out to a parlour with windows that stretched from floor to ceiling, looking out, first on a terrace and then a lawn. I could see a lake in the distance. I wondered if this was the parlour that Hardwar had referred to, above which my mother had starved to death.

Jonas ushered us into an area where there was a three-seater sofa, a low table and two bottle-green leather chairs. The servant followed us shortly after, and placed a tray on the table. He then commenced arranging the items thereabouts. China teapot, teacups, saucers, milk jug, a silver sugar bowl, a selection of cakes. Emily immediately lunged for the cake stand, grabbed the biggest cake and shoved it into her mouth whole.

'I do apologise for my sister; she forgets her manners. And in truth, she is starving.'

'Not at all,' said Jonas. 'Let her feast some more. A healthy appetite is encouraging in a child.'

He bade the servant return with more voluminous cakes. I pictured myself ramming the cakes down Jonas's throat, and watching him choke to death. But I knew I had to be a scholar of patience. We chatted some more as Jonas served the tea.

'How did you meet your wife?' I said.

'Through a mutual friend. In fact, her father was a business associate. He said that he was looking for a suitable husband for his eldest daughter, but I had no interest at the time. He told me of her radiant beauty and of her godliness. But I still wasn't interested. Work and ambition blinded me. I was only hungry for more wealth and more power. My only desire was the pursuit of profit. Then we met at a social function, and the moment I set eyes on her I knew she was the one. God shone through her. I could see the love of God in her eyes. When God took her from me, I was angry with him. I railed with obdurate vituperation. How could a God of love do this harm to me? But then I realised that everything God does, He does for our own good, even though we cannot see it at the time. God sends us tests, as He did with Job. God sends us lessons, as He did with Zacchaeus. Blessed are the pure of heart, for they shall see God.'

'Yes, both Zacchaeus and the rich young ruler were wealthy men, but one was self-righteous and would not give up his possessions, while the other gave his possessions to the poor,' I said.

'You certainly know your scripture,' he said. 'It's good to talk to another man of the cloth.'

I thought about Joseph again, Cathy, how we had made fun of him, but now he was serving me greatly.

'I was like the rich young ruler, but I wanted to be Zacchaeus. God sent Annie to me to teach me the true meaning of love. He took her from me to teach me to be loyal and patient, to be humble and to possess humility. So that I will be rewarded in heaven when we are finally both united again.'

How these religious zealots bored me, Cathy. Scratch away the brocade and gold leaf, and what we had before us was another Joseph, thinking only of how he might feather his nest in the next life.

More cake arrived. Emily commenced to stuff her face, cream and jam and sugar smearing her cheeks; she washed it down with great gulps of sugary tea. I could get used to this, I thought, as I reached for another cake myself. This was only what I deserved. Hadn't I suffered enough under Hindley's boot? I pictured you with your feet under the Lintons' table, already accustomed to drinking from fine bone-china cups.

'All is good in God's kingdom,' I said. I didn't even really know what I meant by that but it was the sort of nonsense men like Jonas lapped up.

'Have you served the Lord long?' he asked.

'When our parents died, we were both so grief-distraught, June and I, that we didn't know what to do with ourselves. Nothing seemed to matter any more. Nothing made sense any more. I kept thinking about their life's work, unfinished.'

He nodded gravely.

'And what was that work?'

'God's work, sir,' Emily said.

'The orphanage, I take it?'

'Yes, they were raising money for the venture up until the evening of their death.'

Mr Bold reached into his waistcoat pocket and pulled out

a gold chain, on the end of which was a locket. He opened the locket.

'This is a lock of Annie's hair. Her hair was like silk. It shone like a buttercup in the midday meadow. Just like yours, June. Here, look.'

He beckoned Emily over to where he was sitting on the sofa and she sat down beside him. He held up the lock of hair to Emily's head. In fact, it was a good deal darker than Emily's, but I didn't correct his error. He put the lock of hair back in its place and secreted the locket in his waistcoat.

'Can I hold your hand?' she said to Jonas.

He held out his pudgy hand and she gripped it firmly. For a moment I thought she was going to do her trick and I tensed. Now wasn't the time and we'd agreed that we needed a different game to fix Jonas.

'Annie has been watching over you in heaven, as our parents have been watching over us. She sees you. She's watching you now,' Emily said.

I looked at Jonas Bold. He was sitting forward on the edge of his seat, staring at Emily, transfixed.

'I have tried to do as Annie would have me do, all this time since she passed over. I have persevered with many philanthropic endeavours since then. I want her to be proud of me. That's why I set up the medical dispensary. It is only by helping those less fortunate than ourselves that we do good in God's eyes. This is what my love hath taught me. I want now only to devote the rest of my life to doing charitable work. My days of greed and acquisition are over. I no longer serve Mammon, I serve only our Saviour, our Lord Jesus Christ.

Whose love for us was so great that He died to save us from eternal damnation.'

'And Jesus said that it is easier for a camel to pass through the eye of a needle than for a rich man to enter the kingdom of God. But you are a godly man, Jonas,' I said. 'And one day you and Annie will embrace once more. Then you will be united for eternity. You two will never part in heaven.'

I looked at Jonas. There were tears rolling down his cheeks. We sat opposite and watched him weep. We'd been right about him. He was a soft touch.

I stood up and went over to the window. I watched the wind shake the burnished leaves and the sparrows flit from one branch to another in search of insects. I saw a throstle on the lawn, digging for a worm. He dragged one out, as thick as a rope, and gobbled it down. We had our own juicy worm sitting right here, crying his eyes out.

'I'm afraid,' said Jonas, taking out a fogle and dabbing his eyes. 'Terribly afraid.'

'You have nothing to be afraid of,' I said.

'God loves all His children,' Emily said.

'Not this one.'

'That's silly talk,' Emily said.

'She's right,' I said.

'I . . . you . . . I've done things.'

'God forgives our sins, as long as we repent. And you have repented. Remember that God forgave those who gave their wealth away.'

'My whole life now is an act of repenting. And yet, I'm afraid I do not have enough years left to repent sufficiently for the things I have done.'

'God looks down and sees who you are now,' I said.

'You are good people,' he said. 'But you don't know the magnitude of . . . Is God's grace infinite, do you think? Does it know no bounds?'

'Christ is a great saviour,' Emily said.

He dabbed at his eyes again with his fogle. He stuffed it back into his pocket.

'I'm a rather fond old man. Forgive me . . . Do either of you need further refreshment?'

'A cup of tea, please. Five sugars. And some more cake,' Emily said.

Jonas rang a bell and when the servant arrived he gave him the orders. Then he poured Emily another cup and sugared it using a silver spoon. He handed her the cup. She held it like a porridge pot and slurped greedily.

'Do you require anything else?'

She shook her head.

'We three all know the pain of loss.'

'Indeed we do,' I said. 'But we also know that we will be united with our loved ones for all eternity, when the time comes. When God chooses.'

'But what of that other place?' Jonas said, almost whispering. He looked frightened again.

'It's reserved for those who do not repent,' I said. 'Now, we have burdened you too long with our company and it's time we were on our way, isn't it, June?'

Emily nodded.

'Really? You must go so soon?'

'It's been a great pleasure. We are very grateful for your kindness.'

'Please don't go yet. There is more to discuss.'

'I'm afraid we must.'

'But you'll come back?' he said, desperation in his eyes.

I nodded.

'I'll have my driver take you both back into the village.'

'Please, don't trouble your driver, the day is fine and the walk will do us good. If God had wanted us to drive across the country instead of walk He would have fitted us with wheels not legs.'

Jonas laughed. 'In which case, let me give you something before you go.'

He reached into his purse and pulled out three guineas.

'This is too generous, sir.'

'Buy some food for you and your sister. I won't have you starve.'

'God will provide,' Emily said and nodded sagely.

'Please, take it.'

He pushed the guineas towards me.

'We couldn't possibly—'

'I insist. Take them. It will make me happy.'

I took hold of the coins and pocketed them.

'You will come back next Sunday, won't you?'

I nodded. Emily nodded.

'Please, I implore you.'

Vying the Ruff

We strid back over meadow and moor, dean and dale. We approached the edge of the forest. The leaves were already turning from green to gold and from gold to red. When we got back to our camp, I explained to Emily that we now had too much money to carry about our persons. My breeches weighed down like wet bags of sand. We dug a hiding place under the mantrap and buried a bag of coins. When we'd finished we sat back with ferns as our cushion and rested.

'We're rich,' I said.

'Not rich enough,' she said.

'No, you're right. Not rich enough to get the best education.'

'We need to acquire a lot more. Legal training doesn't come cheap.'

'What do I need legal training for?'

'To get what's yours — why else would you need it? I've been thinking of the best way to get to Hindley, and that's where it really hurts him.'

'How do you mean?'

'Wuthering Heights.'

'But how?'

'I've not worked that one out yet. But I'm thinking. And I need more for the shop. I don't want some shithole. I want a proper counter and a big window. I want cloches and silver cutlery like Jonas Bold. We need to think about where you will go to get tutored.'

'We've burned our bridges there,' I said. 'We can't go back to Liverpool or Manchester town.'

'True enough.'

'In any case, I wouldn't know who to ask, or even where to go.'

'All good things to those who wait,' Emily said. 'For now we still have work here.'

'What are you thinking?'

'You heard what he said. The old man is weak. His grief has weakened him further. His conscience is troubling him. Everything is set. He's an easy target. He's made himself fabulously rich by exploiting others. Now he has turned to God. And God hates greed but loves a sinner. All the old man wants now is to be reunited with the love of his life and reconcile his past with the Lord.'

She was thinking along the same devious lines as myself.

'Will we have time though,' I said, 'before word reaches Kirby?'

'We only need one more week,' she said. 'If we vie the ruff properly, we can get at least half what is his. Then you can have his head on a pike.'

~

Life in the forest was about death. Each place was a different grave. The forest floor itself was rich with decaying matter. The branches of trees breaking up and softening. Like bones turning into meal. The leaves that had turned copper and gold were falling slowly through the autumn air, making ghosts of themselves. The mushrooms were pecked and cratered by slugs and maggots. Everything was diminishing. Even the light, filtered through green and gold and copper tones, was an ageing version of itself. The forest smell sweetened and deepened. Time crept by slowly, at the pace of a snail. Summer's heat was fading. We spent less time bathing in the pool and more time sitting by the fire. We played cards and gathered what food there was.

I tried to keep my mind from dwelling on those who were actively pursuing us. Searching every street. Looking down every lane. Asking of our whereabouts in every ale-house. I hoped Emily was right. Kirby was a remote village, that was true, but word had travelled from Yorkshire to Lancashire, from Manchester to Liverpool. I tortured myself with thoughts of our capture, but banished the thoughts by concentrating on our card games. My game was improving and I was becoming a worthy opponent, winning as many games as I had previously lost. The nights were the hardest part.

Emily's nightmares were diminishing. She would still wake screaming from time to time, but I could usually soothe her and she would go back to sleep again. Then, with Emily sleeping beside me, I would spend hours unable to drift off, the night engulfing me. The blackness was all-encompassing. Whether you opened or closed your eyes it made no difference. Black or black. The colour of nothing. The deepest shade of the abyss. Black – the sky's ink, thief of light. The mind abhors a vacuum and in the blackness horrid images filled my head. Of what the men had done. Of what pain my mother had suffered. To end her life in that way was such an act of desperation. I would hear a vixen scream but in my nightmares it was my mother, pleading for them to stop. Pleading for them not to take me. Pleading for them not to hurt her. I would hear an owl cry but in my nightmares it was my mother crying. Lost. Alone. Confused. Desperate. Around and around the images went. I would lie on my back and pray for daylight.

~

Out foraging we came across a meadow of wild flowers that bloom into autumn: red campion, meadowsweet, harebell and marigold.

'I've got an idea,' Emily said.

'Go on.'

'What were Annie's favourite flowers?'

I smiled.

'And what flowers bloomed the day after she died?'

My smile widened.

'We dig these marigolds up, roots and all, and we plant them in front of Jonas's bedroom window, so that when he wakes and draws his curtains, they will be the first thing his eyes encounter.'

I helped her dig them up, careful to retain their delicate root system. Then, under the cover of dusk, we walked with them to Bold Hall, climbed over the wall and crept beneath Mr Bold's bedroom. We carefully planted the flowers. Dozens of them.

'Let's see what he thinks of that,' Emily said.

The following Sunday we found Jonas waiting for us outside the chapel. He was standing to the side of his coach. His big round face was cut in half by his smile when he saw us. We drove back to the estate. Jonas was in an excited condition and chattered away to both Emily and I about how our meeting last Sunday had inspired him. How his feet had barely touched the floor. How he had felt Annie's presence in bed that evening, then again when he was out walking a day or two later, then again during the sermon. How fired up he had been in church, feeling that, through his words, he was receiving God, bringing his congregation directly in touch with divine love.

'Then, a few days ago, the most extraordinary thing happened.'

'What's that?' I said.

'When I went to my window and opened the curtains, there before me, twenty, maybe thirty, maybe more . . . beautiful, large, rich yellow flowers.'

'Really?'

'They were marigolds.'

He paused and waited for us to respond. But we both knew it was better for him to lead.

He smiled. 'Don't you see? They weren't there the day before. It was Annie. She'd put them there. I know it.'

We both nodded.

'I had the most extraordinary sensation this morning,' he said. 'When I was washing my hands. I was standing over the washbowl, the soap in my grip, looking out of the window, watching Annie's flowers sway in the breeze, like they were waving at me. And then I felt her presence in the room. The light from the sun was striking the taps, making them sparkle. It was then that I felt her warmth behind me, and then a sublime calm. I could hear her come closer, then her hand on my shoulder. I didn't want to spoil the moment. I knew she would go as soon as I turned around. So I stood there in my nightshirt, with the dawn sun pouring through the window, feeling the warmth of her hand on my shoulder and her sweet breath on my neck. I barely dared breathe. I knew the spiritual connection was wavering, and then it was gone. It was all over. The bridge between our world and the life everlasting had evaporated.'

Emily rolled her eyes behind the man's back.

'Then I turned around and do you know what I saw?'

'No. What did you see?'

'A single white feather, suspended in a sunbeam, floating down to the ground.'

Emily shook her head.

'Don't you see? It was an angel. Annie's angel. I've been giddy ever since. I feel like a boy again. Rejuvenated by Annie's love. I tell you, it was like when we first met – I've got butterflies in my stomach and I can't stop smiling.'

He laughed a boyish laugh and patted his wig. Emily yawned. I mostly nodded and let him prattle on; it was all favourable to our plan. I looked over to Emily and winked at her.

When we got to the house Jonas led us into the dining room and we saw that the table was replete with sandwiches, cold meats, cheeses, fruits and cakes. We ate several platefuls of grub, glugging it down with plenty of sweet tea. Then we went back to the parlour.

~

We returned three days later on Jonas's insistence. He wanted us to have a proper meal, he said. By now I was becoming ever more anxious. Time was ticking by and the risk of word spreading was increasing by the day. But Emily allayed my fears, reassuring me that it would all be worthwhile in the end. We were seated at the dining table and Bold's servant filled our plates. This time there was roast widgeon with plum sauce. Afterwards we ate poached pears and peaches in syrup.

Jonas wiped his chops with a napkin and turned to me.

'Tell me more of your life as an orphan, Adam? I'm interested to know the details.'

So I told him a tale. It was easy to elaborate, as I had lived the truth of the story. I just had to make up the names and the places. But the feelings were the same. Afterwards, I could see that Jonas was moved by my account. He nodded solemnly and was quiet, staring up at the painting of his beloved.

As we set off back I turned to Emily. 'I'm getting impatient. When do I get to put my hands round his throat?'

'Not long now,' she said. 'You'll see. What was he talking about as we were leaving?'

'Eh?'

'A piece of music. Said it was Annie's favourite.'

I tried to think.

'He was talking about her playing it on the harpsichord. He used to listen to her play.'

'Don't tell me you've had another idea?'

'Come on,' she said, and grabbed my sleeve.

We doubled back. We climbed over the wall and crept to beneath the music room. I took out my knife and forced the latch open. I nudged the window enough for Emily to crawl in.

~

The next time we visited, Jonas was in an ebullient mood once more. As the servant ladled out the soup, he told us of the latest development.

'Annie has been here again,' he said.

'In what way?' I asked.

'When I went through to the main hall yesterday morning I noticed that the music book above the harpsichord was open.'

'Is that so strange, sir?'

'I distinctly remember closing it. But that's not what is strange about this tale. I called one of the servants and I asked him whether he had opened it, perhaps when he was cleaning? He was adamant. The book had been closed. But now it was open. Not only that, it was open on page thirty-seven.'

I shrugged.

'That's the page where the music for "Au Clair de la Lune" is printed. Annie's favourite. She would often sit at that instrument, pleasantly playing its melody.'

'Incredible,' I said.

Emily nodded.

He smiled and took some soup onto his spoon. We ate in silence for a spell. As we snacked on smoked cheese and grapes, Jonas turned to us and said, 'I had a dream last night.'

I nodded.

'Me too,' Emily said. 'I dreamed I was a mole and I couldn't find my mole hat. I mean, moles don't even have hats, do they?'

Jonas was in his own world. He didn't seem to even hear Emily. He was staring up at the portrait.

'In my dream, Annabel came to me and she said that she had something to tell me.'

'What was it?' I asked.

'She said that she had spoken with God.'

I nodded again, this time more gravely.

'She said that God told her that the vast wealth I have accumulated is tainted.'

He put his teacup on the table and stared at the floor. 'It is hard indeed for the rich to enter His kingdom. Many are turned away at the gates and have to suffer the flames of eternal damnation.'

'Is that what God told Annie?' Emily said.

'It's what I know in my heart,' he said. 'My riches are tainted.'

He took out the locket from his waistcoat and furled his fist around it. I watched his knuckles turn white.

'I'm sure it isn't as bad as you make out,' I said at last.

'They are the result of misery and human bondage.' He was still staring at the floor.

'Who do you speak of?' I asked.

'I saved them from barbarism. I brought them up from the animal level. I introduced them to the Bible and the word of God. But only by force. God doesn't want that. He wants His children to come to Him of their own free will.'

'And if they won't? Is it not still godly to show them the light?' Emily said.

'God told Annie in my dream that if we are to be together in eternal bliss, I must give my wealth away. Only then can I be pure in the eyes of the Lord, and only then will He open the gates and we will be truly as one. "Keep only what is essential to your earthly existence, Jonas, my love – the rest must be gifted to those in need." That's what she said.'

'And what did you say? In this dream?'

'I said, "I'll do it, my love. Earthly riches are no reward. Trinkets mean nothing to me."'

He got to his feet with difficulty and took hold of his stick. Emily and I watched him as he walked over to the painting of Annie. He stood beneath it, staring up. The face in the painting was much bigger than Jonas's, making Annie look like some deity staring down from the heavens.

'When I woke I felt as though I had been somewhere else,' he said. 'I had been somewhere else. In sleep I had found a halfway place between the dead and the living, and that is where Annie spoke to me.'

Jonas suggested we take a walk in the gardens. He opened the glass doors of the conservatory and we strolled across the terrace and past a fountain, along ornate flower beds that were mostly withering, ready for winter, until we entered a wooded area. A path meandered down to the lake. We sat on a bench by the water and watched martlets dive and scoop. The summer guest gorging on the last of summer's harvest. The leaves were copper, bronze, gold and every other burnished hue. Emily went to the water's edge and picked up a stone. She skimmed it across the mirror of the lake's surface.

'Is it all right if I have a paddle?' she said.

Jonas nodded. 'Please do.'

She took off her boots and stockings. She rolled her dress up in a knot so that it rested just above her knees. She waded in. Jonas was unusually quiet. He stared deep into the green-blue water. There were still some late blooms by the waterside but mostly it was fretted by green reeds. The last of the dragonflies hovered about.

'You seem troubled,' I said after an interval.

'Aye. That I am, Adam.'

'Is there anything I can do to soothe your fevered brow, sir?'

'Yes, there is.'

'And what is that?'

'You have lived on the streets. You have gone days without a meal. You know what it is to go hungry. I have never known an empty belly. I have never been without a bed or a roof over my head.'

'We each have our crosses to bear,' I said.

'And June. She has known great privation also. Oh, I'm not saying I have never suffered hardship of any kind. It was hard sometimes in Jamaica. It is a wild and mountainous place. Full of mutiny. We had an agreement with the Maroons.'

'Who were they?' I asked.

'Runaway slaves. There was a peace treaty. As long as they brought back future runaways, we would leave them alone.

Which they did. But the fear was always there. Having an army of unpredictable Africans all around you, it was hard to sleep some nights. I had to be tough. I had no choice.'

As I listened to him talk I wondered if Hindley justified his own malicious conduct with the same self-serving story.

'There were thousands of them and only hundreds of us, you understand?'

I nodded.

'I was in charge of forty-two slaves. Do you think they accepted their submission gracefully?'

'No, sir, I suspect not.'

'During that first year, do you know, I didn't see another white person for weeks on end. I wasn't even thirty years old. So you see, I had no choice.'

'I don't know what you mean.'

'I'd never been, you know, before I came to the island. I wasn't a brute. I was an educated man. A lover of books. Do you know, I have a library containing more than a thousand volumes?'

Emily waded back out of the water and walked over to where we were sitting.

'I thought I saw a pike,' she said.

'That's entirely possible,' Jonas said. 'There is indeed an old pike in there.'

'It's a big one, nearly had my leg off.'

'Well, let me see, must be about eight pound now. Not the biggest there is, but a decent size. Why don't you have a walk in the orchard just over there?' he said to Emily, pointing to the right of the pond. 'The apples need collecting. I think there's a basket thereabouts.'

She looked at me for affirmation. I felt that Jonas was opening up and that it would be beneficial if the two of us could talk some more so I nodded to Emily, to say she should go.

'I'll have a look,' she said, and wandered off again.

'It was a dangerous world, Adam. I was responsible for everything on the pen: housing, clothing, feeding, the lot. The things I had to endure: blisteringly hot sun, hurricanes, floods. But I learned very quickly how to make the land fertile and thus profitable. It began in me a lifetime's passion for horticulture. Plants, roots, cuttings, saplings.'

He rambled on about gardening matters for some time, before going off on another tangent. I tried to steer the conversation back on course.

'Forgive me, sir, but why are you telling me all this? Is something troubling you?'

'I . . . I just wanted you to know . . . I've made mistakes.'

'We all have, sir. I'm sure.'

'Fieldwork had to be synchronised with the mechanical processes. Cane that takes too long to be crushed and processed rapidly deteriorates, you see. Timing between the field and the factory was a very tricky business. And if the slaves weren't pulling their weight . . . I had very little experience at this stage, you understand. There were enormous pressures on me.'

'I'm sure you did what you could.'

Jonas grabbed hold of my arm and turned to me, his eyes pleading. 'Yes, but is that how God will see it, Adam? That's what I need to know.'

He stared deep into my eyes. There was something manic and desperate in that stare. I just shrugged.

At last he said, 'Forgive me, Adam. I shouldn't burden you with all this. But like me, you are a man of the cloth. Our job is to bring the sinner closer to God.'

'In truth, sir, I have not yet been accredited.'

'No? But I thought you said—'

'I did. I mean, I fully intend to be, but I am not experienced enough yet. I am, in all honesty, barely literate and numerate. There is much I need to learn. And I have not the wealth to educate myself.'

'I see,' said Jonas, sitting back on the bench. 'Let me think on this matter,' he said. 'Will you come back another day?'

'Well, I—'

'You must, I insist. Tomorrow maybe?'

'Not tomorrow,' I said.

'Then the day after?'

'I'll see what I can do,' I said at last.

All I wanted to do was grab him by the scruff of his neck and push his head under the water. To hold it there as he thrashed about, until he thrashed no more. But I thought again about our plan. We were almost there. Patience.

I went to find Emily. She was gathering apples and had a dozen or so in the basket. I explained that we were leaving. We walked back to Jonas and thanked him for his hospitality. He made us promise that we would return in two days' time.

As we walked back to the forest, I turned to Emily and said, 'So what next?'

'He's a worm on the end of our hook,' she said. 'We just need to dangle it a little longer. Here, have one of these,' she said, handing me an apple. I bit into the flesh. 'What do you think?'

'Nice,' I said. 'A bit tart.'

'I meant, what do you think we should do next?'

I shrugged.

When we got back to the shelter, we built up a fire and played a game of havoc. We talked about how we were going to manipulate Jonas, until we agreed that we should see what transpired on Tuesday and take it from there. I could feel growing unease in the pit of my gut. I pushed the feeling away and concentrated on my playing hand.

We made two more visits to Bold Hall before we had any kind of breakthrough. Jonas had sat us around the dinner table and asked us to tell him more about our parents' thwarted plans to build the orphanage. He seemed fascinated by every detail. So I wasn't entirely surprised at the end of that final visit, after the table had been cleared of crockery and the port had been served, when Jonas turned to us both and said, 'I've been spending a lot of time with Annie in the garden.'

We both nodded. I sipped my port.

'You two coming into my life. The harpsichord, the marigolds. Annie has sent you. I'm sure of it. I've told her all about you both and about the orphanage. I've told her about your plans to get accredited. I could feel her presence all around me. The leaves in the trees rustled with her spirit. She knows. She hears. She listens. I've been thinking as well that June needs an education. I want the very best for you,' he said, turning to Emily. 'And after a lot of thought, a lot of ruminating, a lot of talking with Annie, I've come to a decision.'

'And what decision is that then, may I ask, sir?'

'I want you to have a portion of my wealth. I want you to use it to complete the orphanage and what is left I want you both to use to secure your futures and keep from want. I will retain that which is enough to keep me in a modest fashion till I end my earthly days. That is all I require.'

'But that is too generous, sir,' I said.

'We are not worthy of such a gift,' Emily said.

'You are more than worth what I have,' he said. 'Don't try and dissuade me. It will do no good. I'm a stubborn old mule. Ask Annie. Ask her about the caffoy. Too lavish, she said, but I insisted.' He pointed up to where the painting was hanging. 'Stubborn as an ox. That's what she used to say. Once I've made up my mind, there is no dissuading me. So don't even try. It will do no good, I assure you.'

'Well, if you are sure this is the right thing to do, sir?'

I could feel the knot in my gut dissolve. I tried to contain my relief. At last, the old man had taken the bait, the plan had worked. It had been a huge effort – as much an effort of will and nerve as that of skill – but he had cracked. I tried not to show my joy, and instead smiled inwardly.

'Mankind is in a state of guilt. There is a sense of dread of divine displeasure.'

He was looking down at his empty plate.

'From the most learned philosophers down to the greatest savages, subject to such remorse as makes them wish for some method of expiating their offences. The minds of even the most enlightened men, who have the highest standard of moral perfection and the quickest sense of duty.'

He looked over to where Emily and I were seated.

'There has to be atonement. I've never been more sure of anything in my life. My wealth is like an iron cloak, dragging me down into the mire. It is a millstone round my neck, pulling me under to Beelzebub's domain. I thought that by purchasing human chattels from a godless land and transporting them to my own plantations, where they could be occupied with honest toil, and receive the word of Christ, that I was doing God's work, but I've seen the error of my ways. Annie came to me in a dream again last night. My dearest Annie. And I wish only to do what is propitious by Annie and my Lord Jesus Christ. Everything else in my life is dust. This is my mission on earth. Perhaps my philanthropic actions will be an example to other men like me, who have made their riches from the blood, sweat and tears of bonded labour. God wants only free men. Iron cuffs and shackles anger Him. Neck braces and manacles offend Him. Collars and chains provoke His wrath. The block repels His love, as does the whip. He has made man in His image to be free to devote his life to God. To use our free choice to love Him. To serve Him by force is not to serve Him at all. Only the devil wants bonded slaves. Annie and I made an Eden here, in order to replicate that Eden that seated man before his sin. With an orchard for pear and apple, woodlands and water. Beds of flowers and beds where every one of God's vegetables grows.'

He took out the locket containing the lock of hair from his waistcoat and gripped it in his fist.

'I have done things. Things that cannot be undone. Many refused to eat. They had to be force-fed. They would have died otherwise.'

He took out the lock of hair and stroked his cheek with it.

'So soft. My Annie's hair was like her temperament. So soft. God made both the lion and the lamb.'

He put the lock of hair to his lips. He stared off, out of the window, dreamily.

'You know, on my first voyage I saw a man flogged for committing sodomy with a sheep,' he said and laughed bitterly.

'That's disgusting,' Emily said.

'No, June, that is man at his most base. We each have that baseness in us. That ship was infested with rats, and slaves lay in their own uncleanliness. The smell was overpowering. On our homeward journey the ship was terribly damaged by a storm. We lost food and livestock overboard. We were doomed, or so I thought, but some force guided us to safety. And I now know what I didn't know then. That there is a God who hears and answers our prayers.'

I let a respectful silence descend before I responded.

'I find it hard to locate any error in what you say, sir. I'm moved by your heartfelt sentiments. It marks you out as a man of great compassion and divine devotion.'

'I've never been so sure of anything before. Thanks to my dearest Annie. Next Sunday you will come to my house and I will give out my wealth. I then intend to spend what time I have left working on the minds of men who think it is acceptable to buy and sell human chattels.'

You might find that plan is thwarted then, I thought, as I pictured his head on a pike. Inside I was chuckling. We had him. This was it, Cathy. Everything we had worked for was almost in place.

'Very well, sir. You have chosen a righteous path. I am honoured that you have selected me as your servant in this matter.'

'And I am deeply touched,' said Emily, 'that you would do such a good thing for us both.'

He took hold of Emily's hand and kissed it tenderly. Then he turned to me and looked me in the eye. We shook hands.

As we walked back to the forest, I felt as light as a butterfly. I was hardly aware of the cold wind blowing at my cheek. Inside I was warm and content. I laughed with joy and Emily joined in. She chatted beside me.

'That couldn't have gone any better,' she said. 'We've only gone and cracked it.'

'I know,' I said. 'I can't believe it. Just four more days before we get to pick up the rewards of our labour.'

'Do you think he's off his rocker?'

'How do you mean?'

'The way he talks about Annie, it's like she's in the room. Sometimes I think he's forgotten that she's dead and thinks she is standing next to him.'

'Who knows where the dead go when they die?' I said. 'Maybe they do walk by our side. Maybe they follow us wherever we go and sleep in our bedchambers when we sleep.'

Emily carried on chatting about Jonas as we traipsed across the moor, but my enthusiasm waned as my thoughts returned to my mother. I kept picturing in my mind what Jonas had done to make his guilt lie so heavily on his conscience. He had left her to die in a darkened room. Dragged from the place of her birth, pulled from the bosom of her family. Made to travel overseas in a boat where they were stuffed like figs in a barrel. Made to lie in their own ordure. Sleep in a box not big enough to move about. Brought to a plantation where men would use her for their own purposes. The thought sickened me all over again. Men like Jonas were able to live an immoral life for whatever length of time they pleased, just as long as they repented before they breathed their last breath. What kind of God was it that looked down at us from His throne in heaven? What kind of maniac was He to think that this was devout work?

The next day, Emily checked the snares and brought two rabbits back. I filled the pot from the beck and picked some mushrooms. I sliced them up and put them into the stew. I found some greens to add to the concoction and watched Emily gut the animals.

'I tell you what – I'll be glad to see the back of rabbit stew,' she said, as she slopped the discarded offal onto the forest floor.

'Just another week, Emily. Then no more rabbit stew for us. Only sirloins of roast beef, venison, duck and partridge.'

'And cakes.'

'If you like.'

We talked some more about what we would do with our wealth, until Emily started one of her coughing fits. I didn't say anything, but secretly my concern deepened. I thought about my namesake again, William Lee. How quickly he had gone from a playful boy to an invalid. And how quickly he had dwindled from that point on, to his grave. I resolved to consult a physician as soon as our plan had come to fruition.

~

We were travelling in Jonas's coach, speeding to his estate. It was Sunday and my axe and knife were secreted in my surtout. I had spent the morning sharpening them, ready for my revenge. We would get Jonas's worldly goods, then I would gut him like an eel. It was a fine autumn day, red and gold leaves falling in our wake, but Jonas was quiet during the journey and there was a darkness in his eyes that disconcerted me.

'Is everything set?' I asked.

He just nodded gravely and stared out of the window at nothing in particular. I had a growing sense of unease, but I tried to push it from my mind. It is a big day, I told myself. He is about to take a life-changing step, one he can never reverse. Of course he must be apprehensive. It's perfectly natural. In fact, it would be stranger if he were not in this dark mood. But nothing could assuage the knot of foreboding in my gut.

The coach pulled up outside the front door and we alighted. We went into the dining room. The table was bare, in stark contrast to our previous visit. So, there's to be no feast, I thought. No matter. Jonas stood beneath the painting of his deceased wife. We stood waiting for him to speak, but he folded his arms and remained silent.

'Are we waiting for someone, sir?' I enquired.

'Let's not be hasty,' he said.

'Is something the matter, sir? I couldn't help noticing that throughout our journey here, your mood has been somewhat melancholy.'

He nodded slowly but said nothing. He turned to the portrait and stared up at it.

'I've heard that sometimes dark devices show us their light reflection, in order to gain our trust.'

'You confuse me, sir. For sure, your words are riddles.'

'Yesterday I ordered my servants to collect a significant portion of my wealth from the vaults and to box it up in wooden chests, ready for collection. Shortly after they had carried out the task, there was a knock at the door. I wonder if you can guess who the visitor was?'

I looked at Emily. I could tell from the way she was rubbing the hem of her frock with her thumb and forefinger that she didn't like where this was going. I didn't like where this was going either. I tried to retain my composure.

'I've no idea, sir.'

'It was a man who introduced himself as Dick Taylor, a man with only one hand. He told me how he had lost his other hand, and how he had lost his dear companion, who was murdered in his bed a few weeks ago, while he still slept. A coward's way of killing a man, I'd say. He told me of my old business partner, Mr Hardwar, and how he had been tortured and mutilated in the office of his Custom House. And how he was left to bleed to death. He also told me about a girl with white-blonde hair, who he knew to be a witch and who was in league with the devil himself. Then he showed me this.'

He reached into his frock coat and pulled out a folded sheet of paper. He unravelled it. He held up the wanted notice.

I felt ice-cold water run through my veins.

'I see,' I said.

I looked at Emily again. Her pale face had blanched even paler than before, so that her skin was even whiter than that of the painting of Annabel Bold. I had my knife on me and the sharpened axe. I had come here to rob him, then to butcher him. This Jonas was old, fat and out of shape, he would present no difficulties. I would just have to do the deed sooner rather than later.

'You are nothing more than a thief, a liar and a killer,' Jonas said, warming to his theme.

'I am the son of Lilith,' I said. 'My mother who you drove to her death. Who died under your very roof in the attic above this room. And now I have come back to put right your terrible crime.'

Jonas raised his eyebrows in surprise. I was getting ready to pounce, when the door to the parlour opened and in walked Mr Bold's two servants, alongside an officer of the law and Dick Taylor, who was brandishing a pistol with his one remaining hand. They stood next to Jonas Bold beneath the portrait. We were outnumbered five to two. The door we had come through was a good ten yards distance. The lead ball in Dick's pistol would outrun us. There was a large bay window behind us. That was another possible escape, and the door the men had come through, which led to the parlour, also at least ten yards away. None of these options were particularly hopeful.

'Look what the cat dragged in,' Dick Taylor said, his skull grinning.

Jonas nodded. 'So, you're Lilith's son. The brat she spent six years grieving over. Why she thought she'd have been able to keep you I don't know. But I'd heard you'd survived her. Didn't hear much else – I left your dispatch to Mr Hardwar. He was short of money at the time, put you to work in his kitchens as far as I recollect. I didn't want to know the details. As long as the problem was sorted. Your father was out of his depth, of course. A bloody tyke from the sticks. I don't know what hold she had over your father, but he had a special agreement to use her exclusively. That was, until Mr Hardwar got tired of him.'

'How well did you know my mother?'

'Once Mr Earnshaw was out of the picture, your mother became one of my favourites,' Jonas said. 'We called her Negro Number Twenty-nine. Twenty-nine times a night. I was sad to see the light die in her eyes. Watching her in this house dwindling by the day. I did what I had to do. Now I'm going to do what I have to do again.'

We had the table between us and the men. There was no time to think any further. As fast as I could, and using all my strength, I flipped the table over and grabbed Emily, but a shot rang out and as I pulled her down, I saw that she was bleeding.

No time to go to her aid. I leapt up, brandishing a chair, and threw it across the room at Dick Taylor. It crashed into him, knocking his gun to the floor. The officer now held a pistol, which he fired. I ducked behind the table again, then seeing that the bullet had missed me, I ran from behind the table at the officer, who held his gun towards me. It was a race to get to him before he could take aim. Just as I reached him, holding my knife ready to stab him, he pulled the trigger. But the gun misfired and I plunged the knife into his neck. He went down. I yanked the blade out of his severed windpipe and thrust it deep into his heart. Once, twice, three times. The man crumpled at my feet.

The two servants just stood there, fixed to the spot as though they had been planted there by Jonas, evidently not fighting men. Dick had reached for his gun and was busy reloading it, but with only one hand it was slow work. I gripped the throat and belly of the axe and ran at him as fast as I could. He was about to pull the trigger, but I grabbed his arm so that he fired the shot at the ceiling. Then, still holding onto it, I held the axe aloft and brought it down with great force, chopping through the meat and bones of his wrist, so that I now held his hand as though it were a glove. I threw it onto the floor, with its fingers still clutching the gun. I plucked the pistol from the hand and held it against Dick's forehead.

'Please, don't,' he said. 'I'm sure we can come to some arrangement.'

He was kneeling before me, blood pumping from the wound. I fired the pistol into the middle of his forehead. Flesh and bone exploded. I could feel hot spittles of blood freckle my face. The room reeked of gunpowder. He was thrown onto the floor. Next I ran at the servants, who were making their way to the door. I grabbed the first by his hair and plunged the knife between his shoulder blades. He stopped in his tracks and fell to his knees. I took the knife out and slit the man's throat. He fell to the floor, blood gurgling from the gash. I lunged at the second servant, who held the door handle in one hand and had the door ajar. I stabbed him in the neck. He cried out, falling against the door and closing it in the process. I stabbed him in the cheek, then in his liver. He fell to the floor. I leapt onto the man and stabbed him indiscriminately in his guts and chest, in his face again. But I was stabbing a corpse, panting with the effort.

I turned around. The parlour door was open and Jonas had escaped. I ran into the parlour but there was no Jonas. The door that led to the kitchens was also open and I ran over to it. I found Jonas at the back, near the sink, and close to the back door.

'Not so quick,' I said.

He turned around, absolute fear in his eyes. He picked up

an iron pot and threw it at me, but it was a weak throw and fell short a few feet from where I was standing. He grabbed a meat cleaver that was lying on a wooden board.

'We don't have to do it this way,' he said. 'I want to give you everything I've got. Killing a man will bring you no satisfaction, either in this life or the next. There is time for you to save your soul. Give up your weapons and God will forgive you.'

'That's where you're wrong,' I said, walking slowly towards him. 'I don't want God's forgiveness.'

'I know people. Important people. Magistrates, judges, lords and politicians. Powerful people. I can get you off. You see if I can't.'

'I thought you wanted to be with your wife, dear, sweet Annie? I only want to give you what you desire,' I said.

I lunged at him as he came at me with the cleaver. I slashed at his arm and the knife cut deep. He dropped the cleaver and tried to shield himself with his arms. I threw the knife down, then the axe as well, so that both lay on the kitchen floor. I punched him in the face and the blow knocked him back against the wall. I grabbed him by the hair, forgetting it was a wig, and it came off in my hand. I threw it onto the ground and grabbed him by the few hairs he had left, growing at the back of his head. I smashed his face into the stone top, knocking his teeth out of his head, throwing him onto the floor and pouncing on him. With both thumbs, I gouged out the jellies of his eyes. I put my hands around his throat and squeezed the life out of him. His florid complexion purpled. He stopped struggling and collapsed. I crouched over the corpse, panting like an animal.

Suddenly, I remembered Emily. I ran back through the kitchen, through the parlour, into the dining room. Emily was on the floor, holding her hands close to her chest, trying to stop the flow of blood from the shot wound. I ran across to her and held her up so that she could breathe more easily.

'Emily, Emily. Can you hear me?'

Her eyes were open but they had glazed over and were staring at nothing.

I shook her gently.

'Emily, please, stay with me till I get some help.'

She looked up at me for the first time. I ripped a sleeve from my shirt and tied it tight around her chest, to staunch the flow of blood. I picked her up in my arms and carried her out of the house, to the coach that was still with horses.

'I'm going to drive us back to the village. I'll get a physician. He'll patch you up. You'll see.'

I opened the coach door and lay Emily across the seat. As I did, she grabbed hold of my neck. She pulled me towards her.

'My dad . . . My dad . . .' Her voice was weak and I had to lean in closer to hear what she was saying. 'He was a bad man, William Lee. He's gone to hell. Am I going to hell?'

I shook my head. We're all going to hell, I wagered. I thought about my mother. Was she going to hell? Aren't those who take their own lives condemned to the fiery pit? Wasn't that what Joseph said? Very well, I'd see her then some day.

'You don't understand. My dad. He did some bad things.'

'I know. You've told me. He was a murderer.'

'Worse than that, William. He was worse than that.'

I stroked her hair. 'Don't talk. Rest. We need to get you to the doctor.'

'He didn't see me, William. I looked at him, but he didn't see me.'

She looked deep into my eyes, with a pleading expression. I waited for her to continue but instead she released her grip and was flaccid once more.

I sat on the cold stone step and wept.

I railed against the world. I cursed God and I cursed humanity. There was no good in the world, only an ocean fleet of evil. I lay on the floor and beat my head against the stone. I lay there for a long time, unable to move. I'd lost the only person, apart from you, Cathy, that I'd ever really cared about. I'd reneged on my promise to keep her safe from harm, as you reneged on your promise that we would always be together. You said that I was more you than you were yourself. That our souls were made of the same thing. I cursed promises.

Eventually I became aware of myself again. I stood up and walked back to the coach. I lay Emily neatly across the seat and gently closed her eyes. I wiped away the blood from her face with the pilfered fogle. I shut the coach door. I went back inside the house, past the bodies of the men I'd killed, until I came to Mr Bold's study. Inside the room were two large wooden chests. I opened the first. It was full to the brim with diamonds, sapphires, rubies and other jewels. I went over to the second: it was stuffed with guineas and gold sovereigns. He must have had his servant fetch them from his vault before encountering Dick Taylor.

I was a rich man. But what good were my riches now? I sat by the boxes, thinking things through. I owed it to Emily, as well as to myself, to make something of my life. If not, then two people had died in vain, Emily and me.

I thought back to what Emily had said in the woods, about an education being the key to taking revenge against Wuthering Heights. I would use this wealth to get an education and become a gentleman. I would become an expert in the legal acquisition of personal estates. I would go back to Wuthering Heights and take everything from Hindley. I would not stop until he was completely destroyed. I would destroy his wealth, I would destroy his power, I would crush his spirit, so that death would be a sweet release from his torment. And you, Cathy, why should you have it easy? You might be married, living a life of luxury, but I would come between you and Edgar. I would see to it that your soul would be in constant torment. I would make sure that you would never be happy. Just as you had ensured that I would never be other than cast out and alone.

I stood up and closed the lids of the chests. I looked at my reflection in the mirror on the wall. I was covered in blood, my forehead was cut open and blood oozed from the wound. My shirt was ripped. I looked more like a beast than a gentleman. But it was easy to change from one thing to another. No man becomes a gentleman through honest toil. There was only ever one way to get money and that was to steal it from those who stole it from others. I would return one day to Wuthering Heights, in tailored garments and in a chaise. Mark my words, Cathy.

The wooden chests were a great weight and cumbersome to shift. It took a huge amount of effort, but eventually I heaved the first one over to the coach and loaded it up next to

Emily's body. I went back for the second. I had one last look around the house. I went into the study and furtled through the drawers in the desk. There were ledgers and account books. Certificates of purchase and receipts. Above the desk was a shelf, and along this shelf a neat line of black books with dates written on the spines. I pulled the first one out and flicked through it. It was a journal. Each page was headed by a date, underneath which was a short description of the day's events. To-do lists. Records of stocks and sales. Appointments and meetings of various sorts and short summaries of events. I took another journal from the year before, 1779. I flicked through it. I put it back. I counted through to 1764. The year of my birth.

With some trepidation, I lay the book on the desk and opened it. More dates. Times. Figures. Meeting with so-and-so. Appointment for this and that. But then, as I turned the pages, my eyes could hardly believe what they saw. Further on, the journal was a meticulous account of each and every sexual congress during his years on the plantation. Where and when, with whom, how often. 'Above the wall head', 'right hand of the river', 'towards the negro ground'. 'The floor', 'north bed foot', 'east parlour'. I turned the next page and saw the word 'Lilith'. I slammed the book shut, afraid of what I might read next. I didn't want to know. I wanted to know. I thought about my mother. Clothes torn. Held down. A girl not much older than Emily. Men all over. Whip and boot. Crying out. Pleading. Alone. In agony. At least now her pain was over. I took hold of the book and several others and placed them inside the remaining chest. I would learn more of my history. No matter what misery it wrought. Then I dragged the chest out of the building and over to the carriage. I heaved it up next to its partner, untethered the horses, mounted the cab and cracked the whip.

When I got back to camp, I dug up the money we had buried and put it with the rest of my wealth. I removed the ferns from the entrance to the mantrap we had constructed and placed Emily at the bottom. I scooped up heaps of earth and poured it over her body. I kept doing this until she was buried under the mound of fresh soil. I patted the earth down.

I looked around at the makeshift camp that had been our home these past few weeks. I dismantled the shelter and took the tree branch that had been used as the main support. I dug out my knife and sharpened one end of the wood, then fixed it into the ground like a stake. I gathered the rest of the branches and twigs and piled them around. I took all of our other possessions, including the blankets that had kept us warm, and Emily's other dress that she had been saving for a special occasion, and gathered them in a heap around the stake. As I did I noticed a brightly coloured object close to our former shelter. As I got closer I saw that it was the deck of cards, fastened with some string. I untied the deck and shuffled the pack. I took out a joker and placed it on the soft mound where I had buried Emily, then I re-tied the deck and tucked it into my coat pocket. Save them for another day. I had a game I was going to teach Hindley.

Then I took the flint and used my knife to start a fire. I watched the flames lick the fabric of the frock and turn the edges black, before catching more thoroughly. The smoke was thick and black due to all of the leaves on the branches, and the wood still wet with sap. For a time the fire was obscured by its own thick fog. The wood hissed and crackled. But then the smoke cleared and the wood stopped hissing. Big red flames consumed the pile. I could feel the heat burn from where I was standing.

I walked back to the carriage. As I climbed up to the driver's seat and took the whip in my hand, I looked back at the grave for the last time. The fresh mound rising up as though the earth was pregnant. 'You have not died in vain,' I said. 'I'll make sure of it.' And I allowed hot tears to prick my eyes once more.

The fire was raging. I cracked the whip. The horses galloped. It was over. It had begun.

1783

You have been travelling for nearly a week. Last night you stayed in a coach house and feasted at an eating establishment of the highest quality. You dined on a leg of boiled mutton and caper sauce, turnips, broccoli, a roast duck, a semolina pudding, cheese, punch and brandy. You are travelling along a coach road in a brand new chaise. You have been on this road before, three years since, only that time you were heading west, now you are heading east. You are wearing your new black leather boots. They have been specially designed so that each heel has a cut-out piece.

In the distance, on a steep hill, you see the silhouette of a gibbet cage suspended from a gallows. You beckon the coachman to halt and you dismount your carriage. You approach the tarred corpse that hangs in the gibbet cage. The stench of rotting flesh is pungent. You stare at the black figure within, mesmerised by this mummified form. The wind is gentle and the gibbet rocks like a cradle. The bough of the gallows creaks. Iron rungs bind the corpse. Its arms pinned to its side. Its head fixed by metal plates, so that as the corpse swings in the breeze, its face stares across the moor unseeing. The tar hasn't reached the top of his head, so that one eyeless socket peeps out. Flies dance around the hole.

Two farm labourers, carrying scythes, walk by. You urge them to stop.

'Excuse me, I don't suppose you know how this poor unfortunate wretch met his end, by any chance, do you?'

The labourers bow deferentially and doff their caps. 'Why, good sir, he was hanged by the neck, three weeks since. Then he was tarred and transferred here shortly after.'

'And for what crime?'

'Treason, sir,' says one.

'He got caught,' says the other. 'He organised a meeting in the woods. He wanted to raise wages and improve conditions for the mill workers of Keighley. Haven't you heard?'

'And for that he hanged?'

'Oh yes, sir. It is a capital offence to organise labour round these parts.'

You thank the men for their information. You hand them a shilling each. They trundle down the hill with the blade of their scythes jutting out behind them. You stare at the corpse swaying in the wind. You think about Sticks. Running to something or running away from something, that's what he said all those years ago. You wonder if he ever stopped running and if so, where he is now. You place your hand on the cage to stop it from rocking. You are aware that you should feel something but you feel nothing. You let go of the gibbet cage and it starts to sway once more. You climb back into the coach and shout from the window to the coachman to carry on up the road. There are many miles yet to go and the roads are slow going.

As you ride there are two moments you return to again and again. The first night at Wuthering Heights. Mr Earnshaw had collapsed in his chair by the fire, fatigued by his long journey over marsh and moor. His boots by his side clagged with mud. Mrs Earnshaw had supper prepared for him but he was too tired to eat it. He complained about his feet. He soaked them in a bowl. He had a blister on his heel. Mrs Earnshaw gave his supper to you instead. And you sat by the fire watching the flames turn the peat black and the coals orange. You chewed through a crust of bread, a slice of ham, a wedge of cheese and a boiled egg, and as you did, you thought, maybe it won't be so bad after all.

Hindley was standing in a corner, watching you. 'It's his fault,' he said to Nelly. 'What's his fault?' she said. 'This.' And he'd held aloft a fiddle that was snapped nearly in two at the neck. 'It was an accident,' she said. 'Accidents happen. It's no one's fault.' 'It's his fault,' Hindley repeated. 'If Father wasn't with him he'd have been more careful. It's his fault it's broken.' You are glad that the fiddle is broken and you look across from your plate of victuals and smirk at this Hindley. He's glaring at you in the darkness of his corner with just the flame from a lamp to light his features. But you know that look. It says, I'll pay you back for this.

And he did pay you back. Many times. So that now you are his debtor. It is your turn to pay him back. Everything runs in a circle, the river and the rain, the moon around the earth, the earth around the sun, even revenge. You noticed Cathy looking at you curiously with none of the malice of Hindley. She had spat at you earlier when Nelly was scrubbing you, but now she has returned with renewed interest. When you make eye contact she looks away, but as you chew the crusts, you see her watching you. Later, after you have finished eating and the dog is licking your empty plate, she comes closer. 'Do you want to play?' she says, producing a box of wooden soldiers. You don't play games, but for her you make an exception. She opens the *box and lays the toys on the ground. A dozen men in uniform, carved out of wood. You pick one up and turn it around. It is engraved and finely painted. 'That one's a foot soldier,' she says. 'You can keep it if you like.' You soon become friends. Till Linton gets in the way.*

Which brings you to your other abiding memory. Cathy cosy in Thrushcross, sitting by the fire, a goblet of brandy in her hand. You outside in the dark and the cold. The many candles of the chandelier, casting warmth and light all around the room. She'd hurt her leg. Just a cut. She hadn't broken a bone, just the skin, and yet she spent five weeks there. It didn't take five weeks for the skin to heal and for her to recover from that injury. Five weeks. Just an excuse. You suspected that then and you know it now. She had wanted to be there. She'd made out the injury was worse than it was so that she could stay in that palace of crimson and gold. Velvet and silk, cut glass and cut flowers. Fine bone china, silver platters, crystal glasses. You'd stayed at the pane for a long time that night, until the chill went into the marrow of your bones. As you walked back, you came across the corpse of the dog you'd throttled earlier. You prefer dogs to people, and yet you felt no sadness for this beast. It was Linton's pet and therefore it was a part of Linton. It felt good to destroy something that he owned.

Now you are returning after three years away, a changed man. You are travelling in a one-horse chaise along a coach road, but the chaise has no value to you. Once you've reached your destination, you'll sell it and pay the coachman off. You have no attachments. Perhaps you'll burn it on the moors to show how little it means to you. You are wearing a suit cut in the latest fashion, but of dark brown woollen cloth. You have forgone any trimmings or embroidery. The waistcoat is styled short and single-breasted with small, neat lapels. Your breeches are high-waisted. Long over the knees, and tailored for a slim silhouette. You wear a plain muslin scarf around your neck, knotted at the front. The look is 'no frills'. In your waistcoat pocket is a gold watch, but it means nothing to you. The watchmaker asked if you wanted it engraved with your name. But you still don't know your name. You might give it to a beggar, or a thief, or else throw it in the bog. The things you want can't be bought.

As you are driven through a familiar landscape other memories come back to you. How Hindley's already apparent hatred of you had soon grown bitter and brooding. That time Mr Earnshaw had brought back two colts from the market. He gave one to you and one to Hindley. But your colt had fallen lame and you had gone to Hindley and told him he must exchange horses, and if not, that you would tell Mr Earnshaw about all the thrashings. You had bruises as proof. Hindley had called you a dog but given you his horse anyway.

You think about Emily. You want to feel something. But you feel nothing. You are in mourning for an absence of feeling.

You have imagined the day you would come back to Wuthering Heights many times. You imagine the look on Cathy's face. But as you get closer to home, it is not that look that possesses you, but rather the feelings that the thought of seeing her again brings forward. You are surprisingly nervous. Your stomach turns over and your heart aches. Your guts feel as though they are being ground in a quern. It's just as Sticks had said all those years ago. Like in all the songs, where some temptress puts a spell on a man that he can never break. Somehow Cathy has put a spell on you, and despite what you feel, the anger that is still raw, you want to be the apple of her eye, not Linton. You want her to say that she loves everything you touch, loves every word you speak, loves everything about you. Three long years and you feel the familiar sickness rise inside your stomach, a *sense of helplessness, a feeling you can't control or assuage; instead, it boils up like unattended milk. You thought after all this time the wound would have scabbed over and healed, leaving just a faint scar in its place. In fact, it is as open and as raw as the day you left, and as fresh, and as wet.*

Once it would have degraded her, but now you are a gentleman and a man of wealth. Just maybe. It's as much as you can think before you kick the thought out. To feel is to weaken. But perhaps. You can't bear to think about it now. Your love must be a black-hearted one. And like a bird of bad omen you are returning to the nest that once cast you out into the storm. To crush the eggs beneath your feet. You are the devil Hindley named you. Half-man, half-monster. Between Aire, Wharfe, Nidd and Swale. Between shrike, snipe and ouzel. Between dipper, piper and wagtail. Between martin, stoat and weasel. Between shank, coot and teal. Between gout-weed, goat's beard and witch hazel. The devil has his own spells.

You are wearing your new black leather boots. They have been specially designed by a cordwainer in York. He'd laughed at your audacity, when you'd instructed him on the design, but carried out your wishes anyway, asking you again to be sure . . . A cleft in the heel, you say, sir? All your boots now have cloven hooves.

Acknowledgements

This book would not have been possible without the help, encouragement and expertise of many people. To these people I offer my thanks and gratitude. They are:

My editor, Clio Cornish at HarperCollins, who has been a massive help in getting the story ready for publication and made many valuable creative contributions along the way.

Lisa Milton at HarperCollins, who first showed interest in the book and set the publication wheel in motion.

The rest of the team at HarperCollins, who have worked so hard to bring this book to life.

My agents, Jemima Forrester (literary) and Clare Israel (script), who have both offered so much help and advice throughout the process and gone way beyond what a writer can expect from an agent. Much respect.

Lisa Singleton, who read the first draft and encouraged me to persist with it.

Amanda Whittington for the reading suggestions.

Fellow writers who read drafts at various stages and gave me invaluable advice: Gary Brown Simon Crump, Steve Ely, Jim Greenhalf, Anne Heilmann, Matt Hill, Christina Longden, Leonora Rustamova.

I would like to thank the following people for their help and expertise: Zoe Johnson at University of Huddersfield Library; Harriet Harmer at the archives and special collections, University of Huddersfield; Paul Ward, Historian; Mary Chadwick, Historian; The Liverpool Maritime Museum; the slavery archives at Liverpool City Library; Margaret Daley at the Liverpool Record Office; Alexandra Mitchell at the Peel Group; Michael Powell at Chetham's Library in Manchester.

And the following publications:

Aldred, J. *The Duke of Bridgewater*
Ashton, T.S. *An Economic History of England: The 18ᵗʰ Century*
Ashton, T.S. *The Industrial Revolution: 1760–1830*
Atkins, W. *The Moor: A Journey into the English Wilderness*
Baines' Flora of Yorkshire
Basker, J.G. (ed.). *Amazing Grace*: *An Anthology of Poems About Slavery 1660–1810*
Billett, M. *Highwaymen and Outlaws*
Brandon, D. *Stand and Deliver!: A History of Highway Robbery*
Brears, P. and Wood, S. *The Real Wuthering Heights: The Story of the Withins Farm*
Brontë, A. *The Tenant of Wildfell Hall*
Brontë, E. *Wuthering Heights*
Cameron, G. and Crooke, S. *Liverpool: Capital of the Slave Trade*

Carrington and Miall. *Flora of the West Ridings*

Costello, R. *Black Liverpool: The Early History of Britain's Oldest Black Community 1730–1918*

Gifford, T. *Pastoral*

Goddard, C. *The West Yorkshire Moors*

Green, J. *Slang Down the Ages*

Griffin, E. *Liberty's Dawn: A People's History of the Industrial Revolution*

Haining, P. *The English Highwayman: A Legend Unmasked*

Hart, A. and North, S. *Historical Fashion in Detail: The 17th and 18th Centuries*

Hett, C.L. *A Glossary of Popular, Local and Old-fashioned Names of British Birds*

Hochschild, A. *Bury the Chains: The British Struggle to Abolish Slavery*

Lynch, J. (ed.). *Samuel Johnson's Dictionary*

McFarlane, R. *Landmarks*

McFarlane, R. *The Old Ways*

Mingay, G.E. *The Agricultural Revolution*

Rhys, J. *Wide Sargasso Sea*

Ribeiro, A. *Dress in Eighteenth Century Europe*

Sutherland, J. *Is Heathcliff a Murderer?*

Taylor, G. *The Problem of Poverty*

Thompson, E.P. *The Making of the English Working Class*

Walvin, J. *The Trader, The Owner, The Slave*

Whitaker, J. *The History of Manchester*

Wilson. E. G. *Thomas Clarkson: A Biography*

The 18th century travel writing of Arthur Young

The online version of The Oxford English Dictionary

During the writing of the book, I have walked hundreds of miles across the Yorkshire Moors. I also walked from Top Withens, the inspiration for the location of Wuthering Heights, to Liverpool docks, re-enacting the walk that Mr Earnshaw took in 1771, which resulted in him returning with Heathcliff. The moors surrounding Haworth and further on have been a massive inspiration and continue to be so. They are a place of freedom and refuge.